BOSTON BLACKIE

BOSTON BLACKIE

JACK BOYLE

BOSTON BLACKIE

Published by Wildside Press LLC.
www.wildsidebooks.com

CONTENTS

CHAPTERS   PAGE

I   Boston Blackie   9

II   Boston Blackie's Little Pal . .   12

III   Boston Blackie's Code . . .   26

IV   The Cushions Kid   36

V   One Week to Live   46

VI   "Not to Snitch on a Pal" . . .   57

VII   The Woman Called Rita . . .   66

VIII The Miracle   76

IX   Fred the Count   90

X   The Price of Success   101

XI   The Spirit of the Cushions Kid .   115

XII   A Problem in Grand Larceny .   127

XIII The Shot in the Dark   141

XIV The Mystery of the S. S. Humboldt   149

XV   Missing Gold   159

XVI   The Frame-up   173

XVII The Third Degree   184

XVIII An Answer in Grand Larceny .   196

XIX   Alibi Ann   205

XX   Boston Blackie's Prophecy Comes True   217

XXI   The Love of a Woman . . .   231

XXII For Fifteen Years   246

XXIII The Revolt   255

XXIV First Blood   265

XXV   Boston Blackie's Mary . . .   277

XXVI "Play for Me 'Little Squirrel'" .   285

XXVII Trapped   299

XXVIII Man to Man   308

CONTENTS

FOREWORD

THE great fire that followed the San Francisco earthquake had burned itself out. Half the city was a seared waste of smouldering ruins. Though the sky by night still reflected the red but dying glow of the wall of flame that had leaped from block to block like a pursuing creature of prey, the undevastated remnant was safe.

Those of us who had lived through the four unforgettable days of chaos just passed, began to look about us once more with seeing eyes. Men smiled again, as amid the ruin, they planned the reconstruction of a city more beautiful than the one they had lost. The indomitable spirit of a people united by a great and common disaster rose undaunted and hope mastered despair.

For the moment all men were equal. Gold had lost its value. Food, first of all necessities, was not for sale, and master and servant, banker and laborer, millionaire and beggar, waited together at the relief stations for their equal daily ration.

Every park, every square, every plot of ground was covered with the improvised camps of the refugees. One hundred thousand people had fled from their homes before the incredibly swift sweep of the fire. They had fled with only such possessions as they could throw together in a moment and carry on their backs. With this inadequate material men built such makeshift shelters for their families as individual skill permitted. Each man was "on his own," the sole protector and provider for his mate and children.

Out in Golden Gate Park one Sunday afternoon— the fourth after the earthquake—I came upon a rude but comfortable refuge with a blanket forming each of three walls and a tarpaulin for a roof. Before the uncurtained entrance a man sat cross-legged with a little child on his lap. With masculine clumsiness he was trying to fashion a rag doll from a torn piece of sheeting and a bit of blue ribbon. The tot on his knee watched, smiling, with eyes wide with excitement and pleasure. Nearby, three other kiddies—the eldest not older than six or seven—sprawled on the grass, playing contentedly.

Something prompted me to pause. The man looked up and smiled.

"Some job for a mere man, this is," he said, indicating the caricature of a doll on which he was working.

"Not so bad, evidently, from your little girl's viewpoint," I answered, with another glance at the glowing eyes of the waiting child. "But maybe her mother will improve on it."

"I'm the only mother there is in this camp," he answered. Then, as if he sensed my curiosity: "You see, pardner, none of them is mine."

"None of them yours?" I echoed in amazement.

"Not one. I picked them up, lost and crying— poor, little stray lambs—during the fire. And now it's up to me to take care of them. I'm hoping their folks, if they're alive, will wander by my nursery and find 'em. If they don't—well, I guess we'll stick together, eh, little pals."

That was my first meeting with the strange but, to me, wonderfully human character I have tried to picture with photographic accuracy in the following story. I have hidden his identity under the name "Boston Blackie." To the police and the world he is a professional crook, a skilled and daring safe cracker, an incorrigible criminal made doubly dangerous by intellect. To the world "Boston Blackie" is that and nothing more. But to me, who saw him in the park, caring, tenderly as a mother, for the forsaken little children the fire had sent him, "Blackie" is something more—a man with more than a spark of the Divine Spirit that lies hidden somewhere in the heart of even the worst of men. University graduate, scholar and gentleman, the "Blackie" I know is a man of many inconsistencies and a strangely twisted code of morals—a code that he guards from violation as a zealot guards his religion. He makes no compromise between right and wrong as he sees it. Principle is, to him, a thing beyond price. Today "Boston Blackie" would go, smilingly content, to a lifetime behind prison bars rather than dishonor the conscience that guides him.

And shall we judge him, you and I? When prompted to do so, inexorably there rises in my mind the picture of a man, grave faced and kindly, sitting cross-legged on the grass and making a rag doll with loving hands for a lost and homeless little child. It was Christ who said: "Suffer little children to come unto Me" and "Even as ye have done unto the least of these so even have ye done unto Me."

With these words before me I halt, leaving the verdict to God Himself.

JACK BOYLE.

March 1, 1919.

BOSTON BLACKIE

CHAPTER I

BOSTON BLACKIE!

BOSTON BLACKIE . . . in the archives of a hundred detective bureaus the name, invariably followed by a question mark, was pencilled after the records of unsolved safe-robberies of unequalled daring and skill.

The constantly recurring interrogation point was proof of the uncanny shrewdness and prevision of a crook who pitted his wits against those of organized society and gambled his all on the result of the game he played—for it was in the spirit of a man playing a vitally engrossing game against incalculable odds that Boston Blackie lived the life of crookdom. The question mark meant that the police suspected his guilt—even thought they knew it—but had no proof.

The name, Boston Blackie, was an anathema at the annual convention of police chiefs. The continually growing list of exploits attributed to him left them raging impotently at his incomparable audacity. He neither looked, worked nor lived as experience taught them a crook should. Traps innumerable had been laid for him without result. Always, it seemed, an intuitive foreknowledge of what the police would do guided him to safety. In short, Boston Blackie, safe-

9

cracker de luxe, was the great enigma of the harried, savagely incensed guardians of property rights.

Though detectives never guessed it, the secret of Boston Blackie's invulnerability lay in his mental attitude toward the law and those paid to uphold it. In his own mind he was not a criminal but a combatant. He had declared war upon Society and, if defeated, was ready to pay the penalty it inflicted. Undefeated, he felt the world could not hold a grudge against him. The laws of the statute books he discarded as mere "scraps of paper." He saw himself not as a law-breaker but as a law-upholder, for he lived under the rigid mandates of a crook-world code that he held more sacred than life itself. A guilty conscience proves the downfall of most prison inmates. Blackie, his conscience clear, played the game winningly with the zest of a school-boy and the joy of a gambler confidently risking great stakes.

Boston Blackie was no roystering cabaret habitue squandering the proceeds of his exploits in night-life dissipation. University trained and with a natural predilection for good literature, his pleasures were those of a gentleman of independent means with a mental trend toward the humanitarian problems of the day. His home was his place of recreation and in that home, sharing joyously the perils and pleasures of his strangely ordered life was Mary, his wife— Boston Blackie's Mary to the crook-world that looked up to them with unfeigned adulation as the chief exponents of its queerly warped creed.

Mary was Boston Blackie's best loved pal and sole confidant. She alone knew all he did and why, and, knowing, she joined in his exploits with the wholeheartedness of unquestioning love. Together they played; together they worked and always they were happy in good fortune or evil. A strange couple, so unusual in thought and life and habit that detectives, judging them by other crooks, were forever at sea.

Seated in their cozy apartment in San Francisco which for the time was their home Blackie suddenly dropped the current volume on mysticism which he had been reading and looked across the room to Mary, busy with an intricate piece of embroidery.

"We need a bit of excitement, Mary," he said with the unconcerned air of a husband about to suggest an evening at the theatre. "We'll take the Wilmerding jewel collection tonight."

"I'll drive your car myself if you're going out there," she answered with the faintest trace of womanly anxiety in her voice.

"Well, then, that's settled."

Boston Blackie resumed his reading and Mary her embroidery.

CHAPTER II

THE room was faintly illumined by the intermittent flame of a wood-fire slowly dying on the hearth of an open grate. The house was silent dark, seemingly deserted. Outside, the dripping San Francisco fog clung to everything in the heavy impenetrable folds that isolated the residence from its neighbors as though it stood alone in an otherwise empty world.

Inside the handsomely furnished living-room, and opposite the fire which now and then leaped up and cast his shadow in grotesque shapes against the ceiling, stood a man intently studying the paneled walls—a man with a white handkerchief masking his face and a coat that sagged under the weight of the gun slung ready for instant use beneath one of its lapels.

The man was Boston Blackie. Concealed behind the oaken panels he inspected so painstakingly was a safe in which lay the Wilmerding jewels—a famous collection.

For two generations San Franciscans had eyed them with envy. Handed down from mother to daughter they had played their part in the social warfare of the city of the Golden Gate for half a century. And Blackie was there to make them his own.

12

He ran acutely sensitive fingers—sandpapered until the blood showed redly below the skin—over the woodwork, seeking the hidden spring he knew was there—for an incautious servant's remark had traveled up through the underworld until it reached Blackie, the one in a thousand expert enough to use it. Quickly his questing fingers located the key panel, and the door rolled noiselessly back, disclosing a steel strong-box.

"Ah, neatly arranged!" murmured the safe-cracker in an inaudible and satisfied whisper as he stooped and gently turned the combination-knob. It revolved without perceptible sound, but science is an impartial ally —the ally of able crooks as well as of those who war upon them. Blackie laid a tiny metal disk against the combination. Wires led from it to a transmitter he hooked over his ear. Then he turned the dial-knob again slowly and with infinite care. The audion bulb within the transmitter—science's newest device for magnifying otherwise imperceptible sound—carried to his ear plainly the faint click of the tumblers within as the dial crossed the numbers of the combination that guarded the jewels. One by one he memorized them, slowly but surely reading the combination that, once his, would enable him to open the safe, take the gems, relock the strong-box and depart without leaving behind the slightest outward evidence that robbery had been done. The cracksman smiled contentedly as he worked. Already he reckoned the Wilmerding collection of jewels as his own.

A faint sound from behind caught his ear. He straightened quickly, dropped the audion bulb into his pocket and slid the panel noiselessly back into place.

"A step on the stair!" he whispered in sudden alarm. "And I was sure the house was empty except for the two servants asleep below-stairs—I counted them out one by one; and yet there's some one coming down from above. Coming down slowly, stealthily, too!"—as he heard a second cautious step. "Too bad! In another five minutes I'd have been gone."

He drew his mask higher over his face and stepped backward into the shadow of the drapery before the window he had prepared for a quick exit in an emergency. Then he waited, listening with every sense alert, every muscle rigid.

Again he heard the step, now close to the doorway. Then in the dim firelight a small tousled head appeared—the head of a little child who stood irresolute outside the room.

The boy—a mere baby of four—hesitated on the threshold of the dark room, evidently trying to summon courage to enter. The safe-cracker from his refuge saw and read a conflict between fear and determination in the wide eyes of the little intruder. For a full minute the child hung back; then suddenly with a low cry, half fearful, half courageous, he ran across the room to the window and tumbled straight into the arms of the safe-cracker, of whose presence he had no inkling.

Blackie, fearing an outcry, spoke quickly, sooth-
ingly, but the boy neither screamed nor cried. He
stared wonderingly for a moment into the kind eyes
that looked down into his, and then with a faint sigh
of relief involuntarily nestled closer in the protecting
arms that held him—a lonely, frightened child finding
comfort and consolation in the unexpected solace of
human companionship.

"Who is you?" lisped the little fellow, smiling con-
fidingly up into Blackie's perplexed face. Then with
suddenly increased interest: "You isn't Santy, is you?
No, you isn't Santy 'cause that on your face is a hanky,
not beards." He had reached up and given the par-
tially disarranged handkerchief mask a gentle, inquir-
ing tug.

Blackie smiled back at him.

"No, I'm not Santa Claus to-night, little man," he
said. "Who are you?"

"I'm Martin Wilmerding, Junior, and I'm four
years old," the boy said proudly.

"You are! Well, well! And where is your mamma
and your papa?"

"Papa's gone away, Mamma says, and Mamma's
gone to a party; and w'en Mamma was gone, then
Nursey went out too, and said she'd spank me if I
told. John and Emily is downstairs s'eeping, and
I woke up an' it was dark, and I was 'fraid—a little."

"So they've all traipsed off and left you alone for
me to entertain, have they!" said Blackie, his eyes
narrowing grimly as understanding of the situation

came to him. "But what were you coming, downstairs for? Looking for Mamma?"

"Oh, no—Mamma won't come for ever and ever so long. I was all alone and 'fraid, and I came down for Rex."

"Rex—who is he?" asked Blackie quickly.

"He's my doggie, my woolly doggie. See, here he is."

The boy squirmed out of Blackie's arms and pattered in bare feet to the window-seat, where he resurrected Rex from beneath a cushion. Then he hurried back to Boston Blackie and climbed to his lap with the toy dog clasped in his arms.

"Rex s'eeps upstairs with me," the child informed his new-found friend. "But to-night Nursey forgot him, an' I woked up an' 'membered where he was, an' it was so dark an' I wanted him so bad, so I comed downstairs for him. I isn't 'fraid when I has Rex, 'cause I can hold him close an' talk to him, an' then we bofe goes to s'eep. See, isn't he a dear little doggie?"

Unconsciously Boston Blackie's arms tightened around the soft little body nestling contentedly against his breast.

"You poor, abandoned little kiddie!" he said softly. "You poor little orphan! You're a little man, too, for it took real nerve to come down here after your pal Rex—far more nerve than I had to use to get in here."

"I likes you. You're a nice man," said the boy with

childish intuitive understanding that the man in whose arms he lay was a friend.

Blackie looked at his burden in puzzled indecision. He hadn't the heart to desert his new-found pal, and yet he was a safe-breaker in a strange house, with each passing minute doubling his risk. Even the sound of their voices, low-pitched though they were, was an imminent danger. The boy, quiet and content, cuddled close to him, hugging his precious woolly dog.

"Hadn't you better run back to bed, Martin?" said Blackie gently at last. "Nursey will be back soon, and she'll be cross if she finds you down here."

The child clutched the arms that sheltered him.

"Y-e-s," he admitted slowly. Then wistfully: "It's awful dark and quiet upstairs. If you come up and tuck me an' Rex in bed, we'll be good and go right to s'eep. P'ease."

"Of course I will," said the safe-cracker a bit huskily. "I'd do it if the whole house were full of coppers."

He rose with the boy still in his arms.

"You must show me the way, Martin," he said. "And we mustn't make any noise and wake John and Emily. Now we'll go."

They climbed the dark stairway together and, the child directing, came to the open door of a big deserted nursery. A little empty bed revealed the refuge from which Martin Wilmerding, Jr., had begun his perilous adventure in search of Rex and companionship. Blackie laid the boy down and covered him gently as a mother might have done.

"Good-night, little pal," he said. "I'm glad I happened to be here to-night."

The boy clutched his hand.

"P'ease stay and hold my hand," he pleaded. "I's going right to s'eep if you will. P'ease, 'cause it's awful dark."

Boston Blackie sat on the edge of the bed and took a tiny hand in his. The boy with a sigh of perfect contentment nestled snugly in downy comforts.

"Goo' night," he said drowsily.

"Good night, little pal," answered Blackie. Silence descended over the nursery as Blackie with aching throat waited hand in hand with the little Wilmerding heir, who was learning too soon that life's problems must be mastered alone and unaided.

Five minutes passed, and Blackie, looking down, saw the boy was fast asleep with baby lips parted in a peaceful smile, and Rex's fuzzy head tightly clasped to his breast. The safe-cracker gently withdrew his hand and smoothed the covers.

"Poor little chap!" he said. "Everything in the world that doesn't count and only one real friend—Rex. Poor, lonely little chap!"

The safe-cracker crept noiselessly down the stairs to the room that contained the purpose of his visit. The fire had died to a few glowing embers. Again he rolled back the paneled door and exposed the safe. Again he adjusted the audion bulb and began anew the task of deciphering the combination. And again with his work but half finished there came a startling interruption—a short and a long blast from an auto-horn that sounded from somewhere out in the fog.

"Mary's signal! Some one's coming," he reflected disgustedly. Quickly he drew a damp cloth from his pocket and mopped off the door of the safe and the woodwork to destroy the possibility of telltale finger-prints, then once more closed the panel. He drew back into the comparatively safe shelter of the win-dow-hangings, and waited.

"I'm going to have those jewels to-night if I have to stay here till morning," he murmured resolutely. "I wonder who this can be? The nurse who slipped out on her own business and left the poor little kiddie alone, I suppose."

The faint purr of a motor stopping before the house reached his ears.

"That doesn't sound like a nurse to me," he thought. "If it's the mother of that boy, she'll be here, likely enough, with all the lights on in a minute. Well, anyway, we'll wait and see what happens. The window's ready for a quick get-away, and all the coppers in town couldn't get me once I'm outside in this fog, with Mary and the machine ready. We haven't lost out yet."

The whir of the motor died, and voices sounded outside as steps ascended from the street.

"Two are coming—a man and a woman," mur-mured Blackie. "Matters are growing interesting."

The outer door opened and closed softly. In the darkness the safe-cracker sensed two dim forms in the doorway; then an electric button clicked, and the room was flooded with light. Blackie saw a brilliantly handsome woman, cloaked and in evening dress, and an equally handsome man similarly garbed. The woman let her wrap slip to the floor as she turned to her companion.

"What is it, Don?" she asked apprehensively. "What is troubling you so? Tell me."

"The same thing that always troubles me," he answered, stepping toward her and taking her hands in his. "My love for you, Marian!"

The man drew her closer to him gently but irresistibly, and his arm dropped to her slender waist.

"Your own heart tells you all that is in mine— it must," he added quickly. "Marian, dear, this torture must end to-night."

For a second, with his arm around her, she swayed toward him. Then slowly she released herself and drew away.

"Don't, Don, please!" she begged tremulously. "You know we agreed not to discuss things that— that can't be remedied. Is this all you had to tell me? Is this why you have brought me home now from the dance where at least we might have forgotten and been happy for an hour?"

Her face, as she looked up at him, was a strangely mingled contradiction. There was reproach in her voice; there were tenderness and regret in her eyes,

but behind them lay an instinctive womanly shrinking
from something to be feared.

"Yes," her companion said, studying her face, "that
is what I have come to tell you to-night: first that
I love you; then that I am going away. Marian, I
sail for Honolulu to-morrow morning on the *Manchuria.*"

"Oh, no, no!" the woman cried, springing to his
side and catching his arm in a movement imploringly
detaining. "Oh, Don, you wouldn't! You couldn't!
Tell me it isn't so. You say you—you—care; and
yet you would leave me to face an empty life here—
alone—in this house."

To Blackie, watching from within the window-
embrasure, the sweeping gesture of hate that accompanied her final word was as revealing as a diary.
It seemed to picture the luxurious home as a prison
in which love and a woman's illusions had slowly
stifled and died. It seemed the signed confession of
an unhappy and embittered wife. And also, in its
resentful recklessnes, the gesture explained the man
she called "Don"—the man who now gently drew her
into his arms and tilted her head till she faced him
squarely.

"It is true that I am leaving on the *Manchuria,*" he
said, "but it is not true that I am leaving you. Because"—as she stared up at him in breathless wonder
—"Marian, dear, you are going with me."

A slowly rising flush colored her white cheeks, and
for just a second her eyes answered the fire and ten-

derness in his. Then she laid trembling hands against
his breast and slowly pushed him away as she bowed
her head.

"It can't be, Don," she said, speaking so low the
man stooped to hear her. "What you ask is impossible. I can never do that—never."

"And why not?" he answered. "Is it because of
what our friends here will say? That for them and
their gossip!"—snapping his fingers. "For a week
idle tongues will buzz over teacups and cocktail
glasses. Well, let them. You and I will not be there
to hear. We will be together far out on the Pacific
under a warm sun and a blue sky, with heartache
forever dead and buried beyond the horizon, and a
lifetime of perfect happiness rising before us as you
see the islands rise out of the sea. Hawaii is a beautiful land, dearest—a land that has no yesterdays.
Are we to miss all that awaits us there, all that makes
life worth living, because we fear chattering tongues
two thousand miles behind us? No! Dear one, we
must both sail on the *Manchuria.*"

He stopped, seeking a glimpse of her averted face.

"Why must you go?" she asked, her head still
bowed.

"There is serious labor-trouble on the sugar planta-
tion. Michaels cabled me this afternoon. It is absolutely imperative for me to return at once, and the
Manchuria to-morrow morning is the only steamer
this month. I have taken passage, and I can't—I
won't—leave you behind. Will you go, Marian?"

Slowly she shook her head.

"This, then, is the end, Don," she said. "You know I can't go and you know, too,"—her voice now was bitterly resentful,—"that life will be a hideously empty thing to me after the *Manchuria* sails in the morning. But I can't go. I am tied here with bonds that can't be broken—by me."

"Do you mean that, Marian?"

She hesitated and brushed a hand quickly across her eyes—then nodded silently.

"If you do," he continued, betraying the bitterness of his disappointment, "it proves one of two things. Either you are a coward afraid to risk a momentary sacrifice to buy a lifetime of happiness, or deep in your heart you still love your husband. Which is it? Do you care for Wilmerding? Has my love been no more than a toy to amuse you in idle hours?"

"How can you ask that, Don?" she answered quickly. "You know it hasn't; and as for my husband—" She stopped and stood staring down into the fire, her face altering with each of many swiftly changing emotions.

At last she looked up and into the eyes of the man beside her.

"I did love Martin Wilmerding once," she said. "Sometimes I have thought that if the past two years could be blotted out,—forgotten,—I might love him again even yet; but now, to-day, to-night, I do not love him. That is my answer, Don Lavalle. To-night I do not love him."

"How long has it been since you thought you might care for him again?" Lavalle demanded jealously.

"Since you came into my life and taught me to care for you."

He stooped over her eagerly.

"You tell me that, and expect me to leave you here!" he whispered. "Never! In saying you love me, you have decided. Come, Marian, come."

For a second their eyes met. His were eager, ardent, passionately tender. To a woman grown reckless through neglect, they pleaded his cause better than words. She crouched by the vanishing fire, weighing her problem. Behind her Lavalle, intuitively avoiding speech, awaited her verdict. From his hiding-place Boston Blackie watched, forgetful for the moment of why he was there.

Minutes passed—minutes in which Marian Wilmerding, choosing her future at diverging crossroads, relived her life.

The years behind her flitted one by one through her mind—years she saw as a nightmare of steadily growing disillusionment. She had loved big, handsome, debonair Martin Wilmerding when they were married. As a suitor he had stood out alone among the many men who had asked her hand. They had been very happy at first, were still happy when their boy was born. When and how had the present gulf between them grown? Memory told her. It had begun when she found the romance-haloed suitor she had married, slowly altering into a husband who regarded her love as an irrevocably given possession requiring neither attention nor the refreshing nourishment of tender response.   Time widened the breach. She had been morose, petulant; he had not understood and had withdrawn more and more into a cycle of interests in which she had no share.   She, hiding her wound, retaliated by plunging into the feverish gayety of ultra-smart society.   For many months they had lived as strangers, never meeting except occasionally at dinner.

And now she was facing the inevitable result—listening to the plea of a man for whom she had confessed her love, urging her to leave home and husband.   What was the answer?

CHAPTER III

HER throat tightened in an aching pain as her eye fell on the thin gold band that encircled a slender finger. Martin Wilmerding had stooped to kiss that hand and ring on the day it first was placed there.

"Dear little wife," he had said, "that ring is the symbol of a bond that never will be broken by me. Throughout all the years before us, whenever I see it, this hour will return, bringing back all the love and devotion that is in my heart now."

Recollection of the long-forgotten words swept her with a sudden revulsion of feeling, and she sprang to her feet. In that instant she realized for the first time why she had come to love Don Lavalle. It was because in his fresh, ardent, impulsive devotion he was so like the Martin Wilmerding who had kissed her hand and ring with a vow of lifetime fealty that had left her clinging to him in tearful ecstasy.

"Don," she said, "if you really love me, go—now, now."

Lavalle's arms, eagerly outstretched toward her, dropped to his side. It was not the answer he had awaited so confidently. A vague resentment against her tinged his disappointment with new bitterness.

26

"That is final, is it, Marian?" he asked.

"Yes, yes. Don't make it harder for me. Please go," she cried almost hysterically.

He slipped into his overcoat.

"Perhaps you will tell me why," he suggested with increasing asperity.

"Because of the boy and this," the woman said brokenly, laying a finger on her wedding-ring.

"Nonsense," he cried angrily. "What tie does that ring represent that Martin Wilmerding has not violated a hundred times? You have been faithful to it, we know, even though you admit you care for me. But has he? I have not the pleasure of your husband's acquaintance, but no man ever neglected a wife like you without a reason."

"Go, please, quickly," she pleaded, shivering.

"I will," he said, instinctively avoiding the blunder of combating her decision with argument.

He caught her in his arms, and stooping quickly, kissed her on the lips. She reeled away from him, sobbing.

"Our first and last kiss. Good-by, Marian," he said gently, and left the room.

She followed, clutching at the walls for support as she watched him from the doorway. He adjusted his muffler and caught up his hat without a backward glance, and she pressed her two hands to her lips to choke back a cry. Then as he opened the outer door, the crushing misery of her loneliness swept over her, overpowering self-restraint and resolution.

"Don, oh, Don!" she pleaded, stumbling toward him with outstretched arms.

In a second he was at her side, and she was crying against his breast.

"I can't let you go," she sobbed. "I tried, but I can't. Take me, Don. I will do as you wish."

From his hiding-place Blackie saw them re-enter the room. The woman stopped by the fireplace, drew off her wedding-ring and after holding it a second between shaking fingers, dropped it into the ashes.

"Dead and gone!" she said. "Dead as the love of the man who put it on my finger."

"My ring will replace it," said Lavalle tenderly, but with triumph in his eyes. "Wilmerding will want a divorce. He shall have it, and then you'll wear the wedding-ring of the man who loves you and whom you love—the only ring in the world that shouldn't be broken."

"Don, promise me that you will never leave me alone," she pleaded falteringly. "I don't ever want a chance to think, to reflect, to regret. I only want to be with you—and forget everything else in the world. Promise me."

"Love like mine knows no such word as separation," he answered. "From this hour we will never be apart. Don't fear regrets, Marian. There will be none."

"My boy," she suggested, "he will go with us. Poor little Martin! I wouldn't leave him behind fatherless and motherless."

"Of course not," he agreed. "And now you must get a few necessaries together quickly—just the things you will require on the steamer. You can get all you need when we reach Honolulu, but there is no time for anything now, for under the circumstances it is best that we go aboard the steamer before morning. Can you be ready in an hour?"

"In an hour!" she cried in surprise. "Yes, I can, but—but—how can we go aboard the steamer to-night? We can't, Don. Your passage is booked, but not mine."

"My passage is booked for Don Lavalle and wife," he informed her smilingly.

She turned away her head to hide the flush that colored her face.

"You were so sure as that!" she murmured, with a strangely new sense of disappointment.

"Yes," Lavalle answered, "for I knew love like mine could not fail to win yours. Will you pack a single trunk while I run back to my hotel and get my own things together? I can be back in an hour or less. Will you be ready?"

"Yes, I will be ready," she promised wearily. "I will only take a few things. I want nothing that my—husband ever gave me. I shall only take a few of my own things and the jewels in the safe that were in Mother's collection. They are my own, and they're very valuable, Don. It will not be safe to risk packing them in my baggage. I'll get them now and give them to you to keep until we can leave

them in the purser's safe to-morrow. Be very careful of them, Don. They couldn't be replaced for a
fortune."

Boston Blackie saw her hurry to the wall—saw the
sliding door roll back; with a quickly indrawn breath,
he watched the woman fumble nervously with the
combination-dial. The safe-door swung open, and she
rapidly sorted out a half-dozen jewel-cases and re-
closed the safe.

"Here they are, Don," she said, handing the gems
to Lavalle. "I have taken only those that came from
my own people. And now you must leave me. I must
pack, and I can't call the servants under these circumstances. I must get the boy up and ready; and
also,"—she hesitated a second and then added,—"I
must write a note to Mr. Wilmerding telling him
what I have done and why."

"Don't mail it until we are at the dock," warned
the man. "Where is he—at his club or out of town?"

"He's at the Del Monte Hotel near Monterey—or
was," she answered. "The letter won't reach him
till to-morrow night."

"And to-morrow night we will be far out of sight
of land," Lavelle cried. "That is as it should be. I
am glad I never met him, for now I need never do
so."

He stuffed the jewel-cases into his overcoat.

"I'll be back in my car in an hour," he warned.
"Hurry, Marian, my love. Each minute until I am
with you again will be a day."

He caught up his hat and ran down the steps to the street, where his car stood at the curbstone.

As the door closed behind him, Marian Wilmerding sank into a chair and clutched her throat to stifle choking sobs. Intuitive womanly fear of what she was to do paralyzed her. For many minutes she lay shaking convulsively as she tried to overcome the dread that chilled her heart. Then the dismal atmosphere of the masterless home began to oppress her with a sense of wretched loneliness.

She rose and with hard, reckless eyes shining hotly from behind wet lashes, ran upstairs to pack.

As Donald Lavalle threw open the door of his empty car, a man who had slipped behind him around the corner of the Wilmerding residence stepped to his side.

"I'm sorry to have to trouble you for my wife's jewels, Lavalle," he said.

The triumphant smile on Lavalle's face faded, and he shrank back in speechless consternation.

"Your wife's jewels!" he ejaculated, trying to recover from the shock of the utterly unexpected interruption. "You are—"

"Yes, I am Martin Wilmerding; and the happy chance that brought me home to-night also gave me the pleasure of listening from the window-seat of the living-room to your interesting tete-a-tete with my wife."

A gun flashed into Boston Blackie's hand and was jabbed sharply into Lavalle's ribs.

"Give me Marian's jewels," the pseudo-husband cried. "Hand them over before I blow your heart out. That's what I ought to do—and I may, anyway."

Lavalle handed over the cases that contained the Wilmerding collection of gems.

"Now," continued his captor, "I want a word with you."

A gun was thrust so savagely into Lavalle's face that it left a long red bruise.

"I have heard all you said to-night. I know all your plans for stealing away my wife," the inexorable voice continued, "and I've just a word of warning for you. You are dealing with a man, not a woman, from now on; and if you phone, write, telegraph or ever again communicate in any way with Marian, I'll blow your worthless brains out if I have to follow you round the world to do it. Do you get that, Mr. Don Lavalle?"

"I understand you," said Lavalle helplessly.

Again the gun-muzzle bruised the flesh of his cheek.

"And as a last and kindly warning, Lavalle," Blackie continued, "I suggest that you take extreme precautions to see that you do not miss the *Manchuria* when she sails in the morning; because if you are not on board, you won't live to see another sunset if I have to kill you in your own club. Will you sail or die?"

"I'll sail," said Lavalle.

"Very well. That's about all that requires words between us, I believe. Go, and remember your life is in your own hands. One word of any kind to Marian, and you forfeit it. I don't know why I don't kill you now. I would if it were not for the scandal all this would cause when it came out before the jury that would acquit me. Now go."

Lavalle pressed the button that started the motor as Boston Blackie stepped back from his side.

"I've just one word I want to say to you, Wilmerding," Lavalle began, his foot on the clutch. "It's this: You have only yourself to blame. Don't accuse Marian. You forced her into the situation you discovered this evening, by your neglect of the finest little woman I ever met. I was forced into it by a love I admit frankly. Don't blame Marian for what you yourself have caused. I won't ever see or communicate with her again."

"That's the most decent speech I've heard from your lips to-night," said the man beside the car, dropping his gun back into an outside pocket. "I don't blame her. I've learned many important facts to-night—one of which is that the right place for a man is in his own home with his own wife. I'm going to remember that; and the wedding-ring that was dropped into the ashes to-night is going back on the finger it fits. Good night."

Lavalle without a word threw in the clutch, and his car sped away and was enveloped and hidden by the fog.

Halfway down the block, Boston Blackie came to another car standing at the curb with a well-muffled chauffeur sitting behind the wheel. As he climbed in, the driver, Mary, uttered a low, thankful cry.

"No trouble. I have the jewels here—feel the packages; and a whole lot happened," said Blackie with deep satisfaction. "I've a new story to tell you when we get home, Mary. It's the story of a big burglar named Blackie and a little boy named Martin Wilmerding and a still littler woolly dog named Rex, and a woman who guessed wrong. I think it will interest you. Let's go. I have several things to do before we go home."

When they reached the downtown district, Blackie had Mary drive him to the Palace Hotel. There he sought out the night stenographer.

"Will you take a telegram for me, please," he said. Then he dictated:

" 'To Martin Wilmerding, Del Monte Hotel, Monterey:

" 'The boy needs you. I do too. Please come.
                                          "MARIAN.' "

Though there was a telegraph-office in the hotel, he summoned a messenger-boy from a saloon and sent the message.

Then he went to another hotel and found a second stenographer, to whom he dictated a second message.

" 'Mrs. Marian Wilmerding, 3420 Broadway, San Francisco:

" 'The packages you gave me were what I really

wanted.   Thank you and good-by.

"D. L.' "

Summoning another boy, he sent the second message from a different telegraph office.

"Those telegrams, and how they came to be sent,
will be a mystery in the Wilmerding home to the end
of time," he thought, deeply contented.

"Let's go home, Mary," he said then, returning to
his car and climbing in.   "I think I've finished
my night's work, and I don't believe I've done such
a bad job either."

He was silent for a moment.

"I've given a wife to a husband," he said half to
himself.   "I've given a father to a child; I've given
a mother the right to look her son in the face without
shame; and I've played square with the gamest little
pal I ever want to know, Martin Wilmerding, Jr.,
and his dog, Rex.   And for my pay I've taken the
Wilmerding jewel-collection.   I wonder who's the
debtor."

CHAPTER IV

BOSTON BLACKIE dropped the paper he had been reading, a satisfied smile lighting his face. Two months had elapsed since the evening, still treasured in his memory, on which he had met and comforted his "little pal" at the Wilmerding home. And now in the daily column of society notes he read "Mr. and Mrs. Martin Wilmerding, accompanied by their son are leaving the city for a month at their country home in Monterey County."

"It succeeded," he cried joyously to himself. "It couldn't help it—not with a boy like that drawing them together. I wish Mary were back. This news will make her even happier than it has me."

Impatiently he began to pace the floor, visions of a tiny youngster in nightclothes and with a woolly dog, filling his mind as he waited for his wife. A step sounded in the corridor.

"Mary at last!" exclaimed Blackie in tones caressingly tender.

Then his ear caught the sound of a second light step on the stairway. He listened with every faculty strained and abnormally alert. His hand, which instinctively, at the sound of the strange footfall, had sought the revolver which lay nearby, let the gun slip back to its place.

36

"A woman with her," he added. "Strange! But she comes for a good reason, if she comes with Mary."

He rose and unbarred the door at the light, distinctive rap of the elect among crooks. Mary threw herself into his arms and clung to him, sobbing. Behind her entered a second woman, with the face and figure of a young girl, but with eyes old and tired and world-weary from heartache and suffering. She too was weeping, but quietly, hopelessly, as women who love do for their dead. Blackie recognized her at once.

"Why, it's little Miss Happy!" he exclaimed, using the name with which crookdom had rechristened her when she was first introduced to its circles by the Cushions Kid, youthful pal of Blackie in bygone days. "What's wrong, little girl? What's happened to the Kid?"

The girl covered her face with tiny hands, frail and thin and almost transparent, and sobbed silently. Mary released one arm from Blackie and encircled the thin shoulders that seemed so pitifully childish for the burden of grief they bore. The girl's head fell on Mary's shoulder.

"Oh, Blackie," cried Mary, "the Cushions Kid is in Folsom Prison, and he's sentenced to—to—" Her lips failed as she strove to speak the dreaded words.

The other girl raised her head and laid her hand on Boston Blackie's arm.

"The Kid's sentenced to be hanged, Blackie," she

said, forcing out the words slowly, one by one, as
though each tore her heart. "Only fourteen days
left, Blackie. Only fourteen little days! Oh!" Her
voice rose as self-restraint snapped. "Day and night
I see him standing on the trap, bound and helpless. I see the black cap sliding down over his dear
face. I see—the—the" She covered her eyes as
though thus she could shut out the picture imagination seared on her brain.

"I love him so, Blackie. I love him so," she
moaned. "You won't let them kill him. You'll save
him for me, won't you, Blackie?"

Her blind confidence in the power of a hunted
crook to wrest her lover from the hand of the law
was as a little child's belief in the omnipotence of a
father.

"Make her some coffee, Mary," he said, "and
you're going to lie here and tell me all about it. You
look terribly sick, child."

"I've been starving myself. I needed every dollar
I could make for the Kid's mouthpieces" (lawyers).
"Every day they wanted more jack, more jack, more
jack" (money), "and there was no one but me to
make it. The Kid's pal turned out a rat, you see."

Boston Blackie raised himself and stared at the girl,
his eyes aglow with admiration. He had felt the
agonizing torture she had chosen to endure for the
sake of a love that knew no higher law than sacrifice
and service.

"Game little girl!" he muttered. "The worst

of us see the day when we thank God for our women.
Tell me about the Kid's fall, Happy," he added
aloud. "Why wasn't it in the papers?"

"It was. They were full of it, but he called himself Jimmy Grimes, and the coppers never made him.
They don't know who he is yet. It was the express-
car robbery on the overland rattler at Sacramento.
The messenger was killed. But Blackie, the Kid
didn't do it. He wasn't even in the car, though he
was in on the job. Whispering Malone bumped the
messenger and tossed the package and jack and
jewels to the Kid, who was waiting for them at the
river bridge. They got the Kid at the hop-joint that
night with the stuff still on him. Malone blew, after
the pinch—the yellow-hearted rat! And now the
Kid's up at the Big House with a death-sentence that
isn't coming to him because he's too right to snitch
even on a rat."

The girl lifted herself on her elbow and raised one
frail hand as though taking an oath.

"So help me God," she cried, "I'd go straight to
the coppers and tell them who killed that messenger,
I'd tell them how the job was pulled, I'd tell them
everything,—enough to put Whispering Malone
where my poor boy is now,—but if I did, the Kid
would quit me. You know he would, Blackie. That's
all that stops me. You may say I'm a copper at
heart, but I can't help it. I would! I would!" The
girl's voice rose as emotion mastered her.

"But I can't," she added with a hopeless gesture

and dropped back on the couch, whimpering like an animal wounded by the jaws of a trap. Blackie laid a comforting hand on her thin arm.

"You haven't a wrong drop of blood in you, child," he said gently. "You wouldn't snitch to the coppers, no matter whose life depended on it. We men who play the crooked game must pay some day, and while we pay behind bars, our women suffer, like you, outside them. It doesn't seem right, but it's true. It's part of the price of loving men like us—like me or the Kid—who—"

"Stop," interrupted the girl. "Don't say that. The only happiness I ever had was with the Kid. The only happiness I ever want is his love. Do you think that if I could, I'd forget what we've been to each other? I suffer, because I'm afraid for him. It's thinking what these terrible days and nights must be to him that—that drives me wild.

"You can imagine what it is to count the days, the hours, the minutes, of life that are left you—to face them alone and helpless like a trapped rat. I see him led from the death-cell young, strong and full of life, and then in just one little minute, lying white and cold and—and—"

The girl sprang suddenly to her feet, wringing her hands.

"They must not; they shall not," she cried. She dropped on her knees and held out two fragile arms, imploring Divine mercy.

"Merciful God, help us now," she prayed. "Don't

let him die. He is so young, and you know he didn't kill the messenger. He was so good to me. He never, never betrayed a friend. O God, it isn't right that he should die for Whispering Malone. The time left is so very, very short. Please, please, O God, help Boston Blackie to save him. Amen!"

Mary was on her knees as little Miss Happy finished. Boston Blackie's head was bowed. The girl, still kneeling with arms imploringly outstretched and tears streaming down her face, strained her eyes upward as though to speed her prayer to its destination. The intense, unmistakable sincerity in the plea that came from the overburdened heart of the child-woman—a wife in fact but not in name—seemed to chasten and sanctify the air of the room and the hearts of the trio within it.

Vividly Blackie pictured the Cushions Kid, still a boy in the first days they had been together. Chicago, Denver—a dozen places flashed to his mind where they had pulled off jobs—Blackie, the master, and the Kid his protegee—and then that night in K. C. where the Kid had risked everything for him.

What he was Blackie had made him. Every trick and stall was Blackie's own. Love akin to a father's was in his heart for him. The Kid was "right."

Boston Blackie, husky under the stress of the feeling Happy had fanned into a flame of determination, broke the silence.

"What have the lawyers done?" he asked. "Have they been to the Governor for a commutation?"

"The appeal was denied long ago. They have just come back from the capitol. It took my last two hundred dollars to send them. The Governor refused to interfere unless we show the Kid is innocent and turn up the right man. Boss Tom Creedon turned us down, too. You're the last hope, Blackie. The mouthpiece is through."

The girl searched the man's face for some sign that would stimulate into new life the hope that her love would not let die.

"I suppose you had to raise the money for the trial, too," Blackie said. "How did you do it, Happy?"

The girl looked into his questioning eyes frankly.

"I'm working at the Spider's dance-hall," she said without embarrassment, though no place bore a more unsavory reputation. "I dress like a school-kid and sell more drinks than any two of the girls. No,"— in answer to the query in his eyes,—"I'm not like the rest of the girls. I promised the Kid I wouldn't be. I went to the Spider's joint as a last resort when the lawyers said they'd quit the appeal if I didn't raise money. I'd been filling in as a stall for Red-Eye, Costigan's gun-mob, but they're a cheap, worthless lot—not our kind, Blackie—and my bit wasn't enough to keep the lawyers going. So I went to the dance-hall. There was nothing else to do. I had to have money to fight the Kid's case."

"Poor, brave little woman!" said Mary, putting an arm protectingly around the girl and kissing her gently. "I know what you have gone through, dear."

"I stood it better at first, when I knew that every time I sold a drink or begged luck-money after a dance I was earning a dollar that might save the Kid," she said. "Lately, since the mouthpieces told me they don't see any hope, it has been worse than hell itself. Mary, Blackie, I've sat there pretending to drink with strangers while the picture of my boy in the death-house blinded me. I've laughed and joked while I counted how many hours, how many minutes, even, are left him. I've danced with men, knowing each step was cutting my poor boy's life another second shorter. Ugh!" she shuddered, "how I hated the touch of their hands, the look in their eyes, the words on their lips. I hated the music; I hated the crowds; I hated the lights and the laughter, for always I could see the Kid lying alone in the dark, waiting, waiting, waiting! But I laughed with the rest, for the lawyers wanted dough, and it takes a laughing face to get the money at Spider's."

Boston Blackie, without a word, rose from the pallet and switched on the lights.

"How much money have we, Mary?" he asked.

Mary, whose face was white and drawn, delved into a trunk and handed him a big roll of bills. It was the money which meant escape from all the dangers that threatened them. Blackie counted it; then he divided it into two piles.

"That's for you, Mary, in case anything happens to me—in case I don't come back," he said indicating

the smaller package of bills. He stuffed the larger
roll inside the breast of his soft shirt. "This I'll
'take with me. Money is the right kind of ammunition for a job like this, and there's eight thousand
dollars here. It's enough."

He slipped the revolver on the table inside the
waistband of his trousers. He took a second gun in
a holster from a desk drawer and slung it under
his left armpit. Then he turned to little Miss Happy
and with gentle hands laid on her shoulders stilled the
convulsive shudders that shook her body.

"You stay here with Mary," he commanded.
"You've done your bit for the Kid, little woman.
No more of the Spider's for you. Everything a man
can do for him is going to be done—providing the
coppers don't get me first. Don't despair, and don't
hope—too much. Just pray as you did a moment
ago. I'll be at Folsom by noon to-morrow."

Mary slipped to his side and clung to him. He
looked into her face and kissed her gently, as though
in renunciation.

"I'm sorry, dear one," he whispered. "Happiness
seemed our very own this morning. Now—who
knows? But you know I must go. You know I must
try even if I fail."

"Yes, yes, go. I want you to, dear. I knew you
would, when I brought her here. There is no other
way. But oh, my dearest, why is life so very, very
cruel and hard? Blackie, I am only a woman."
There was no break in Mary's voice, no tears in her

eyes. Instead, in them Blackie saw and recognized the same spirit of willing sacrifice with which women sent their men to the trenches "somewhere in France" and watched them go with smiling lips, brave eyes—and breaking hearts.

Blackie stooped and kissed her.

"You see now, dear," he said with deep conviction, "why I felt held here. Now we understand why." Once more he kissed her; then with a cheery word to Happy he was gone.

Mary covered her face and choked back a sob as the door closed. Happy knelt beside her, and the two women clung together, united by misery, for each knew the life of the man she loved was at stake now.

"If all men were like Blackie, there wouldn't be any like him," Happy cried; and paradoxical as it sounds, that was precisely what she meant.

CHAPTER V

FOLSOM PRISON is tucked away in an isolated nook in the lower foothills of the Sierra Nevadas. The prison is built on a small, level plain, barren, brown and treeless, that lies in the shelter of a semi-circle of hills. The gray, squatty buildings are a bleak and unlovely blot on the scenic grandeur that surrounds them.

Behind the prison flows the American River between low, sandy banks. On the other three sides, dotted every hundred yards by watchtowers manned by gun-guards, stretches a broad, glaring white line. It is the dead-line of the prison, for Folsom has no walls and needs none. Within that line men in stripes pray or curse as they choose, while they work out the stunted measure of life that the law has left them. To step beyond the line—even one step beyond it—is death, for the guards in the towers are ordered to ask no questions, to wait for no explanations, to shoot to kill. Many times, on turbulent prison-days, they have obeyed that order with unerring aim. Convicts call the dead-line the River Styx.

From the second-story window of one of the buildings in the prison inclosure a man looked out through barred windows toward the far-away mountains

46

whose snowy peaks glistened and gleamed in the rays of a setting sun. His face was young and boyish, but his eyes were hard, desperate and aged, for he was counting the sunsets that still remained to him— just six. Early in the gray dawn of the seventh day before the sun peeped over the mountains now before his eyes, his life was to be blotted out.

Through the partitions in the death-house the sound of hammering reached his ears. He shuddered and gripped the window-bars more tightly in spite of the years of training that had taught him that there is no dishonor for such as he but weakness and a babbling tongue. He knew the hammers were building the scaffold on which he would stand for a few brief seconds before a sea of morbid, curious enemy faces, until the world ended in sudden blackness. He hoped they would be quick, mercifully quick, when the final moment came, for he wished to die with a smile and a jest on his lips, according to the tradition of his kind.

He looked at his hands and moved them. He touched his eyes, his lips and pressed a hand over his heart to feel it beat. Hands, eyes, lips were all a part of him now, and responsive to his will. In six days, they would all be dead clay responsive to nothing. And what of the will that controlled them now, that consciousness of self, that awing individuality called "I" that has its home in the innermost recesses of the brain? Would it too be merely a thing dead and done? Or—

The snap of bolts turning in heavy locks and the clang of a door in the corridor dragged the mind of the prisoner back to the present. The door of the cell was unlocked, and a guard stepped in, followed by a convict carrying a tray covered with a newspaper. The Cushions Kid swept a pile of magazines from the one small table, and the convict set the food down. The latter looked toward the condemned man, caught his eye and then, with his back toward the guard, who stood within three feet of them, spoke rapidly in the prison language that makes no sound.

"Stiff" (letter) "in orange," he said. "Key in newspaper, page four, column four." The man laid his hand on the paper that covered the dishes and raised it as if to see whether he had slopped the food about in carrying it. "Page four, column four," he repeated. Then he turned and went out. The guard followed him and shot the lock in the cell door.

The instant the clanging corridor door informed him he was alone, the Cushions Kid picked up the orange that lay on the dinner-tray and examined it with eager eyes. It was not until he had gone over the entire surface inch by inch that he discovered a circle in the skin outlined by an all but imperceptible knife-mark. He pried out the inside of the circle and found inside the orange a pellet of paper protected by tinfoil. In case of unexpected interruption, he cut up the orange to destroy any evidence it had been tampered with, and smoothed out the paper, his heart beating high with hope of he knew not what.

The writing was not Happy's, as he had hoped; it was Boston Blackie's. He recognized the well-remembered chirography at once. This was what he read:

Cigarettes have often saved men's lives, though physicians declare the ash from the burned paper is injurious to the health, as it forms a black deposit on lung-tissue or anything else it touches. This easily can be proved.

That was all. There was no signature to the cryptic message, but it needed none.

"Boston Blackie is framing something for me," the Kid thought, trembling like a child in the wild joy of new-born hope. "With the old chief outside, there's a chance, even for me."

He scraped the dinner into his slop-bucket. He couldn't eat, but to avoid possible suspicion, it was necessary to get rid of it.

"Now we'll see what's what," he said.

Once more assuring himself that he was alone in the death-house, he picked up the newspaper that had covered the food. He turned to the fourth column of the fourth page. It was a column of society notes. Peeling off several of a packet of cigarette papers, the Cushions Kid touched them with a match and watched them burn to curling crisps of charred ash. He spread the note on the table before him and poured the ashes of the paper on it.

"We'll see what cigarette-papers do to the lungs, Blackie, old pal," he said, rubbing the ash lightly into the paper. Nothing appeared but a gray smudge.

Smiling like a schoolboy bent on mischief, the Kid turned the note over.

"Maybe it's the back of the lungs and letter that are affected by burned cigarette-papers," he said to himself as he repeated the operation.

His guess was right. As his finger-tips gently spread the black ash over the paper, characters outlined in black began to appear.

"Perfectly scandalous what cigarette-papers do to a man's lungs, ain't it, Blackie?" he whispered as he worked the ash evenly over the page until its entire surface was a dirty gray on which, outlined in pure black, were long rows of figures. They had been written with oxalic acid mixed with milk, and were absolutely invisible until the fine ash of the paper adhered and turned them black. When the Kid's work was done, the first line of Blackie's message looked like this:

2-6, 8-4, 6-1, 6-1, 10-1—9-4, 2-1, 3-5, 5-3, 4-2—
11-1, 7-3, 20-8, 2-1.

Burning with impatience, the boy turned to the designated column of the paper. The first of Blackie's line of figures was "2-6." The sixth letter of the second word in the column of type was *h*. The Kid jotted it down beneath the figures. Next was "8-4." That proved to be an *a*. The "6-1" repeated proved a double *p*. Then came *y*.

"Happy," repeated the Kid, working in an agony of fear. The next word was "sends."

"Thank God, she's all right," he breathed with

quick relief. "Ah—'love!' 'Happy sends love.' Dear, dear little girl! Right and true always! And good, thoughtful old Blackie, to guess that even now that's what I'd want to know first."

He worked on, slowly turning the tiny lines of figures into letters and words. As the words became sentences, his breath came in quick, strained gasps, for Blackie's message outlined a plan of escape that could scarcely fail, barring mishaps.

The Cushions Kid was told that on the following night he would find a ball of black thread in the banana that would be served with his dinner. He was to weight the end of the thread and lower it from the window of the death-cell after dark. At midnight the convict runner who delivered hot coffee to the watch-tower guards would tie a cord to the slender invisible thread, and at the end of the cord there would be a package containing a revolver, a gimlet, a fuse and caps and a bottle of nitroglycerin. Raising the cord with his thread, the Kid could pull up this precious package and find himself armed and provided with enough explosive to blow out the window-casement of the death-cell.

With this avenue to freedom open, the drop to the ground would be simple and safe, for in the midnight coffee served the guards on the night set for the escape, there would be enough chloral hydrate to leave them safely unconscious for many hours. The Kid was not to try to cross the quarter-mile of open ground between the death-house and the river, for there was no way of disposing of the night captain and the extra guards in the executive offices. Instead, he was to dodge to the end of the death-house, where a steel grating usually padlocked covered an airhole into the prison sewer, which led direct to the river and was sufficiently large to permit a man to crawl through it. In place of the iron padlock he would find a painted wooden one. Through that sewer the Kid was to go to its mouth on the river, where Boston Blackie would be waiting, with the huge steel bars that guarded the exit already open for him.

The rest should be easy. They had then only to let the current of the river carry them down as far as the railway bridge, where a track velocipede commandeered from the Folsom section-house would be hidden to carry them over the twenty miles of rails to Brighton, the railway junction, from which there was a freight before daylight that, if all went well, they would ride to the city of Stockton and safety.

The plan was flawless. As he comprehended in its entirety the road to freedom that was opened to him, the Cushions Kid realized what fearful risks had been undertaken in his behalf. He wondered how Blackie had managed to smuggle the gun and liquid dynamite and chloral into the prison. He wondered how he had dared even to visit the prison, for it was apparent he had visited it and secured co-operation from the inside.

If he had known that as Blackie in a miner's garb

sat in the prison visiting-room three days before, he had looked straight at a glaring poster which contained his likeness and an offer of a thousand dollars reward for his arrest, the Cushions Kid would have had some idea of the peril which Blackie had faced. If he had seen Blackie in the presence of a guard talking commonplaces to a convict, interspersed by inaudible instructions in the lip language—the Kid would have had an even clearer idea of what the risks had been. Louisiana had undertaken the task of arranging all details inside the prison—undertaken it without a second's hesitation, though he knew well he was risking a frightful punishment and additional years of servitude for a man he had never seen. That he was Blackie's friend, however, was enough.

Smuggling the arms and explosive into the prison had been a delicate and dangerous task. Waiting until the guards present at this interview with Louisiana were off watch, Blackie had re-entered the prison with a crowd of sight-seers. There had been a crucial moment of danger when the guard, before admitting the party, made a perfunctory search of the men for weapons. Had he found the package slung under Blackie's left arm the adventure would have culminated then and there in swift disaster. But the guard didn't find the package.

A half-hour later, as the party passed through the great, noisy, dusty rock-quarry of the prison, Blackie lagged behind, picking up and examining pieces of rock as the miner he seemed to be might be expected to do. One bowlder was marked, not by chance, with a drilling hammer standing upright. Blackie, stooping behind that rock, in one swift motion transferred the package from beneath his arm to an excavation beneath the bowlder and kicked a stone—not there by chance either—into the opening to conceal the contraband. That night in the comparative safety of Louisiana Slim's cell were hidden the gun and nitroglycerine ("soup," the safe-blowers term it) that was to free the condemned man—also chloral for the guards' coffee and a bunch of skeleton keys to release the padlock that barred the sewer-entrance.

Louisiana and his partner, who had carried the package in from the quarry at a risk of which they were well aware, fondled the weapons that opened the way to possible escape with a longing inconceivable to any but men with many long years of imprisonment before them. The gun, the explosive, the keys, the "keeler" for the guards in the tower, were in their hands and pointed the way to escape for themselves. Freedom beckoned and was within easy reach.

Louisiana Slim and his cell-partner stared at each other with glittering eyes that revealed souls tempted almost beyond resistance.

At last Louisiana Slim spoke.

"It jes naturally can't be did, Buddy,' he said. "The Kid's facing the rope. If we use these tools fer our own selves, he'll swing sure. Any time we stepped into a joint on the outside, the gang would

spit on the floor an' holler 'Coppers in the house!'
an' walk out. An' they'd be right. Nix, it can't be
did; but God a'mighty, it's hard— turrible, turrible
hard."

"Pack the junk up, Slim," whispered his partner,
wiping a wet, clammy brow. "Separate it an' pack
it up. I dassent touch the stuff. I've played the
game square for twenty years, but I'm afraid to lay
hands near this."

During the day Slim arranged the delivery of
Blackie's note to the cell of the condemned man.
Then he intercepted Fred the Count, the convict who
carried the guard's midnight coffee and was indis-
pensable to Blackie's plan. The Count was a sleek,
suave bigamist and forger whose specialty had been
making love to trusting women whom he deserted
when he had stripped them of their wealth. He was
a constant plotter of revolt and was stamped "right"
among his fellows.

Slim asked him to attach the package to the end
of the Cushions Kid's dangling black thread on the
following night and to drop the chloral into the
guard's coffee. As the entire night's supply of coffee
was to be drugged, suspicion after the escape could
not center on the Count, though it was obvious he and
a dozen others would be subjected to third-degree
methods. Slim made no mention of the sewer's part
in the plan; nor did he tell from whom the weapons
of escape had come.

"I'm with you, Slim," the Count assured him.

"I'd go to hell and back and hang in the sack a week
if necessary to save a man from being topped. Count
on me for my part."

The preparations for the rescue were now complete.
With his dinner that night the Cushions Kid received
the silent message "To-night at one."

CHAPTER VI

DARKNESS settled over the penitentiary, and lights winked out from the cell-houses. At eight o'clock one of them—the one that showed in the cell of Louisiana Slim—suddenly went out, then on again, then out and on once more.

"Thank God, things have gone as I planned," cried Blackie, creeping from a hiding-place on the crest of the hill behind the prison as the welcome signal caught his eager-eyes.

In the death-cell the Kid lay on his bunk simulating slumber while his pulses throbbed with excitement and impatience so intense it was a physical pain. A day-and-night death-watch had not been set over him yet, and he was alone. The lights-out bell sounded, and the incandescents died out in blackness. The prison settled into slumber. To the boy lying alone in the darkness with everything staked on a single roll of Fate's fickle dice, the dragging minutes of inaction were almost unendurable. The half-hours between the tolling of the prison bell each seemed a lifetime of suspense. But with eleven o'clock at last came the time for action.

The condemned boy sprang from his couch at the stroke of the bell and groped in his breast for the ball of thread. He tied a stubby piece of pencil to

57

the end of it and lowered it from his window until it
rested on the ground.   Then he knotted it to one
of the bars and crouched in the darkness, waiting.

It was nearly an hour—it seemed centuries to the
waiting Kid—before a quick, furtive step sounded on
the gravel beneath the window.   The step paused;
and the prisoner's finger, laid on the. thread where
it was fastened to the bar, felt a gentle tug that proved
the man below had found its dangling end.   There
was a second of silence; then the gravel crunched
under footsteps that died away around the corner of
the death-house.   The bell tolled midnight, breaking
the stillness with a sudden shock that was like a blow.
The Cushions Kid crept to the window and looked
out into the prison yard, lighted by a dozen flaring
arc-lights.   It was deserted, as he knew it would be
while the guards were eating.   He raised the thread
slowly and began to pull it in with infinite caution.

Before the cord to which the thread had been tied
reached his trembling fingers, the added weight on
the tiny string told him the package below was swinging clear of the ground.   Meanwhile he was forced
to pull the thread over the rough stone of the window-
ledge — stone that, because of the weight below,
threatened to sever it.   Would the thread hold?   A
life—his life—hung swaying in the balance on the
end of the inadequate strand of linen.

Inch by inch the thread came up.   At last the end
of the knotted cord appeared over the angle of stone.
With that in his hands, the danger was over.   The

Kid rapidly dragged up the package, squeezed it through the bars and clutched it to his breast.

Sudden relief from the mastering strain of the past minutes left him suddenly weak, sick, faint. He dropped down on his bunk, caressing the package with eager fingers as though to convince himself that hope was now reality.

From the farther end of the corridor a sound reached his ear. He sprang to his feet as stagnation of mind and body fell from him like a discarded cloak. Bolts were thrown in the locks that guarded the death-house. Some one was entering.

To be found dressed and awake at that hour of the night would be fatal. The Cushions Kid tossed his package between his blankets, drew them over him and closed his eyes with a heart heavy with dread.

The last door was thrown open noisily, proving that no effort was being made to steal upon him secretly. The prisoner took heart. It was scarcely possible that his package had been seen as he dragged it to the window, and yet a visit at that particular hour was a strange and threatening coincidence. Two men were approaching the cell, talking as they came.

"The leak's up here somewhere," the Kid heard one say. "Everything's flooded down below, and getting worse every minute."

The condemned man felt rather than spoke a prayer of thankfulness. They weren't after him or the bundle that nestled in the crook of his knees.

He heard the footsteps outside the door of his cell.

A flashlight roamed its four corners and came to rest upon his face. This was the crucial instant, the Kid felt. He kept his eyes closed and breathed with the deep, even respiration of a sleeper.

"I don't see any loose water round here, but we better make sure," said a voice that the prisoner recognized as the night captain's. A key turned in the lock, and the door creaked on its hinges. "It's a shame to wake the Kid, poor devil, but we've got to find that broken pipe before—"

The Cushions Kid's arms were suddenly seized and pinioned to his sides beneath the blankets. Burly hands caught him by the throat and jerked him from the bunk to the middle of the floor. He tried to fight, to struggle, but it was useless. The blankets were torn from about him; his hands were twisted behind his back; and in an instant, handcuffed and helpless, he looked up in the glare of suddenly lighted electrics and found himself staring with eyes of hate and hopelessness into the grimly smiling faces of the night captain and a guard.

"Come on, boys! We got him trussed up tight as a drum," the captain called, and there was a shuffle of padded feet in the corridor as a half-dozen men, some with revolvers, and some with short-barreled shotguns, poured into the cell. The captain lifted the blankets, and the package that Boston Blackie and the others had risked so much to put into his hands rolled to the floor.

The sight of that precious package in the hands

of his enemies stung the Cushions Kid to furious desperation. Life and liberty were no longer possible, but liberty in a death of his own choosing lay on the floor before him, notwithstanding his manacled hands and watchful captors. In the package on the floor he knew was a bottle of "soup"—nitroglycerin—so refined that any quick jar would explode it. One quick kick, and he would die with the knowledge that the grinning enemies about him had died with him in the sudden overturning of their short-lived triumph.

He sprang forward and aimed a savage blow at the bundle, even as one of the men stooped to pick it up.

Myriads of colored lights flashed through his brain. Then came blackness.

The Cushions Kid slowly won his way back to consciousness with a growing surprise that he was not in another world. Peering down at him were the hated faces of the night captain and the warden of the prison. His hands were still manacled; he was still in his cell.

"What happened?" he asked feebly.

"Your intentions were all right, Kid," the captain remarked, "but my smash to your jaw made your aim bad—which explains why any of us are here."

The Cushions Kid sat up, sullen and silent and inexpressibly hopeless. He had failed again. Nothing awaited him now but the death decreed by law. With difficulty he choked back a cry of despair.

That strangled cry encouraged the warden to begin the work for which he had come.

"Well, boy," he began with an obvious attempt at kind intimacy, "you took a long chance and lost. I can't blame you. But you never really had a chance. You might have blown your way out of this place, yes. But after you were in the yard, what then? You would have been shot down before you had gone a dozen steps. You owe us something for saving your life, even if it is only for a few days."

The Kid eyed him narrowly. Evidently he didn't know of the part the sewer leading to the river played in Boston Blackie's plans—nor of Boston Blackie, either, though it was perfectly evident that there had been treachery by some one Blackie had been forced to trust. The thought that Blackie even now was waiting at the other end of that sewer forced upon him the necessity of diverting any suspicion in that direction.

"If I had made it to the yard, I'd have shown your gun-screws some fancy shooting," he said with apparent frankness. "Once on the ground I'd have walked out from under their rifles."

"Of course your friend on the outside is waiting somewhere just over the deadline for you now," the warden said interrogatively. "But you never would have lived to reach him."

"I haven't anyone on the outside," said the boy shortly.

"I suppose you want me to think that gun and dynamite just grew on the end of that black thread you had out your window."

The warden unwittingly had given proof of the treachery that the Cushions Kid suspected. It was conceivable but not probable that some guard might have seen the package being pulled to the window, but it was absolutely impossible that in the dark anyone could have seen the black thread. Knowledge of that proved definite information.

'It doesn't make any differenc now, but I'm curious to know how that gun got hooked on to the end of your line," the warden continued ingratiatingly. "It wasn't there before dark."

"I'm curious to know the name of the yellow-hearted snitch that tipped you it was there."

"No one snitched. A guard just happened to see you pulling it in," the warden hastened to assure him.

"Well, then, no one put it there. It just grew out of the gravel," gravely asserted the condemned boy. The warden saw he was accomplishing nothing and changed his tactics. He crossed to the bunk, sat down and laid his hand on the Kid's knee.

"Boy," he said, "I'm going to quit beating around the bush and talk straight. I want to know how that stuff got into this prison. I want to know who handled it after it got into the prison. You can tell me."

"Nothing doing, Warden."

"Wait. I hadn't finished. You're going to hang in just four days. Just four days, boy. It isn't pleasant to dangle at the end of six feet of rope. It isn't pleasant to lie in a cell for four days knowing that you're going to dangle. Nothing and no one can save you, boy."

And then after a long pause:

"Unless I do! I'm going to Sacramento to-morrow. I'm going to see the Governor. If I were able to tell him that you aided me in uncovering the men who seem to mistake this place for an arsenal, he might decide to give you a commutation. Do you get me?"

"Nothing doing!"

"Suppose I were to call the Governor up and he were to tell me he *would* grant a commutation under the conditions I have suggested—what then?"

"Listen, Warden." The Cushions Kid turned and looked the official squarely in the eye. "If you were going to hang me in five minutes, and the Governor stood where you are now with a full pardon in his hand and offered it to me to snitch on the men who have taken a chance to help me, I'd hang—hang with my mouth *shut*. That's final. Let's cut the foolish chatter."

The boy's eyes were as convincing as his words.

"You'll hang, all right, you fool," the warden cried, jumping to his feet. "Set a death-watch over him now," he added, turning to the night captain. "Keep his cell lighted and a man sitting in front of his door watching him day and night. Four days isn't long. He won't be so cocky when the time comes to stand on the trap."

When they were out of hearing, the warden turned

to the captain, fuming and fussing because of the narrow escape from a break that would have been hard to explain with credit to the discipline of his prison.

"Will that young fool weaken and talk when his time comes?" he asked.

"No," replied the officer. "I knew from the first he wouldn't squeal. Men able to have and hold friends who will take the desperate chances that were taken for him never squeal. They haven't got it in 'em."

"Has the Count told all he knows, do you think?"

"He has told all he's going to—all it's safe for him to know. I think he handled that package himself, but if he admitted that, he'd have to tell us from whom he got it. And if he did,"—the captain motioned as though his throat were being cut—"he'd do his time quicker than the Kid up there in the death-cell with four days to live."

Back in that death-cell a boy, alone for a few brief minutes before the arrival of the death-watch, flung himself on his face and let an overburdened heart find the natural, human outlet for hopeless grief. The cynical bravado with which he had calmly refused the gift of life was gone. But now for a brief moment he could be just himself—a sobbing, frightened boy facing a certain and terrible death without a kind word or a friendly face to strengthen his shrinking spirit for the greatest of all ordeals.

CHAPTER VII.

THE WOMAN CALLED RITA

SPANISH MICKY, proprietor of a poker-game that enabled him to live in easy affluence on the earnings of the ill-paid guards at the penitentiary, lolled on a couch in his specially furnished room in Folsom Town's one hotel, indolently tinting and polishing the nails of slender fingers, soft and white as a woman's.

Across the room, before a dressing-table that had cost much more than any of Micky's patrons earned from the State in a month, sat Rita the Queen, present partner of the good fortunes that had given Spanish Micky the one gambling-game within reach of an institution with a ten-thousand-dollar monthly payroll. Rita was using a lip-stick and an eyebrow pencil with experienced fingers.

A first glimpse at the pair indicated that Spanish Micky and Rita the Queen were eminently suited to make each other deliriously happy and maddeningly miserable in an endless and delightful succession of emotional tides. Once it had been so. Once love, passionate jealousy and furious anger had alternated in making their life a daily drama worth living—a drama the swift changes of which left no time for ennui. Gradually, however, Micky became secure and satisfied in undisputed possession, and their life had become one of humdrum monotony.

66

"No, there won't be any escape to-night," Micky answered between puffs of smoke.

Rita watched Mickey for a second in her mirror, made a grimace of impatient disdain and returned to her eyebrow pencil with a sigh of utter soul-weariness. She was tired of Folsom, tired of the once-loved man who kept her there, tired of idle, purposeless days without adventure or excitement.

"I've solved the secret of the mystery-man, Rita." Spanish Micky's voice was vibrant with satisfaction as it broke the woman's reverie.

"Yes?" There was interest and curiosity in the inflection.

"He's the fellow who framed the get-away night before last for the guy they're going to hang up at the prison Friday. It would have gone through, you know, if a con hadn't tipped the game off. But that ain't all. This fellow who framed the break wasn't done when his first play went wrong. He's been sitting late into the poker-game every night and taking pains to make friends with the prison guards.

"Larry Donovan, who is on duty in the death-house after midnight, was in the game and blew his pay-check as usual. He tried to touch me for a twenty. Nothing doing, of course. He sure has the card-fever bad. He tried to borrow all round the table and was turned down, nobody but me having checks to spare. Well, he was runnin' around crazy mad to play again, when some one says, after he tries to peddle his watch: 'Gwan out, Larry, and peddle the prison, why don't you? You'll be able to sit in for a whole hour then.'

" 'I'd peddle the prison and everything in it for enough checks to keep me in the game till my luck changes,' he says; and he meant it. I caught the stranger looking at him watchful-like, and right then I had my suspicions. Larry finally goes out to try and make a touch from 'Dutch,' the saloon-man. He's no sooner out the door than the mystery-man says he's tired and cashes in."

Spanish Micky stopped, rolled a cigarette with one hand and struck a match with the other.

"Go on—go on. What happened then?" cried Rita, her black eyes flashing with excitement and deep interest.

"The stranger goes out," Micky continued languidly. "Half an hour later Larry Donovan comes back with money. He's still playing when it comes time for him to leave to go on watch outside the death-cell. Do you get me, Rita? On watch in the death-house, with the stranger's dough in his jeans."

Micky stopped as though his tale were ended. Rita's cheeks were flushed with a tint that isn't bought in boxes, and her eyes were dark, seething pools of emotion. Here at last was what her nature craved—excitement, danger, a last-hour and desperate attempt to save a man already within the shadow of the scaffold.

"And there'll be an escape to-night?" she questioned, lowering her voice.

"No, there won't be any escape to-night," Micky answered between puffs of smoke. "I don't know where the stranger is, but I know where he will be. Behind bars! Inside, looking out, for him!"

He hesitated in momentary indecision as to the advisability of further revelations; then he continued:

"Listen, Rita: You stick around here to-night and keep your eyes open, and you'll see a real rumpus. Your old man Micky has pulled some wise inside stuff, kid. After Larry left last night, I called up the warden and told him what I'd seen. I've been looking for a chance to do him a good turn ever since the town knockers began to howl about my game's keeping the boys from the stir from paying their bills. I told him to call Larry Donovan into his office and throw a scare into him and he'd find out something he wants to know. The warden did it, and Larry spit up everything.

"He was to get five thousand dollars in cash to let this fellow Grimes—that's the one they're going to hang Friday—tie him up in the death-house to-night and cop his keys. The stranger showed him the real money, and Larry—thinkin' how many poker-checks he could buy with it—agreed to stand for the get-away. But there won't be any get-away for Jimmy Grimes or his friend either, for when Mr. Man shows up here to-night, the warden's going to grab him and his five thousand dollars. Planning a jail-break calls for from five to forty years, in this State. Smart Stranger might as well pick out a cell up at the big house right now. And meantime Spanish Micky and the warden are pals. Fine time the knockers will have getting him to bar the boys from my game now, eh, kid? If this mystery-guy carries a gun, and I've got a hunch he does, there's liable to be lead flying to-night, for he's nervy."

If Spanish Micky had been as experienced in reading a woman's mind as he was in reading a deck of cards, he wouldn't have finished his revelation with the smile of satisfaction with which he now turned to receive Rita's commendation. He failed utterly to interpret aright what he saw in the girl's face. He thought it was frightened concern for his safety. Really it was disgust, hatred born of a dead passion, and adventurous resolve.

"Don't worry, kid. I won't get hurt," he said, putting on his coat and hat. "You'll have to eat alone to-night unless the doings are over before dinner-time, for I'm going to stay down in the poker-rooms where the warden's six gun-men are hiding till this bird shows up. So long, babe."

"And I took that thing for my man!" the woman exclaimed with a vicious look at the door through which Micky had vanished. "A copper-hearted rat who ought to be wearing a star and a blue uniform. What a fool I've been to waste six months with him!"

Rita wrinkled her brow into a sudden frown.

"Who knows?" she said, answering the unspoken question in her mind. "Stranger things have happened, and he's class, that's sure, or he wouldn't be taking this kind of a chance for a pal in the death-cell."

Rita dressed for a tramp, picked up a fishing-rod and slung a creel over her shoulder. At the door she turned back and took a revolver and a box of cartridges from Spanish Micky's trunk. Then she went downstairs and sent the clerk to the hotel kitchen for a box of sandwiches—the Folsom House hadn't discovered bellboys yet. All prepared now for the project in her mind, she swung down the dusty road that led to the river and, incidentally, the prison.

Rita reached neither the river nor the penitentiary. At the fork of the roads a mile from town she selected a grassy slope behind a bowlder and sat down to wait for the coming of the man who monopolized her thoughts—though she didn't know his name and had spoken to him but once. But Micky's tale had placed this man as one of the lawless legion who were the heroes of the life she craved. And Rita, being Rita, had no conventions to stay her pretty hand from reaching forth to grasp what it coveted.

At last he came, a dark shadow slipping quietly along the road well after sunset. She rose from the grassy slope almost at his feet—to find a gun against her breast before she could speak.

"It's Rita. Put up your gun," she cried.

An electric flashlight flared in her face. Then it carefully sought out with its beam of light every place of concealment about them.

"I'm alone. You've nothing to fear from me. I've been waiting here all afternoon for you to come."

She thrilled with the joy of that moment.

"Well, what do you want?" Blackie snapped out with scant courtesy.

"I don't want anything," Rita said with careful inflection. "But you do. You want to know, for instance, that in the room behind Spanish Micky's joint there are six gun-men from the prison waiting for you right now. You—"

"What!" cried Blackie. "Are you sure?"

"I am. Micky was suspicious last night when Larry Donovan, the death-house guard, came back into the poker-game with money after you followed him out. He—"

"I told the lying fool he mustn't go back, and he swore he wouldn't. That's a square shooter for you! Go on."

"Micky phoned the warden and told him what he suspected. The warden called Larry in to-day and sweated him. You know the answer to that."

Blackie swore viciously.

"Come over here, and we'll sit down while I think this business out," he said, taking her by the arm and helping her down the bank to her former position by the roadside. "I'm thankful for this service, Rita, very thankful. But I don't quite understand yet why you're here. You're Spanish Micky's girl, aren't you?"

"I was, but I'm done. No man can do what he did last night, and say that Rita belongs to him. I've been taught to hate coppers. If I can't have a man, a real man, I'll live alone the rest of my life."

Blackie suddenly turned his flashlight full into her face and studied her in silence. She flushed like a young girl.

"You believe me, don't you? You trust me? You can. Every drop of blood in me is right."

The girl leaned toward him and clasped his arm with both her hands.

"Yes, I trust you," Blackie answered unhesitatingly. "I'll not forget what you have done for me to-night, either."

"It is because I knew you won't that I did it." A slight pressure on his arm gave added meaning to her words. "You can't go back into the town. What are you going to do?" she asked after a pause.

"Are you absolutely sure Donovan won't be on duty in the death-house to-night?" Blackie demanded.

"Absolutely."

"And the Kid has only one more night to live! Well, I'll stick and keep trying to the end. While he still lives, there's a chance."

"You're going to stay even now when you know you are discovered, know they are looking for you?" Hero-worship intoned every word.

"Sure! Something may happen. You can never tell till you try. Well, Rita, I've got to lie out in the hills to-night, and you've got to get back to town or you'll be missed, if you haven't been already. Good-by. When this business is over, I'll send you our address, and if you're ever in a tight place and need help, you'll get it if you call on me."

The girl noted the plural "our" with a quick tightening of the lips but no surprise.

"That 'our' means his girl," she thought as Blackie rose and helped her to her feet. "I expected that. Such a man as this doesn't travel alone. But she'll have to be some girl to be more attractive and useful to him than I'm going to be—especially more useful."

"I knew you'd be hungry, so I brought you something to eat," she said. "Also a gun and an extra box of cartridges," she added as she handed the articles over. "You may need them before you're safely out of this. Do you know where the little log cabin is in the clump of woods just below the railroad-bridge over the river?"

"Yes."

"It belongs to Micky, and here's the key. You'll find an oil-stove, coffee and blankets inside. Micky is homesteading the land and has to sleep there once in a while. It will be safe and comfortable for you. You couldn't risk making a fire in the open, for they'll be combing the country for you before morning. I'll come at three to-morrow with a basket of food and all the news there is; then you can plan your get-away. You'll meet me?"

"I certainly will, little girl," Blackie assured her with more warmth in his voice. He was astonished at the complete efficiency of her forethought. "I don't understand why you've done all this for me, a stranger, but I want you to know that I'm grateful

from the bottom of my heart—and I never forget
a friend or a favor."

"Maybe you'll understand better after you think it
over," Rita answered. "Good night, and do be careful,"—after a second's hesitation,—"dear."

"Good night!" Blackie slipped away in the darkness, refusing to recognize the revelation in the girl's
final word.

CHAPTER VIII

THE MIRACLE

BOSTON BLACKIE drank Spanish Micky's coffee and ate Rita's sandwiches in pitch darkness. He did not think it prudent to light the lantern he found in the cabin. Then he rolled a cigarette and concentrated his acute brain upon the Herculean problem before him. For only thirty-six hours of life remained now to the Cushions Kid!

The more deeply Blackie studied and analyzed the situation, the more hopeless it appeared. His first plan of escape had offered every chance of success, but a traitor had wrecked it. Spanish Micky had frustrated his second effort—a desperate expedient born of desperate necessity—and roused the prison authorities to double precaution both by day and by night.

And now—what?

An hour later, Boston Blackie slipped out of the cabin and picked his way silently through the brush and bowlders to a point that jutted out into the river above the mouth of the prison sewer—which from the first had been the key of his plans. He was thankful that the unknown traitor within the prison had not been able to reveal that too.

He swam the river noiselessly and landed safely

76

in the shadow of the underground causeway that led to the very foundations of the death-house. Two bars of the great iron grating that protected its mouth were sawed. He had attended to that on the night of the first attempt, when he had lain until dawn beside the sewer, waiting for the boy who never came. Blackie pushed the bars aside, entered the sewer and crawled forward on hands and knees into Stygian blackness.

On and on he went through air that was foul and gas-laden. He lost all sense of time and distance. His hands and knees were bruised and bleeding. The darkness seemed like a blanket that wrapped itself about him and hindered his progress; and the moldy damp underground odor made him think, instinctively, of a grave. He kept on interminably, and at last a faintly diffused glow broke through the wall of blackness. The air grew fresher, and his reeling senses cleared. He was under the manhole beside the death-house.

Kneeling under the grating that covered the manhole, Blackie felt for his guns and the bottle of nitro he carried in his breast pocket. Then he pressed upward on the grating. It creaked but held fast. He pressed harder and still harder without result. Finally he threw his whole strength again and again against the crisscrossed steel covering that held him in. It did not budge.

Once again Chance had intervened to balk him. Not two hours before, a convict employed in the night kitchen had slipped from his post and put back the iron padlock for which Louisiana Slim had substituted a painted wooden one. Believing Blackie must have abandoned all hope of effecting a rescue, Louisiana had ordered this done. It was a final, crushing blow. Fate played too strong a hand for the man crouching below the immovable grating and almost sobbing in an agony of despair.

He scarcely remembered how he made his weary way back through the tunnel, how he swam the river, how he stumbled back to the cabin and threw himself weakly on a bunk, where he lay through the long night haunted by the vision of a boy standing on a scaffold with a black cap being drawn slowly down over his frightened face.

It was scarcely noon the next day when Blackie, gaunt and haggard from exhaustion and seventy-two sleepless hours, heard a motorcar come to a stop on the little-used woodland road that ran along the top of the ridge above the cabin. He slipped out of the log house and into the concealment of a thicket, and unslung his guns. He even hoped the motor contained a posse come to attack his refuge. Anything was better than the maddening ordeal of lying idle and impotent while his watch ticked away the few remaining hours of life left to the boy he had failed to rescue.

A twig snapped on the trail above the cabin, and he saw Rita hurrying toward him with the lithe, swift, graceful movements of a forest animal—a leopard, beautiful but dangerous to any but those she might choose to call her own. She was dressed for city motoring rather than woods tramping, and she carried a suitcase.

He called to her, and she rushed to him with a half-stifled cry of welcome and gladness.

"Oh, Blackie," she cried, dropping on her knees beside him, "I'm so thankful you're here now. I was deathly afraid you'd be off somewhere and I'd have to wait. We've got to get away from here quick. They know who you are up at the prison, and that there's a thousand-dollar reward for your capture. Micky recognized your picture this morning on one of the posters in the warden's office. They've found the sawed bars at the entrance of the se-~er. As soon as they can gather the men, the whole county will be out to hunt you down."

Blackie leaped to his feet, and Rita threw open the suit-case.

"I've brought you clothes, a hat, auto-goggles—all Micky's," she continued. "Dress quickly, dear!" The term fell from her lips quite naturally this time. "I'm going to carry you away from under their noses. And, Mr. Boston Blackie,"—she stepped close to him and looked straight into his face to judge the effect of her words,—"whether Mary likes it or not, you're going to take a nice long auto-drive with another girl—with me."

"How did you know about Mary?" he asked.

"Read about her and you in the paper when the

coppers wanted you, stupid!" she answered. "The second I knew you were Boston Blackie, I knew all about you. I have friends in Frisco who know you and have often told me what a wonder you are. I'm glad I didn't know at first, though. If I had, you might think I fell for you because you are Boston Blackie. Now you will always know that wasn't the reason. It is just because you—are—you."

For once Blackie's ready tongue was bereft of words. He stood looking down at her dumbly while a premonition of impending difficulty shaped itself in his mind. Her laugh broke the silence.

"Dress, Blackie," she cried. "Don't stand there staring at me like that. Wait till we are in the car and speeding toward Sacramento and safety. Then you're welcome to stare as long as you like."

"Will you drive or shall I?" she asked when they stood beside a high-powered roadster ten minutes later.

"You drive. I want to think."

"Of me? If so, I'll drive you round the world and back."

"No, Rita—of the boy we're leaving behind us in the death-cell at the stir—a boy who won't be a boy this time to-morrow unless a miracle happens. I came up here to save him, and I've failed—failed where I would give everything I have or ever will have to succeed."

"You've done everything a right pal could do, and more, Blackie," Rita answered, dropping her banter-

ing spirit for one of deep, comforting sympathy.
"You've risked your life again and again, and you
would have had him out now if it had not been for a
couple of human rats. When your pal dies, Blackie,
it won't be because you failed him."

"He mustn't die, girl," Blackie's teeth snapped
with undying resolution. "He isn't even guilty. He's
hanging because he's too right to squeal on a yellow-
hearted pal. And unless a miracle saves him, he'll
die in the morning. The one last chance is the Governor, and that's not even a chance, for he's already
turned down a commutation."

Blackie was silent as Rita guided the car out of the
twisting hill road onto the broad highway that leads
to the State capital.

"I'm going to Abe Ritter, the lawyer," he continued after a long pause. "He's a politician and
he likes money. He's close to old Tom Creedon,
political boss of Frisco. Creedon elected this governor. I'm going to offer Ritter five thousand dollars
—more if he asks it—to get Creedon to go to the
Governor for the Kid. Creedon could save him if he
would, but—well, he's cold-blooded as a fish, and he
doesn't need money. I can only pay Ritter to try,
and if he fails it's the end."

Blackie's face was anguish itself as Rita turned
her eyes to his.

"You care very, very much to save this boy, don't
you, dear? You'd give anything in the world to do
it, wouldn't you?"

"Anything and everything, Rita. He's almost like a son to me."

Many minutes passed, and the glistening dome of the capitol was in sight above the intervening woodland before either spoke.

"What kind of girl is Mary?" asked Rita suddenly.

"The best in the world—faithful, true, right in every drop of her blood."

A sudden contraction as of pain passed over the girl's face.

"I saw her picture in the paper," she said slowly. "She's pretty, but not prettier than I am when I wish to be for a man I care for. She can't be more loyal than I—if I care. Mary couldn't have served you better than I have when you needed me, could she, Blackie?"

"You did everything any woman could have done, Rita. They would have got me if it hadn't been for you."

"Well, then,"—she turned to him with eyes from which the hardness had vanished,—"is there a chance for me or not?"

Her eyes held his unswervingly as she waited for her answer. Blackie did not dodge the issue or pretend to misunderstand.

"I have Mary," he said. "We've been together in good times and bad, and she has never failed in love or loyalty. I'd hate to be what I would be if I gave her less than that."

"Ah! So it's like that with you." The girl turned from him quickly, and the car shot forward as her foot pressed the accelerator.

"I wonder if Mary knows what a lucky, lucky girl she is," Rita said after a long pause. She sat beside him in silence until the car glided into the city and he directed her to the lawyer's office.

"I'll wait for you. We'll have dinner together?" she questioned as he climbed out of the car.

Blackie nodded acquiescence and disappeared. He returned to find a Rita who had cast off the somber mood in which he had left her.

"What luck and where to?" she queried as he climbed in beside her.

"To Cary's. Ritter is going to 'phone me there. There isn't much hope. Creedon's our only chance. Ritter is going to see him at once, but he doesn't expect good news. I'm afraid the end has come, Rita."

Halfway through the dinner, she suddenly dropped the jesting mood with which she had tried to help him escape the agonizing anxiety that weighted his mind, and leaned across the table toward him.

"Blackie," she said, "I'm done at Folsom. I'm never going back. All my life I have wanted a man like you. Can't you find one little vacant corner in your heart for me? Very little will make me very happy. I don't ask much. I don't ask Mary's place. I just want to be near enough to you to see you sometimes. Will you let me?"

Blackie shook his head. He could not lie to her. "It's no use," he said. "It can't be."

Rita stood up, walked round the table to Blackie and laid her arm on his shoulder.

"I never knew before there were men like you," she said softly with a quickly choked sob. "I wish I had—sooner."

The waiter's discreet rap on the door summoned Blackie to the 'phone. His face, when he returned, told his news before he spoke.

"Nothing doing," he said. "The last hope is gone."

"Oh, my dearest, I'm so sorry," she cried, "—sorrier than you know."

"Will you drive me to the train?" he asked. "I must get back to Frisco before this happens at the prison and try to break it somehow to a little woman I left on her knees praying for the Kid's life. I don't know how to tell her. It would be easier to go along with the Kid."

They rode in silence to the station, and Blackie climbed from the car too distrait for words of any kind.

"Aren't you going to give me your address?" Rita asked. "You promised to in case I should need you some time."

He penciled it on a slip of paper and handed it to her. As the girl took it, she caught his hand between both hers with a pressure that made delicate knuckles show white beneath her skin.

"Anyway," she whispered, "there's one comfort that she can't take from me. I've served you as well as she could. I always will serve you, no matter what it costs me. You'll see. And besides,"—her voice was hard and ruthless again,—"if I had known you first, not Mary or a thousand Marys could take you from me. She's luckier than I—that's all. Goodby, Blackie."

It was early morning—the morning of the execution—when Boston Blackie left the owl-car that had carried him from the ferry, and came to the flat where Mary and Happy had their refuge.

It took all his resolution to force himself to enter and softly climb the stairs. There was no rush from within as he knocked, no door flung frantically open, no faces within, frenzied with grief, to read the death-verdict in his face even before he spoke. He rapped again, and then, a new fear spurring him on, unlocked the door and entered, though he realized he might be walking into a police trap. He half hoped he was.

A swift turn of his flashlight showed him the room was empty. He sat down wearily to wait.

The door below opened and closed, and light, running steps came flying up the stairway. Blackie rose to his feet and switched on the lights. It had come—the moment when he must kill a woman's heart as surely as they were killing the Cushions Kid even now.

The door flew open, and two women came rushing

in. As they saw him, both flung themselves into his arms, showering him impartially with kisses and incoherent cries and sobs of wild rapture.

"Oh, Blackie, Blackie, how did you do it? How did you do it?" cried Happy when at last the power of articulation returned. "My boy is going to live, live, *live!*" In a wildly trembling hand she waved the newspaper she held. "It's a miracle—it's the miracle I've prayed for."

Blackie snatched the paper from her hand as she sank on her knees vainly trying to put into words the prayer of thankfulness that came straight from her heart. He could scarcely believe his eyes as Mary's shaking finger directed them to a telegraph dispatch tucked away in an obscure corner. He read:

Folsom Prison, Oct. 13.—At midnight a telephone-message from Governor Nelson announced the commutation to life imprisonment of the sentence of death against James Grimes, youthful train-robber, who was to have been executed at dawn this morning. It is understood newly discovered evidence convinced the Governor there is some doubt of the prisoner's actual guilt of the murder of which he was convicted. All preparations for the execution were complete when the reprieve reached the prison, no previous intimation that it was to be expected having reached Warden Hodgkins. Grimes was at once taken from the death-cell and lodged with the other prisoners.

"It *is* a miracle," cried Blackie as he comprehended the meaning of the lines. "Mary, Happy, I didn't do this. I didn't even know of it. When I left Sacramento at nightfall the last hope was gone."

"What!" cried Happy and Mary together.

"It's true," Blackie continued. "I was waiting here to tell you everything was over. Three times I framed an escape for him, and each time a last-minute freak of fate stopped it. I tried to reach the Governor through Boss Creedon, and that failed. I came back beaten—and find this." He pointed tremblingly at the few printed lines that had created a new world for four human beings.

"Mary, it *is* a God-sent miracle," he concluded in an awed voice.

He dropped into a chair with the two women crouching at his knees and told them all that had happened at Folsom. When he had finished, they were staring at him with awed eyes and blank, wondering faces.

"It doesn't matter how it happened!" Happy exclaimed at last. "My boy is safe. That is all I want to know. Every night as long as I live I shall thank the good God on my knees for this. And to-night I'm going back to the Spider's to begin to earn the money to get my boy a full pardon—some day."

The child-woman was radiantly happy. That there could be any incongruity in kneeling nightly in a prayer of thankfulness after selling drinks at the Spider's for the sake of the man so marvelously restored to her—that never entered her mind. Perhaps is wasn't incongruous. Who shall say?

Blackie was asleep that afternoon when the woman from whom they rented their flat climbed the stairs to hand Mary a letter addressed to her in a feminine hand. She opened it and read; then she awakened her husband.

"This letter was addressed to me, Blackie dear," she said. "But after reading it I am convinced it is meant for you."

Blackie roused himself and took it from her. Mary stood beside him looking up into his face with a slyly quizzical smile. This is what he read:

Thursday Night.

My dearest:

Mary won't mind my calling you that, I hope. For it's true. You know by now your friend is saved. As I write, the reprieve has been 'phoned to the prison. I hope you are happy as you read this, dearest. I am as I write it.

Do you remember what I said in the restaurant this afternoon? I said I would do more to serve you, risk more to serve you, sacrifice more to serve you, than you know. I'm going to prove that, Blackie dear, to-night.

You said this afternoon that Tom Creedon was your pal's last hope. Your lawyer failed with him. Well, Blackie, I know Tom Creedon too. I met him in Frisco before I went to Folsom, and he fell for me. He's past fifty, but he tries to turn the clock back thirty years when he's with a woman—a pretty one like me. I laughed at him in Frisco.

After you left me at the train I 'phoned him, and he came rushing to me as I knew he would. I told him what I wanted. He objected, denied he could handle the Governor and tried to stall. But in the end he gave in, as men like him always do to a woman.

And so, dearest, I have given you what you said you wanted more than anything on earth—the life of your pal.

Creedon is waiting. I have slipped away for a moment to write this. I am glad and happy, Blackie dear. Are you?

Could Mary do more for you than I am doing? Your answer is my reward—my only one now. Adieu, my dearest.

Yours always,

RITA.

"What a woman!" exclaimed Blackie with a husky catch in his voice. He looked up at Mary, still staring down at him with a twisty little smile on her lips. "But why did she address this letter to you? I don't understand that."

"I know. Any woman would know." Mary sat on his knee and drew his head toward her. "Because she wanted to be quite sure I would see it. And having seen it, if I were foolish and jealous and distrustful like some women, I might quarrel and fuss with you and give her in the end the man she wants—you.

"But I do trust you, and I'm not foolish; and so" —a long pause—"she won't get you."

She kissed him with the wry little smile still on her pretty lips.

CHAPTER IX

FRED THE COUNT

THE day toward which all imprisoned creatures measure time—the day of freedom—had come to Fred the Count. Prison doors opened, and he passed out, jubilant in the intoxicating consciousness of liberty.

A vain attempt to keep on good terms with two wives and the law at the same time had cost him five years in stripes—five years that would have been seven had he not shortened his time at the expense of fellow-convicts. Like everything within the realm of human desire, the Count's shortcut to liberty had a price-tag attached. Ostracism and hatred, bitter and revengeful beyond the conception of the outside world, were the cost of his officially reduced sentence, but as he stepped through the double gates of Folsom Penitentiary and found the world of free men with all its beckoning allurements once more open to him, he felt he had bought cheaply.

He had not always been so certain of this. There had been many months during which the Count, with fear in his heart, had been forced to compute his chances of living to enjoy the liberty for which others had paid with their lives. Two overtrustful convicts with whom he had planned a feasible scheme of escape had slipped from their cells at midnight to be shot to death on the threshold by hidden gun-guards. When a second "break" in which the Count was the leading spirit ended in swift disaster for all but himself, his comrades in stripes began to suspect and watch him. But for a time the bigamist's suave, plausible tongue lulled suspicion.

Then came the betrayal of Blackie's plan to free the Cushions Kid from the death-cell on the eve of his execution. The Kid, as the whole convict world knew, was facing death for the sake of the code that prohibited him from naming the pal for whose act he had been sentenced. The condemned boy was seized in his cell with the means of escape in his hands. The next day the convict colony knew that within it was one willing to barter a comrade's life for his own petty gain.

The elimination, one by one, of those in the betrayed secret definitely fastened responsibility on the Count. From that moment he was a man condemned to death by the prison world in which he lived. With timely intuition he sensed the verdict against him and induced the warden to assign him to duties that kept him well out of reach of the knives which day after day patiently awaited their opportunity beneath a dozen striped shirts.

Though the Count lived for months in an endless nightmare of dread, the hidden knives never found the target of flesh that feared them so.

And now he was free!

His transient regret at the treachery that had endangered his own life slipped from his shoulders as easily as the convict suit he joyously changed for civilian clothes. Remorse he had never felt. Being safe now, he rejoiced whole-heartedly in the unfair bargain by which he profited. Unalloyed contentment was in his heart as he strode down the hill toward the town and the railway.

At the foot of the grade a sharp turn revealed the prison cemetery, weed-grown, unkempt and dotted with wooden headboards. The names on two close to the fence caught his eye. There, side by side, lay the trustful pair he had betrayed to their death, with the grass growing green and strong above their graves. No tremor of fear or regret lessened the Count's buoyant spirit as he noted this. No man need fear the dead, he thought; and as for conscience, that, to him, was a superfluous something which bothers only women and fools—fools like those left behind in stripes, fools like those past whose moldering bodies he was hurrying back to life and gayety and all the joys of freedom.

If there is some good in even the worst of men, as sociologists assert, the Count as a boy must have been kind to his mother.

At the railway station the Count's wary and experienced eye noted with quick gratification that no one who might have a star beneath his coat was waiting for him, as there might have been, for there were many incidents in the bigamist's long career that were not purged by his sentence for victimizing two trustful women who had had more money and credulity than discernment. Time, however, which mollifies and ameliorates everything, even the law, had served him well, and he found no one on the station platform but a young girl.

Admiringly, appraisingly, he noted the trim, childish figure and pretty face clouded by something difficult to interpret. He always eyed women. They interested him to the same extent and in precisely the same way the stock-ticker interests Wall Street speculators—as the obviously easy and only natural avenue to wealth. Their weaknesses, their foibles and follies,—even their virtues,—were as water turning a millwheel that poured the grist of luxury into his ruthless and covetous hands. As he noted the unpretentious dress and unadorned fingers of the girl, his interest died.

"A pretty little *Cinderella* without any *Fairy Godmother*," he thought, and straightway he forgot her. Other things being equal, the Count preferred youth and beauty, but always beauty backed by a check-book.

When the train came, the Count settled himself and forgot even his newborn liberty in the joy of planning the quick turn he intended to make in the crooked money-market. Behind him rode the girl of the station platform—a girl whose childish face, now that she was safe from his observation, was marred by resolute, immutable hatred—hatred consciously righteous and of the sort that never lessens or dies.

Could the Count have known the girl was on that train only because he was, and that the sight and thought of him alone had so altered her sweetly girlish beauty, he would have realized that the hatreds and dangers he thought so safely shackled in the prison behind him had followed him out into the world and were dogging him now, step by step, with implacable, ominous resolution.

That night Fred the Count, ex-convict, landed at the San Francisco ferry and dived, like a rabbit to its warren, into the sheltering purlieus of the city. A week later at a fashionable hotel there appeared in his stead Sir Harry Westwood Cameron, English gentleman, apparently of unlimited leisure and wealth, but whose wardrobe seemed surprisingly new for a man whose luggage indicated an extensive tour.

Sir Harry—it is only fair to accord him the privilege of the name he chose after a careful study of "Burke's Peerage"—lay in his suite reading and rereading a trivial item in the morning's paper. It announced the arrival in San Francisco of Sir Arthur Caveness of London on a secret mission supposed to involve the purchase of vast quantities of war-supplies for the British Government. He had been the guest of honor at a banquet given by the British consul.

Beside this item Sir Harry laid another clipped from the same paper. It related the fact that Miss Bettina Girard, daughter of Sherwood Girard, pioneer Mendocino lumberman, had celebrated her eigh-

teenth birthday with a dance at which the country-
side fox-trotted and one-stepped on the waxed stump
of a single giant redwood tree. The paragraph
added that Miss Girard was the sole heiress of her
father, owner of the largest tract of uncut redwood
in the State.

For a full hour Sir Harry, with mind keyed to its
highest pitch of concentration, conned the possibilities for him contained in the two bits of news. Then
he rose, bowed to his reflection in the mirror, and
went down to dinner, satisfied with himself and the
world.

During the next three days Sir Harry made a
number of preparations with business-like dispatch.
First he wrote a letter to the British consul—omitting the "Sir" from his signature, stating he was an
Englishman desiring to enlist and asking instructions.
He got them, of course, by return mail on consulate
stationery and over the consul's signature. Then,
after nightfall, he visited a dirty, dilapidated little
print-shop located in a single room in an alley near
Chinatown. The sole occupant of the place was a
misshapen little man lying on a couch in a frowsy
dressing-gown. To him—evidently an old acquaintance from their greeting—Sir Harry showed the
consulate letter and asked for duplicate stationery
and a sheaf of checks bearing the same identifying
insignia.

"They'll be ready to-morrow night, Fred," the
little old man wheezed after examining the sample

with a microscope, "and the charge to you will be twenty dollars—which I'll take now."

"Twenty dollars! That's robbery," remonstrated Sir Harry angrily.

"No, no, Fred, no robbery about it," chuckled the hunchback. "I charge one dollar for doing the work and nineteen for forgetting I did it. Cheap enough, when you think it over, ain't it?"

Sir Harry handed him a twenty-dollar bill.

When he received the papers ordered from the print-shop, he bought a plate of glass cut to fit inside one of his suit-cases, and an electric-light extension-cord; then he locked himself in his room and drew down the curtains. On the bottom of the glass he carefully pasted the genuine letter received from the British consul. Next he laid the glass across the top of his open suit-case with a lighted incandescent beneath it. On the top of the glass he laid, one after another, a series of letters he had personally typed on the stationery provided by the printer, and traced on each, with a deftness and accuracy that proved long experience at the task, the exact duplicate of the consul's signature—the light beneath the glass outlining the genuine signature on the blank papers as clearly as though it were written there. These letters, addressed to himself, he mailed and received back again properly stamped by the postal service.

That night Sir Harry Westwood Cameron packed his luggage, paid his hotel-bill, ordered a taxi in time for an early morning train and fell asleep contentedly, in blissful anticipation of an approaching golden harvest.

While Sir Harry slept, an underworld jury of six —four men and two women, grouped round a table in a secluded flat—discussed him with the same consciousness of solemn responsibility with which a court jury debates a death-verdict against a man already adjudged guilty. From the hour of his release from Folsom one or more of the six had been at his heels—following, watching, waiting with silent, purposeful doggedness. Each of Sir Harry's preparations for an approaching flier in high finance had been observed and reported to Boston Blackie, the "mob" chief, who sat at the head of the group, grave and taciturn. K. Y. Lewes, whose hotel-room adjoined the Englishman's, had brought the news that Sir Harry had paid his bill and was ready to leave town. That the time to strike had come was the evident sentiment of the majority. Jimmy the Joke was speaking.

"If he's going to blow town in the morning, tonight's the time to ring down his curtain, and here's the way to do it! There's an eight-inch ledge between K. Y.'s room window and his. Out one window and in the other; a clout over the head with a sap, and a poke with a shiv" (knife), "and he'll be hard to wake when they call him for his train in the morning." Jimmy illustrated with gestures more vivid than words. "Say the word, Blackie, and it'll be all over by daylight."

One of the two women—Boston Blackie's Mary, who sat beside him—shivered slightly. The other, a girl with the face of a child and eyes old with worldliness, stared unseeingly before her as though trying to visualize the scene just described—a sleeping man, a dark shadow slipping through a window, a quick blow, a knife-stab, a groan—and silence. There was no trace of mercy in the set lines of her face, for the man this child-woman loved as only such as she can love was he whom Fred the Count had sought to betray to the hangman and who because of that treachery was still behind prison bars instead of at her side.

They all turned toward Boston Blackie and waited. In all things he was the final arbiter.

"I don't want him bumped off."

A sigh of relief from Mary, and a low gasp of surprise from the rest followed Boston Blackie's words.

"Why, Blackie? Oh, why, why?" cried the girl, asking the question in every mind.

"Because, little Miss Happy, it's too easy, too quick, too inadequate," Blackie answered. "Unless the future holds something worse than death for Fred the Count, he has escaped us. Only years of suffering filled with the gnawing knowledge of *why* he suffers can square the debt this man has taken on himself. Death wont do. We must wait and take him when—" Boston Blackie paused. "Jimmy," he continued after a moment's thought, "pick him up at the hotel in the morning and trail him wherever he goes. It won't be far. He's ready to pull one of his regular capers. He'll take you up to some out-of-the-way place and begin work. The moment he does, wire me. And Jimmy, don't risk one chance —not even one—of losing him."

As the group disbanded mutteringly, little Miss Happy crossed the room and took hold of Boston Blackie's arm.

"You won't let him get away, will you Blackie?" she pleaded. "If I thought there was even a chance he might, I'd—" She stopped short.

"Don't worry, little girl," Blackie answered, laying his hand on her head. "He'll not escape this time—I promise it."

The following afternoon a puffing little logging-train left Sir Harry Westwood Cameron at Sherwood, a mountain village in the heart of California's great redwood forest. Before night he was talking lumber with old Sherwood Girard the pioneer, to whom he had displayed credentials revealing a mission that made him the most honored guest ever received into the lumberman's home, where, in the simple, open-hearted fashion of the mountains, all travelers were welcome.

While Sir Harry talked to her father, Betty Girard, who some day soon would own the vast, unbroken stretches of virgin forest that rolled away ridge below ridge to the horizon, changed the gingham apron in which the visitor had found her, for her most becoming "party-dress" and nervously piled the golden braids of hair that had hung about her shoulders, high on her head in the most womanly coiffure she knew. Sir Harry was the first "real" baronet she had ever seen; and at supper that night, as he noted the flushed face and eager eyes with which the motherless little heiress listened to his stories of an ancestral (and visionary) home in England, Sir Harry exultingly blessed the happy chance that had sent him to Sherwood, for it was plain the aged master of the house, already bound by feebleness to his wheelchair, could measure in months or even weeks the life that remained to him.

In his room that night Sir Harry summed up his prospects with keen elation. Simple-minded, guileless Betty, who judged him by her mountain standards and listened to his stories of London with the fresh zest and perfect belief of a child, would be, he foresaw, easy prey for a man like himself, skilled in the deception of women far more sophisticated than she. When he married Betty,—already an accepted fact to him,—nothing would stand between him and the sole possession of the vast forests on every side but the life of an old man slipping palpably and inexorably toward an early grave. He was thankful there was no mother to combat and convince. Mothers, he had found, were strangely intuitive sometimes.

"It'll be the best job of my life," Sir Harry assured himself delightedly.

CHAPTER X

THE PRICE OF SUCCESS

DURING the weeks that followed, Sir Harry had no reason to doubt the truth of his boast. Detail after detail of his plan of campaign worked like smooth-running machinery. His first step was a call at the Sherwood offices of President Muir of the milling company which turned endless trainloads of Girard logs into sawed timber. To Muir, a Scotchman with all the shrewdness of his race, Sir Harry presented papers, seemingly unimpeachable, accrediting him as a representative of the British Government instructed to purchase vast supplies of lumber. He showed a specification-list detailing sizes and quantities and asked for a bid on the largest order ever placed in California lumber annals. He made but one stipulation—for Government reasons, the entire transaction must remain an absolute and inviolate secret.

Muir considered his visitor with innate caution.

"It's mighty big business ye speak of, Sir Harry," he said. "Who's to pay, and how?"

"A perfectly proper question," Sir Harry answered. "I will pay, and"—he leaned over and tapped the desk to emphasize his words—"in lieu of the usual investigation you, as a business man, naturally would make of my finances, I make this suggestion: If we agree on prices, I will make an advance payment of ten thousand dollars on the day we sign the contract. As the lumber is delivered at the seaboard each month, I will pay spot cash for the shipments before they are moved from the wharves. You get my money before I get your lumber. Is that satisfactory?"

"Ah! It sounds fair and business-like," admitted the Scotchman, and he plunged into a discussion of costs. In this phase of the negotiations Sir Harry further lulled Muir's really groundless doubts of himself by displaying an intimate knowledge of lumber-values and a marked disposition to haggle over every penny. They parted with the lumberman convinced that good fortune had sent him a customer who would keep his mill running night and day for months.

While he continued to argue costs and delivery details day after day with Muir, Sir Harry devoted himself with the skill of experience to winning the second and greater part of the stake for which he was playing—the heart of Betty Girard.

This was an easy task; for to Betty, Sir Harry Westwood Cameron became in a week the dream prince for whom all girls, young and not so young, wait and watch and long—and sometimes really find. He was the personification of romance, the realization of secretly treasured hopes, the fulfillment of desire, for she saw him with eyes blinded by girlish visions of an imaginary Prince Charming. His thin

lips, steely, half-veiled eyes and mirthless laugh were
to her only delightfully "aristocratic." Glibly casual
references to England's best names helped to build
the pedestal from the foot of which she looked up
to him in awed wonder that she, a simple mountain
girl, should have the privilege of intimacy with one
who belonged in such exalted circles. In a word,
Betty Girard was eighteen and motherless.

Sir Harry wooed her with calculated artistry—and
never a word of love. One day he showed her a
photograph of himself lounging on a lawn before
a baronial-looking country home. Betty could not
guess, of course, that it was a picture of one of England's show places that all Cheapside might visit, if
it chose, for a shilling fee.

"Betty, I've wondered very often lately—" Sir
Harry checked himself as if with an effort.

"What?" she urged, studying the photograph with
a new thrill.

"Whether you—" He stopped again and shook
his head as she looked up at him. "It isn't fair to
tell you—now," he continued with a gesture of
pained self-denial.

Betty was too much a woman not to guess the pur-
port of the words he denied her. Why wasn't it
fair to tell her, if he wished to, she wondered. The
possibility that some obstacle might bar a still-uncon-
fessed love helped to fan the flame Sir Harry wished
to kindle and brought her to an inwardly made admission that she did love Sir Harry Westwood Cam-

eron and always would love him, no matter what
threatened to separate them. She cried herself to
sleep.

It never occurred to Betty to ask herself whether
she loved Sir Harry enough to go with him to a
mountain cabin and be happy there in calico. At
eighteen—and sometimes at thirty-eight—women
forget to test their love with such unromantic possibilities.

With the intuitive knowledge of women that is the
gift of such men, Sir Harry kept the girl's mind
always centered on himself—sometimes in doubt,
sometimes in hope, but always on him. At the end
of a fortnight he was satisfied Betty was his for the
asking.

On the day he changed his last twenty-dollar bill,
Sir Harry Westwood Cameron decided he had jock-
eyed long enough with Muir and his lumber bid and
that the time had come to marry Betty, collect his toll
from the village of Sherwood and vanish. Success
now was almost within the reach of his grasping
fingers. And so with a look that thrilled Betty's
hero-worshipping heart, he asked her to take him for
a last drive in her car.

"My work in Sherwood is almost done, Betty," he
said. "I must leave in a few days, and before I go,
there is something I must tell you. I have tried to
keep silent—and failed. Do you care enough to
listen?"

Betty nodded. At last she was to hear the secret

she thought would determine whether happiness or sorrow was to be hers.

Sir Harry was silent until their car stopped on the edge of a rocky promontory which overlooked miles of the Girard forests. Then suddenly he leaned toward her and caught her hands.

"Betty dear," he cried as though an overflowing heart were forcing the unbidden words from his lips, "you know I love you. Love like mine reveals itself without words. You've seen in my eyes and felt in the touch of my hand all that my lips have longed for days to say. Shall I tell you why I have not spoken? Shall I tell you why, if I could, I would have gone away without speaking?"

"Yes," Betty whispered.

"Because I'm going back to England—back to France, where what is left of my regiment is fighting on the Somme front. In one month or six after I reach French soil I may be a maimed cripple—a burden forever to myself and the wife I long for. I have no right to ask you to leave such a home as yours to risk such a future. And yet—when they love—women like you are such willing martyrs to that love that sometimes I have almost dared to hope. Betty, are you brave enough, do you—can you—care enough to go back to England with me and share as my wife what the future has in store?"

Betty, thrilled beyond bounds with the joy of knowing the hero she loved had with knightly magnanimity hesitated to ask her to accept even a share of the sacrifice for patriotism he chose uncomplainingly for himself, sobbed contentedly on his breast and promised she would.

A motor coasting silently down the hill suddenly rounded a turn in the road. Betty Girard sprang away from Sir Harry's encircling arms and vainly strove to smooth her disheveled hair and hide her flushed cheeks. The driver, a woman, gave the pair one quick glance and passed on out of sight without apparent interest.

"She saw us!" exclaimed Betty, hanging her head, blushingly.

"Why should we care, dear? Who is she, anyway? I have seen her a dozen times lately when we've been out driving," Sir Harry answered.

"She's one of a vacation party that has been camped in the woods below our house for the last week or two," Betty replied, stretching out her hands for him to help her to her feet. "Will you drive me home, Harry,"—she used his name for the first time, with a blush,—"and let me tell Dad how very, very happy I am?"

While Betty told her father that night that some day she was to be Lady Cameron, Mary described to Boston Blackie, in his camp within gunshot of the Girard home, the scene on the promontory of rock.

"They're engaged now, beyond a doubt, Blackie," she concluded.

"Which means that she'll be married to him within a week, if he has his way," Blackie added. "Our hour is coming swiftly now, and the price of success is going to be everlasting watchfulness. Isn't this a strange old world, Mary? Think of it—the fate of this innocent little mountain girl we had never heard of two weeks ago depends now on us—a crook mob the world would cage, rightly enough, like wild beasts if it could!"

On the second day after Betty Girard had promised to marry him, Sir Harry Westwood Cameron sat in the office of the mill company reading a contract just handed him by its president. By the terms of the agreement Sir Harry contracted to purchase fifty million feet of redwood lumber, the company agreeing to deliver the timber at the seaboard in monthly lots of five million feet each, with a sharp price-discount as a penalty for delayed deliveries. On his part, Sir Harry agreed to pay spot cash for the lumber as it reached the wharves, with an additional advance payment of ten thousand dollars to stand as a forfeit in case any of the subsequent payments should be defaulted. The contract was a tightly drawn document,—Muir had seen carefully to that, —and there was no conceivable way in which the mill company could lose or be defrauded under its terms.

The lumberman watched Sir Harry narrowly as he read the contract, then turned back and reread it. Somehow, far back in his canny Scotch mind, there still remained his first reasonless but persistent doubt of the Englishman's integrity; but if his customer was satisfied with this contract, Muir conceded he must admit himself wrong. Meanwhile he was on his guard.

"Absolutely correct and satisfactory from my standpoint," Sir Harry announced finally. "As it suits you, Mr. Muir, shall we sign and consider the matter settled?"

Sir Harry scrawled his signature at the bottom of the page. Muir did the same.

"And now except for the matter of the advance payment, our business is satisfactorily settled, I think." Sir Harry drew out a sheaf of checks on which Muir recognized the same consulate insignia he had seen on his customer's credentials and filled out one for ten thousand dollars to the Muir Lumber Company. He flipped it across the table to the lumberman.

"If our deal is as satisfactory to you as I am sure it will be to me," Sir Harry said, "we are both to be congratulated."

He lighted a cigarette, smiling inwardly at the double meaning in his words, and sauntered out to the automobile in which Betty Girard was waiting for him.

Muir indorsed Sir Harry's check and called his cashier.

"Mail this to our bank," he said, "and instruct them to notify me by 'phone when it is honored." To himself he added: "When it's cashed, and not till then, we'll put a night shift to work. Everything seems all right—it can't be otherwise as far as we are concerned; and yet I still have a wee doubt in my head. I wonder why."

Mid-afternoon found Sir Harry Westwood Cameron again within sight of the offices of the Muir Lumber Company. Timing himself accurately, he hurried in just as the mail to go out on the afternoon logging-train was being made up.

"I find I made a stupid blunder when I gave Mr. Muir his check this morning," he said to the cashier. "I drew it on the bank in which the Canadian instead of the British funds are deposited. Has the check gone yet? No! That's fortunate. This is the check you should have had. I'll exchange with you, if you don't mind."

He handed out a new check drawn on a different bank and made out, as the other had been, to the Muir company, for ten thousand dollars.

"Certainly," acquiesced the cashier, opening the letter he had written the bank at Muir's command and handing Sir Harry the first check as he laid the second aside to await indorsement before being mailed. Sir Harry tore up the check in his fingers and let the fragments flutter to the floor.

"Fortunate I happened to discover my error before it passed out of your hands, wasn't it?" he said. "It would have been a beastly nuisance to have rectified it, bound up as I am by red tape. Thanks awfully." And he sauntered out.

Hidden in the palm of his hand was the check returned to him by the Muir company. The one he had torn to bits in the presence of the cashier was an exact duplicate except that it lacked the one essential that gave it value—the indorsement of John J. Muir.

The blood raced through Sir Harry's veins as he turned up Sherwood's boardwalk. The touch of that magic bit of paper, concealed in his hand, was like fiercely intoxicating wine. He knew he needed only to present it at the Muir company's bank, now that it bore the guaranteeing indorsement of the lumberman, to receive without question gold that would buy all he craved in the world of pleasure. And when that gold was gone, there would still be Betty to be cajoled, threatened or abused into giving him more in endless abundance. A single month of freedom had given him wealth!

Nothing remained to be done now but to cash the check when the bank at Ukiah, forty miles away, opened in the morning, and then to disappear, leaving those he had mulcted to count the cost of the acquaintanceship of Sir Harry Westwood Cameron.

Betty, of course, must go with him. Begrudging each moment that still separated him from the actual possession of the money waiting at the bank, he hurried back to the Girard ranch to find her. He showed her a telegram written to himself by himself recalling him secretly and at once to San Francisco to undertake an "urgent mission" and urged her with convincing sophistry to marry him that night in Ukiah.

"This sudden summons to undertake a new mission may mean anything, Betty dear," he pleaded. "It may mean a dangerous trip to the City of Mexico—that was spoken of before I came here; it may mean months of separation; it may—"

Betty laid her hands in his.

"The only happiness I hope for, the only happiness I ask of life, is to share all your dangers and troubles," she said, "I am not afraid—with you."

Sir Harry caught her gently and drew her to him.

"You will go? You will marry me to-night and send me away—if I must leave you—with the comfort of knowing that you, my wife, are waiting for me here and longing, as I shall be, for the happy day when separations are over and we can go home to England—together?" There was a cruelly masterful gleam of satisfaction in Sir Harry's eyes. Once bound to him by a wedding ring, he never intended that Betty Girard should see her mountain home again—never, at least, till he had wrung the last available dollar from her father's rich forests.

"But Dad?" she whispered, stirring in his arms.

"I will explain to him. He will understand and consent," Sir Harry answered.

"Then, if you wish it, I will go." And Betty, who had begun by declaring the idea of an immediate marriage to be impossible, hurried away to pack a suit-case while Sir Harry went to her father. When a girl is eighteen, in love and spells *Romance* with a capital *R*, her own heart pleads with irresistible potency a cause such as Sir Harry's seemed.

Old Sherwood Girard, simple-minded and unsuspecting as Betty herself, had drawn his wheel-chair
to the spot on his porch from which he could best
see the rolling stretches of forest he loved with the
love of one who has met and mastered in their peaceful solitudes the problems of a lifetime. Sir Harry
showed his forged telegram and explained that he
and Betty wished a father's consent to an immediate
and secret marriage.

"Why secret?" the old man asked, studying Sir
Harry's face with eyes, level and keen, though dim-
med by age.

"Because, Dad," said Sir Harry, laying his arm
affectionately round the old man's shoulders, "the
world must not know that I have even been in Sherwood, until the lumber I have bought here for our
armies is safely landed at its destination. Nothing
afloat is safe from the U-boats. The mere fact that
Sir Harry Westwood Cameron, known representative of the British Government, has been in Sherwood, if published, would be ruinous to our projects.
You know what your American newspapers are.
They would make a sensation, with pictures, likely
enough, of the news that our little Betty has
become Lady Cameron. Our wedding will cause
no comment in Ukiah, where I am not known
and shall not use a title that I sometimes regret is
mine. What does it matter when or where we are
married? Betty will return to you to-morrow to wait
here for the day when this new duty to my king

is done and I can return to claim her. Give your consent, Dad. Her happiness and mine depend on it."

Sherwood Girard leaned back in his chair in silence. This sudden wedding seemed uncalled for—almost unseemly.

"And yet," he mused, "I am old, and age is always slow and hesitant in the face of youth. Twenty years ago Betty's mother and I thought a month a year while we counted the days to our wedding. Why should I deny my children now, what they wish?"

He turned to the man beside him.

"Give me your hand, boy," he said, gripping the palm outstretched to him as do men to whom a spoken word and a handclasp are a bond that may not be broken. "It shall be as you—and she—wish. And Sir Harry,"—the old man's voice was tremulous with emotion,—"be very good to my little girl, very good, my boy, and very, very kind. She's only a child."

"I may tell her?" cried Sir Harry, leaping to his feet.

"Yes, and then send her to me. And may God be good to you—as good as you are to her."

"Amen," added Sir Harry with seeming reverence, but smiling at the design in his heart that made the word a blasphemy.

Sir Harry drove Betty to the train in the early evening and left her auto in the village garage. He would follow in it after nightfall, he told her, as

the necessity of keeping his departure absolutely
secret was imperative. Meanwhile she was to go
to a Ukiah hotel and wait. She agreed. Without
a thought of possible evil, she waved him a tremulous, happy *au revoir* and began the wedding journey
the bigamist intended should deliver her irrevocably
into his ruthless hands. With a cruelly satisfied smile
Sir Harry watched her go, and returned to the Girard home to wait, in a scorching fever of impatience,
for the darkness that was to cover his own flight.

That night while Sherwood Girard sat in his
wheel-chair watching the moon rise over his red-
woods and wondering how he could ever endure the
loneliness he would suffer if Betty left him while he
lived, Sir Harry said a brief farewell, took the auto
from the garage, piled in the suit-cases he had hidden by the roadside and turned the car down the
empty, moonlit road that led to Ukiah and the realization of every evil hope he had nursed through five
weary prison years.

CHAPTER XI

THE SPIRIT OF THE CUSHIONS KID

SHERWOOD'S block-long business street was silent, dark and deserted. The one gleam of light in the night was from the incandescent that hung above the big safe in the offices of the Muir Lumber Company.

Examining the strong-box with the calmly critical eye of an expert stood Boston Blackie. He ran his hand delicately over the burnished steel, fondled the combination knobs and turned to the masked man with him who was unpacking a suit-case.

"It's a good box," he said. "Let's get at it. It will take a half-hour to cut into it, and that hick watchman might get back before his time."

Two steel cylinders that just filled the bottom of the suit-case were taken out and set up before the safe. From each a hose led to a metal nozzle punctured by a tiny blow-hole. A heavy curtain of blankets was carefully draped above and around the outfit to cut off from the street the dazzling, bluish light of the flame that was to eat through the solid steel. Boston Blackie took off his mask, replaced it with heavy automobile goggles and then crawled beneath the blankets, which were propped away from the door of the safe by chairs.

"If the copper comes before I finish, don't forget

what I told you," he warned. His companion nodded assent.

From beneath the blankets there began a hissing, spluttering sound, and between them the faint reflection of a blinding light was visible. The second man, armed and masked, stood just inside the front door peering out into the night from behind drawn curtains.

Twenty minutes passed. There was a faint thud as a heavy piece of metal fell to a cushioned floor. The spluttering noise ceased for a moment, then began again. Five minutes, and there was another thud on the floor. Then the light beneath the blankets died, and Boston Blackie, throwing them aside, rose from their folds.

"She's open," he said. "Take a look."

Both doors of the safe were swung back, and a round, gaping hole in each showed where the irresistible heat of the oxyacetylene torch had carved its way through the solid steel as a knife slices cheese.

Boston Blackie drew out a dozen or more unbroken packages of currency and a canvas sack full of silver, and scattered them on the floor.

"It's the pay-roll, Lewes," he reported in a whisper. "I am glad it happened to be here to-night. It would be a nifty little haul, eh?"

So far, Boston Blackie had conducted the business of the evening with skill, dispatch and in all ways as a man of his reputation might be expected to do. Nothing remained to be done to complete a neat job but to bundle the money into the empty suit-case and slip out the rear door. Instead, the safe-cracker began a series of preparations which would have puzzled and amazed others of his hazardous profession.

First he put on his mask. Then he unlocked the front door of the office with a master key he took from his pocket. He opened it and left it slightly ajar. Returning to the safe, he studied carefully the arrangement of the desks and counters, finally indicating one with a jerk of his thumb.

"Get behind there, Lewes, and whatever happens, keep out of sight till I give you the office. Here is your blanket; and be sure you get him on the first throw, for we can't have any noise."

Blackie tossed a blanket to his pal, who obeyed him in silence.

"He isn't due for twenty minutes, but he might be ahead of time, and we mustn't have any kind of a rumble to-night," he commanded as he drew a chair behind the safe and seated himself. He rolled a cigarette and lolled back, waiting, with the unruffled nerves of a man enjoying a quiet evening smoke in his own home.

The lighted incandescent left the dismantled safe and scattered packages of money in plain sight from the half-open door, while the minutes dragged slowly away in absolute silence.

As the clock showed the passing of the hour, a step sounded on the board sidewalk down the street.

"He's coming," whispered Blackie, slipping out of his chair and crouching behind the safe as he readjusted his mask.

The footsteps approached slowly and suddenly stopped before the open door. There was a quick ejaculation of alarm as the watchman saw the wrecked safe and scattered money. He hesitated, fumbling for the revolver he never before had needed, and his eye roamed the room in sudden fear of a bullet from its shadows—a bullet either of the two men hidden within could have sent into his body a dozen times as he stood silhouetted against the window.

But no shot came. Instead Blackie, who had been watching from behind the safe in grim amusement, slowly rose into view with his hands held high above his head.

"Don't shoot," he cried. "You've got me. I quit."

The watchman succeeded at last in dragging out his gun and covered the safe-cracker.

"Keep your hands up," he commanded nervously, advancing on his prisoner. "No monkey business, or I'll pop you sure."

"I don't want to commit suicide," growled Blackie. "You've got me with the goods, and I surrender."

The watchman felt for his handcuffs with his left hand.

"That settles it," ejaculated Blackie disgustedly as

the bracelets came into sight. "I thought I might get a chance to beat it when we got outside in the dark, but now, I suppose, you're going to cuff me to yourself. I'm done for keeps."

"That's just what I'm going to do!" the watchman exclaimed, adopting the suggestion and showing rising excitement as he thought of the reward his night's work would bring him from the lumber company. "Then I'm going to march you over to Mr. Muir's house and keep you safe till he gets the sheriff. You thought you could come up here from the city and blow a safe and get away with it, did you? I guess you know now you can't."

He locked one handcuff over Blackie's extended wrist and snapped the other on his own arm.

"Come on, now. March," he commanded.

"You're some copper." As he snapped out the word "copper," Blackie drew slightly away from his captor. It was the signal for which Lewes was waiting.

The thick folds of a blanket dropped suddenly over the watchman's unsuspecting head. A blow on the wrist knocked his revolver from his hand, and he was thrown to the floor, struggling fiercely but in vain to free himself. With his free hand Boston Blackie snatched a bottle from his pocket and emptied it over the blanket. The captive's struggles grew fiercer, then gradually ceased as the sickly sweet fumes of chloroform tainted the air. At last he lay quiet and inert.

Blackie drew out a bunch of keys, unlocked the handcuff that still bound him to the unconscious man and rose to his feet.

"Neatly done, Lewes," he said smilingly. "He's out. I'll attend to him now. You get the boys and the auto. Be quick, and remember—not a sound from the engine."

Lewes slipped out the rear door and disappeared.

Blackie lifted the blanket and examined the drugged watchman—then dropped it lightly back over his face.

"Not even scratched, and he'll have a story to tell after this night that'll last him the rest of his life," he mused.

A moment later Blackie's quick ear caught the sound of an auto being rolled quietly by hand into the alley behind the building. Three masked men appeared at the rear door. Between them, bound and gagged, was a prisoner at the sight of whose white, rage-contorted face Boston Blackie's lips parted in a singular smile.

The prisoner was Sir Harry Westwood Cameron.

Sir Harry's bloodshot eyes roved in terrified amazement over the strange scene before him—the wrecked safe, the packages of money scattered over the floor, the body hidden by the blanket, and the four masked men who guarded it. When his auto had been stopped at the bridge a half-mile out of town and he himself seized and bound, he had thought himself the victim of a hold-up. But what sort of hold-up men were these, who carried him back to the office of the Muir Lumber Company— the last place on earth he must be at dawn—and held him there now amidst the ruins of a cracked safe?

"I'm going to take the gag out of his mouth. I want to talk to him. If he speaks above a whisper, crack him over the head," said Blackie to his helper.

"What does this mean? What do you want?" gasped Sir Harry as the loosened gag released his lips.

"*You!*" Boston Blackie's eyes hardened into points of steel.

"Me! Who are you?"

Boston Blackie thrust his masked face close to Sir Harry's. Through the slits in the mask, the bigamist felt rather than saw two cold eyes that seemed to bore him through and through with a message of hate and menace.

"Who am I? In spirit I am the Cushions Kid— the same Cushions Kid round whose neck you tried to put a rope to buy your worthless self a few extra months of freedom—the Cushions Kid, who has left his cell at Folsom Prison to-night to teach you, in the hour when you thought you had beaten the world, that a man who plays always pays—and in the same coin."

Sir Harry shrank away in a frenzy of uncontrollable fear from the voice that spoke from behind Boston Blackie's mask, and stared up at him with wide, terror-stricken eyes, scarcely able to believe what they saw.

"And these,"—with a gesture Blackie indicated the other masked men,—"can you guess now who they are? There stands the Kokomo Kid, whom you induced to join you in a break and then deliberately betrayed to his death. Do you remember? You thought he was safely underground in the prison cemetery, didn't you? He isn't. He's here to-night too, in spirit, to watch you pay your debts. Now do you begin to understand why you are here and what is before you—Fred the Count?"

As he heard his prison name flung at him with unutterable hatred by the mysterious man before him, Sir Harry sank on his knees with the fear of death in his heart. Whoever these men were,—whatever they were,—they knew him and all his prison treacheries. He thought he knew what to expect from them. With chattering teeth he pleaded piteously for his life.

"You don't realize even yet what is before you, or you wouldn't beg for life," snarled Blackie in disgust. "You will live to beg for death. Listen carefully, Fred the Count. From the day you left your cell, you have been watched and followed step by step in preparation for this hour. We're not going to kill you. That's too quick and easy. Instead we're sending you back to a cell to stay until they carry you to that cemetery to which you once thought it clever to send other men.

"I let the watchman on the floor there take me in the act of cracking this safe. I let him handcuff me to his wrist. Then we chloroformed him, and now I'm going to handcuff you to him and touch off the burglar-alarm. When Muir and the rest come running down, they'll find you cuffed to the watchman, who will tell them how he caught you. You see the end now, don't you? Safe-cracking to an ex-convict means life, and to make quite sure no mistake will be made, I'm going to put this envelope with your prison photo in one of your suit-cases. The boys up at Folsom will welcome you back, won't they? Ah, you begin to get it now, don't you, Count?"

Sir Harry groaned and groveled on the floor. "You'll learn your lesson well in the years ahead of you."

Boston Blackie stooped and snapped on Sir Harry the handcuff dangling from the still unconscious watchman's wrist. Then he unbound him and turning to one of his silently waiting trio said:

"Bring her in. I promised she should see him."

From the darkness outside the door, a slight, girlish figure with face masked like the rest slipped into the room and stopped before the man on the floor. Suddenly she stooped and looked straight into his face—the face of the now pitiful wreck of a man who but an hour before had boastingly called himself Sir Harry Westwood Cameron, as he hurried toward a bride and a stolen fortune.

"All my life I shall thank God for this moment,"

the girl—little Miss Happy—cried softly to the cowering man. "All my life I shall remember your face as I see it now. Until I die,—if I must go on till then without the Kid,—the years will be less lonely, less hard, because of the picture of you as you are to-night which I shall always have with me, Fred the Count, you traitor. God, I know now, is just."

She was gone as silently as she had come.

Boston Blackie pressed the burglar alarm.

"We're done, Count," he said. "You're the first man I ever helped send to prison—the first man I ever knew whom I think belongs there. Courts don't do the kind of justice we've done to-night. Don't ask mercy of me. Ask it of the men who are in their graves because of you, if you dare."

"It's a job! It's a frame-up! I'll tell the truth about it," Sir Harry screamed, raving and struggling with the desperation of utter despair.

"Tell it all to the judge. I believe you, but he won't," Blackie flung back at him as he slipped out the rear door behind his pals and disappeared.

When the townspeople, routed from their beds by the alarm from the Muir home, came running to the Company offices, they found Sir Harry Westwood Cameron, English lumber buyer, raging like a wild beast and screaming curses from foam-covered lips as he tried to drag the helpless watchman toward the door by a handcuff that cut them both to the bone.

Sir Harry's trial was a short one. A jury of sunburned woodsmen heard the watchman's story, examined the accused man's prison photo, inspected the indorsed Muir check found in his pocket and then, after listening with smiles and covert winks to the prisoner's wild tale of four masked conspirators who had dragged him against his will to the scene of the crime, brought in a verdict of guilty.

*   *   *   *   *

Fred the Count—no longer dapper, well-dressed Sir Harry Westwood Cameron—was on the last stage of his journey back to Folsom Penitentiary. Handcuffed to a sheriff, he crouched dejectedly in the prison van as it slowly climbed the hill that shut the prison from view. As the van turned the crest of the grade, the driver stopped to rest his horses.

Fred the Count looked up. Below him, exactly as he had left it on that morning only a few short weeks before when he went out with the swaggering, self-sufficient ruthlessness of one who thinks himself master of his own fate, was the prison he had never expected to see again. The quarry gang—a group of pygmy figures in stripes—was working among the rocks. One looked up, recognized the Count and called to his fellows.

Tools were thrown to the ground; a score of striped caps were flung high in the air, and cheer after cheer of savage satisfaction floated faintly up from the convicts to the man who was going back among them to do "all of it." It was his own world's welcome "home" to Fred the Count.

Abject and utterly broken in spirit, the Count dropped his head on his manacled hands and sobbed aloud.

"If God is good," he cried, "He will let the knives that are waiting for me down there get me soon. If He is merciful, He will let me die to-night."

Boston Blackie's prophecy was fulfilled.   Fred the Count was praying for death.

CHAPTER XII

A PROBLEM IN GRAND LARCENY

"LIFE is like a lake on a summer day, Mary," said Blackie dropping his tenth consecutive cigarette and twisting restlessly in the easy chair which he had drawn before the glowing grate in their San Francisco apartment. "If you don't drop a pebble now and then, there's never a ripple to break the monotony."

"Fred the Count was a ripple, wasn't he, Blackie?" asked Mary.

"For a moment, yes. But he's safely behind the bars of grim old Folsom and is no longer of any interest to anyone but himself. My mind's getting rusty. I need something to occupy it."

Mary sighed faintly. She loved the quiet and peace of their home but she knew that when the restless spirit of adventure lured him, the man she loved, inevitably must answer the call.

"Diamond Frank is in town," she suggested after a moment's thought.

"Good," cried Blackie. "That's an idea! Frank always has the latest gossip from the north. I'll 'phone him to come up and have a talk."

An hour later the two, from the center of a pall of cigarette smoke, were exchanging news of the hidden world in which each was a recognized leader.

127

"Two million dollars in gold—a truckload—is waiting for anyone smart enough to get it."

Diamond Frank, an ace in the world of crime, paused and shook his head sadly as might an art connoisseur who contemplates a priceless treasure doomed to lie hidden forever from human eyes.

"But it can't be done," he added with regretful resignation. "Not a chance in the world! It's awful, Blackie, but it's true. I know, for I've tried. Think of it, pal! Enough good yellow gold to make any of us rich enough to be worth robbing, and yet a man can't lay hands on it."

"Why?" asked Boston Blackie.

Diamond Frank, lolling back in his chair, summed up the situation with the succinct directness of one who had given his subject painstaking study.

"On the beach at Nome it's in iron-bound, sealed and padlocked chests guarded night and day by gunmen. Not a chance so far. Then it goes into the strong-room of that old floating tub, the *Humboldt*. No guards there, Blackie, but there isn't a stateroom that gives a man a possible chance to cut through to the treasure from top, bottom or sides. The padlock on the strong-room is a double combination that unlocks with two keys, one kept by the captain and one by the purser. It is never unfastened, from Nome to Seattle. A charge of 'soup' would blow it off; but that, of course, is out of the question on shipboard, with the strong-room almost opposite the purser's stateroom. At Seattle it is un-

loaded to a truck guarded by more gunmen. Then
it goes into the First National vaults to stay. There
you are! Three tons of gold unwatched on a steamer
for from five to eight days—and I traveled all the
way to Nome and back on the old *Humboldt* last
fall without finding a thousand-to-one chance of laying a finger on it. It broke my heart, but I had to
give it up."

Boston Blackie lay back in his chair, thoughtfully
silent.

"I should say offhand it would be far easier to
lay hands on the gold than to get it past the Custom
House men and safely away, after I had it," he
remarked at last.

"Jump to it if you see a chance. I'm done," said
Diamond Frank.

"Maybe I will," said Blackie. And though he
dropped the subject as if no longer interested, he
sat alone till dawn, after his friend departed, men-
tally visualizing the treasure room of a tubby, plunging steamer plowing her way southward from the
Nome beaches with a king's ransom locked in her
steel-bound vault.

"It could be done," he said softly to himself.
"And inasmuch as James J. Clancy is president of
the company that owns the *Humboldt*, there is the
best reason in the world why Mary and I should
do it. All the gold the *Humboldt* ever carried would
not even the score we owe old 'Eye-for-an-eye' Jim
Clancy, who identified Mary's father as the hold-up

man who robbed him years ago in Spokane—Jim
found his identification had been a blunder and justified it as 'a regrettable incident but not really a
miscarriage of justice,' for the wrongly convicted
man, now dead, was,' he said, 'one who from his
manner of life could have been no benefit to himself,
his family or the world that is well rid of him.' "

Blackie's fingers were clenched, and his eyes were
cold and steely with determination as he quoted the
words that had been Clancy's epitaph to the memory
of the man he had wronged.

"Yes," he added to himself grimly, "the man who
could say that of big, open-handed, kindly old Dayton Tom, is a man whom it will be a pleasant privilege to rob. We'll do it."

Three weeks later the *Humboldt* lay off the shore
whose golden sands made a thriving city of the once-
deserted Nome beach. At intervals, above the mo-
notonous surf-roar, the sound of high-pitched laughter and broken bars of dance music floated faintly
out across the water. The last homeward-bound
steamer of the season was ready to sail, and all Nome
was celebrating.

The *Humboldt's* upper deck was deserted except
for one passenger—a girl who leaned over the after-
rail intently watching the labor of seamen who were
lowering weighty, carefully guarded chests of gold
from a jutting pier to small boats that were to carry
them to the strong-room of the waiting ship off-
shore.

The girl, off guard in the safety of her solitude, watched the movement of the treasure with almost proprietary solicitude. Because of that jealously guarded gold she was a passenger on the *Humboldt*. Because of it there lay on her forearm, hidden by the sleeve of her traveling suit, a tight fitting bracelet a dozen times more precious to her than its weight in diamonds. Often and involuntarily her fingers slipped beneath her sleeve to caress softly the circlet they found there. It represented a difficult adventure skillfully accomplished. It was confirmatory proof of the logic of the master-mind that had set itself the seemingly impossible task of rifling the steamer's treasure vault. It was an instrument of revenge infinitely precious to the daughter of the man the world had called "Dayton Tom."

The boats, each with a shotgun guard idle but watchful in the stern seat, put off from the wharf and drew up beside the *Humboldt*. A whining cargo engine lowered a rope net to the bobbing carriers, and one by one, with infinite care, the treasure chests were swung to the steamer's deck and piled there in ten rows, each four boxes high. Forty chests of gold—forty iron-bound storehouses of vast, illimitable power!

The boxes were counted, checked and recounted and then wheeled down the companionway to the ship's strong-room. Inside the steel-bound vault, with guards barring the doorway against the curious, the chests were counted once again and each of their heavy seals examined by Captain McNaughton, Purser Dave Jessen of the *Humboldt* and the Nome manager of the express company that was guaranteeing the treasure's safe delivery in far-away Seattle. Every seal was intact, every chest in its place; and with a sigh of relief as his responsibility ended, the express manager accepted the receipt signed jointly by the ship's captain and the purser, for two million dollars in gold.

At a command from the Captain, a dozen or more trunks, boxes and treasure parcels intrusted to the steamer for safe-keeping by passengers, were wheeled into the strong-room and checked off the purser's list. All were there. The *Humboldt's* treasure-room was in order. With a final, sweeping glance of satisfied security, the Captain's eye roamed the interior of the steel-lined room. Then he stepped out, pulled shut the great steel-barred door and put in place the giant padlock that guarded it. The Captain's key turned softly in the lock. The purser's followed it with another gentle click of hidden ratchets—and the treasure was as safe as human ingenuity could make it.

Purser Jessen, with a sigh of relief, locked his key in a secret compartment of his private safe. Captain McNaughton hid his key in the money belt that girdled his waist and never left his body night or day. Then he opened a panel in the wall above his berth and threw on an electric switch that turned a death-dealing current through the steel plate in the floor just within the strong-room door and connected, also, a series of alarms that would rouse the ship if the treasure-room door were opened so much as an inch.

"Well, that's well off my mind!" the Captain murmured, and went on deck to direct his final preparations for sailing.

A shrieking blast came from the steamer's siren. A score of small boats and launches, each crowded with passengers, put off from the pier. An hour later they swarmed over the *Humboldt's* decks by hundreds, and the *Humboldt,* with a final siren blast, slowly swung her prow seaward and began her long homeward journey.

Nightfall found the girl who had watched the loading of the treasure with such interest standing alone against the after-deck rail abstractedly watching the steamer's foamy wake fade away into the darkness of an empty sea. On the passenger list she was registered as "Miss Marie Whitney, Chicago," a name that cloaked the presence on the *Humboldt* of Mary Dawson—Boston Blackie's Mary— able assistant of the husband for whom she was waiting now, tense and eagerly expectant, to surrender the circlet on her wrist against which her fingers lay protectingly.

A step on the deck behind her caught her ear. From the darkness a voice spoke softly.

"Mary," it said.

The girl stirred in a revealing movement of love,

joy and pride in her own well-accomplished task. Without turning her head she stretched two hands behind her and grasped the man's eagerly.

"I have it, Blackie," she said, speaking in a whisper. "Absolutely perfect, too! It's on my left wrist. Take it quickly—and oh, my dear, do be careful of it. It couldn't possibly be replaced now. The door is wired, as you thought—alarms ring all over the steamer if it is opened. The wires run out through the upper left wainscoting of the companionway. Everything is arranged as you planned."

"The man who said this trick couldn't be turned didn't know my Mary," whispered the voice behind the girl's head, as strong deft fingers slipped the bracelet over her wrist with a caressing touch as thrilling to her as rare wine.

"Your work is done,—well done,—dearest," he said. "Take no more risks whatever. No matter what happens, neither recognize nor communicate with Lewes or with me again. With this bracelet in my hand the gold already is ours."

"Do be careful, Blackie dear," she urged under the stress of the natural, ever-present fear of a woman for the man she loves. "I've had a queer feeling —a sort of premonition—"

"Sh-h-h!" interrupted Blackie. "Someone's coming."

Silently as a shadow he glided away across the darkened deck.

A man's firm, heavy step approached, and as Mary

leaned across the rail and stared again in seeming
idleness toward the disappearing wake beyond the
steamer, a blue uniform appeared at her side, and
Dave Jessen, the *Humboldt's* purser, stooped and
peered into her face.

"It is you, Miss Whitney. I knew I couldn't be
wrong even in the dark," the young officer said,
betraying with each word the deep and deferential
interest which had grown steadily during the weeks
since the *Humboldt* had left Seattle with "Miss
Marie Whitney" among her passengers.

"I'm the unfortunate bearer of bad news, Miss
Whitney," he concluded seriously.

"Bad news?" repeated the girl, looking up
quickly.

"I fear so," he continued. "You know how
crowded we are this trip. Every stateroom is sold,
and we're even bunking some of the miners down in
the crew's quarters; but even so, I was sure until
the last moment that I could keep your double stateroom for you alone. But I can't. An hour before
we left Nome, Captain McNaughton received a wireless from Seattle that forces us to make room for
express company detectives and—"

"Detectives!" echoed the girl.

In the darkness her slender hands clutched the rail
until the knuckles whitened. With a quick, fierce
effort of will she mastered her fear and looked up
at him with a smile that invited confidence.

"How exciting!" she exclaimed. "But what have

detectives to do on the prosaic old *Humboldt?*"

The man bent toward her and lowered his voice.

"The Seattle police have been informed by one of their spies, a woman, that two crooks—top-notchers with an international reputation, the wire said—are on board the *Humboldt* for the purpose of looting the treasure-room on the trip home," he said. "That, of course, is impossible; the strong-room is absolutely burglar-proof. But with two millions of gold on board, precautions even against the impossible are necessary. So I had to turn over a state-room opposite the treasure-room to the officers, and must ask you to permit me to give you company on the return trip. I'm sorry, but—"

"Whom are you putting in with me?"

"A Miss Nina Francisco. She's a Californian, an exceptionally likable young woman, I think. She has been in Nome all summer, visiting mines in which her father is interested, she told me. Do you mind sharing your cabin with her, Miss Whitney?" he finished with unconscious tenderness.

"Certainly not," Mary answered. Then, spurred to the necessity of obtaining further information by Blackie's danger, she looked into the officer's face with parted lips and eyes that were bright with an excitement which she had no need to feign.

"A robbery planned on this ship!" she cried. "How wonderfully exciting! Are these crooks being watched? Will they be arrested here on the *Humboldt?*"

"Probably not, unless they really make an attempt to break into the strong-room," Jessen replied. "We have their names and a description, but they are using aliases, naturally, and we haven't been able to identify them yet. But it really doesn't matter, for now that we have been warned, there isn't a chance in a million for them to accomplish anything on shipboard; and at the dock in Seattle, officers who know them will take them into custody as they go ashore."

The girl's body stiffened, and her face, protected by the darkness, grew suddenly white and infinitely careworn. Imminent danger threatened Boston Blackie, for she knew he would use without delay the circlet she had given him but a moment before. She must warn him at once of his peril.

"I think I'll go below," she said. "It's growing chilly."

She shivered, but not from cold.

"I may have Miss Francisco's baggage moved into your cabin?" asked the purser, steadying her with a gentle hand as they returned across the deck.

"Of course—and thank you for your courtesy," Mary answered with cordiality that quickened the pulse of the bronzed, clear-eyed young officer beside her. "As you have chosen her as my companion, I am sure Miss Francisco and I will be congenial, and I am so excited over your news about the—the—crooks. You'll let me know if anything exciting happens, won't you, please? Why, it's all just like a movie, with all of us playing a part in it!"

She laid her hand on his arm and looked plead-
ingly into eyes as innocent and straightforward and
free from guile as the sea winds that had tanned his
cheeks.

"You know I will, Miss Whitney. Good night,"
said Jessen, his voice revealing what he feared to
put into words.

"Good night—and don't forget your promise," she
said with a smile that gave no hint of the anxiety in
her heart as she disappeared toward her stateroom.

Mary penned a hasty note telling Blackie the cru-
cially important news, and slipped out of her stateroom to rap in the code of the crook-world at his
door—under which she slipped the note when an answering rap came from within.

During Mary's absence a young woman, tall, dark
and voluptuously handsome, entered and stood eyeing
curiously the cabin to which her baggage had just
been moved. On the table she saw the tablet on
which Mary had written, with a freshly used pen
beside it. Without hesitation she stepped to the
table and held the paper to the light. On the sheet
beneath the one that had been used, and which Mary
in her hurry had neglected to destroy, a few words
were visible.

" '*Seattle* ..... *wireless* ..... *treasure-room* ..
....*detectives!*'" the woman read with widening
eyes at each telltale word. "So she knows the secrets of the wireless room, does she?" she mused.
"And she was talking with a man out on that dark

deck when the purser went for her! Ah! She hurried down here and wrote a note and evidently has gone to deliver it. I'm lucky to have stumbled across this. I think the delightful Miss Whitney who so obviously has turned that simple-minded purser's head is not quite what she seems."

Once more she picked up the tablet and strove to decipher further information from the few faint words imprinted there.

As she bent over the paper, Mary entered. The newcomer laid down the tablet without a trace of embarrassment.

"Miss Whitney, I presume?" she said, extending a jeweled hand languidly. "I was just admiring the tint of your stationery. You have guessed, of course, that I am Miss Francisco, whom you have so kindly permitted to share this cabin."

The women's eyes met in a long, appraising glance, during which each tried vainly to hide beneath smiling lips a surging flood of hostility based on feminine intuition rather than reason.

"I'm sure we shall have a delightful trip together," said Mary in slightly strained tones, as she picked up the tablet and tossed it carelessly into a drawer. Her quick eyes had caught the words at which her new companion was staring as she entered, and she realized that her momentary carelessness had doubled the gravity of her problem.

"A spy!" she decided instantly. "A spy put here to watch me, but I'll not let her know that I suspect."

"She sees the words imprinted on that sheet of paper and knows I have read them," thought Miss Francisco. "She's on her guard now, but can't possibly guess that I know who is on this steamer and why he is here. I'll win her confidence, and maybe—"

She turned with a smile to her new friend. Ten minutes later the two went arm in arm to the music-room.

CHAPTER XIII

THE SHOT IN THE DARK

AS the *Humboldt,* plowing steadily southward beneath sunny skies, neared Seattle, the tension in the stateroom occupied by Miss Whitney and Miss Francisco increased until it became a tangible something as vibrant as an electric current. Neither woman for an instant relaxed her ceaseless watchfulness, and neither betrayed it; yet each knew that as she spied, she was being spied upon. Mary, in the light of her knowledge of the crucial situation on shipboard, found much in her gay companion's conduct to deepen her suspicion that Miss Francisco, if not actually a detective, was an emissary of those whom she knew were on board.

On the days following the woman's first appearance in Mary's stateroom, Nina spent much time in the steamer's wireless station—where, apparently, she flirted flagrantly with the operator—a role in which she proved herself decidedly adept.

"Camouflage to cloak her anxiety for further news from Seattle that will enable the officers to identify Blackie and Lewes," was Mary's inward comment as for the hundredth time she studied her fellow-passengers with the hope of determining the identity of the police officers she knew to be among them. The detectives were lodged close to the treasure-room,

141

the purser had said; and gradually her suspicion centered on an Englishman—Sir Arthur Cumberland on the passenger list—who, with a secretary-companion, was ostensibly making the Alaskan trip as part of a round-the-world tour.

Cumberland was a big, blond Britisher with a long, drooping mustache, an accent that was joyfully mimicked by other passengers in the salon, and a decided weakness for the American bar below decks. His secretary was a keen-eyed little man named McDonald whose burr suggested the Clyde.

Just why she doubted Cumberland, Mary herself could hardly have explained, except that she felt he was too obviously in dress and personal appearance what he seemed—too perfectly the familiar, titled Englishman of the American stage. A chance word crystallized her suspicion into certainty on the night she hid herself in a secluded nook behind a lifeboat to win for a moment the relief of being off guard. The Englishman, smoking, stopped beside the boat. Almost immediately he was joined by the secretary.

"What have you learned?" demanded Cumberland.

"Haven't located anything yet," answered McDonald.

"You must—quickly; for I'll have them before we sight Seattle or my name's not—" He stopped, glanced round as if fearing eavesdroppers and laughed at his own caution.

"Be careful," warned his companion as they strolled on.

From that moment Mary assiduously courted the company of the pair—an easy task, for a pretty face was the open sesame to Sir Arthur's good will and interest. She had no definite plan, no specific hope, but hour by hour prayed for inspiration.

Miss Francisco had scarcely noticed the Englishman until Mary adopted them as deck companions. From that moment, however, she managed to make herself an inseparable member of the party.

One night after too-frequent visits to the buffet, Cumberland dropped an *h* now and then and lapsed occasionally into an accent not at all suggestive of Regent Street. Mary, looking up as she caught this falsenote, found Nina Francisco studying her curiously. McDonald also was keenly aware of his chief's incriminating bit of forgetfulness, for with ill-hidden anger he managed to separate him from the ladies, and the pair vanished into their cabin.

That night when they were alone in their stateroom Miss Francisco, to Mary's surprise, began to discuss and speculate upon Sir Arthur Cumberland and his business.

"Did you notice anything peculiar in our friend the baronet's language this evening?" she asked innocently.

Mary, busy at her dressing-table, flashed a quick look into the glass and met her companion's eyes in the mirror.

"She's wondering whether her detective friends have betrayed themselves to me," she thought.

"It was peculiar for a titled Englishman," she said aloud. Then, after a moment's thought in which to weigh her words, Mary added: "But it was nothing that I was not fully prepared to expect from him."

Again the women studied each other furtively.

"So you think as I do that our titled globe-trotter may be—" began Nina.

"I know just as you do," interrupted Mary with increasing emphasis on each word, "that Sir Arthur Cumberland is playing a part for a purpose. I think even you will admit he plays it badly."

Nina tucked a drooping lock of her raven hair into place and toyed with a powder-puff before answering.

"You're quite right," she said at last. "Sir Arthur would play any game rather badly, I imagine— very differently from you, my dear."

"And from you also," added Mary, following the words with a look that accentuated their inner meaning.

"Does that mean necessarily that we—you and I —must play at cross purposes on the *Humboldt?*" asked Nina.

"You can answer your own question far better than I," said Mary.

"Thanks," replied Nina. "You have clarified the atmosphere for both of us, I think. Anyway, in seventy-two hours we will be in Seattle, and then—"

Mary without replying threw herself on her berth and switched off the lights to save herself the ordeal of parrying Nina Francisco's coldly analyzing eyes. In seventy-two hours the *Humboldt* would be in Seattle, she had said pointedly—in Seattle, with detectives waiting at the dock, she meant, and a prison looming large and certainly in the background. Mary's clenched fingers bit into her palms at the thought. Her fears were not for herself but for the man she loved. With the robbery still uncommitted,—for in the light of the information she had given him she had no thought that Blackie would persevere in his attempt to secure the gold,—Mary knew there would be little or nothing on the *Humboldt* that would justify a prison term; but she knew, too, that with a man of Boston Blackie's crookworld prestige in their toils, the police would find or invent something for which he could be imprisoned.

Without realizing that she had slept, Mary was suddenly awakened to full consciousness by a stealthy movement near her in the pitch-dark cabin. She listened with every sense keyed to superlative alertness. The sound, a soft, slippered step, was repeated, and she felt a faint fresh breeze stir her hair. Instantly she realized its significance. The door of the stateroom, locked when she retired, now was ajar. Silently she raised herself and stared into the darkness. Her eyes detected a blacker blotch just within the cabin door, crouching furtively like an animal ready to spring. Now and then in the faint light that filtered in through the open porthole she caught a reflected glint of bright metal near the figure at the doorway. She recognized that changing, intermittent flash. A person within the cabin, watching the companionway—down which twenty steps distant was the door of the treasure-room—held a revolver.

Noiselessly as an Indian, Mary drew herself over the side of the berth till her feet touched the floor. She slipped into her dark-colored dressing-gown and with eyes still fixed on the figure in the doorway, felt beneath her pillow till her fingers grasped the butt of a revolver.

As she rose with slow caution, a faint sound reached her from the companionway—the gentle creak of a heavy door moving on little-used hinges. As if that were an awaited signal, the form in the doorway straightened and glided silently as a shadow out of the cabin into the pitch dark companionway. Mary, a second silent shadow, followed.

With eyes accustomed now to the darkness, Mary detected two forms in the narrow passageway which branched at right angles just beyond the treasure-room. One—the one that had been within the door of her cabin—was slinking inch by inch along the wall with the stealth of a jungle cat stalking its prey. The other was bent over the lock of the treasure-room door. In the absolute silence Mary heard the man's fingers gently moving over the steel plate.

A faint ejaculation of astonishment came from the man before the strong-room. Then a tiny ray of light illumined the door for a fraction of a second. By its flash Mary saw that the massive padlock that should have guarded the gold was gone.

As the light winked out into absolute blackness, the figure stalking the man by the door moved quickly forward. Mary followed close behind.

Then a dozen amazing things happened at once:

From the cross companionway beyond the strong-room, a third figure rose apparently from the floor and seized the man before the door. There was a fierce struggle, followed by a deafening splintering of wood as they crashed against the cabin partitions and fell to the floor. From between the struggling forms the sharp crack of a revolver followed a brilliant flash of flame which for a second lighted the faces of the fighting men. By the flash Mary saw them clearly.

The attacker, who had risen from the floor beyond the strong-room, wore a crook's mask. The man who had fired the revolver for which both were now struggling desperately was Sir Arthur Cumberland.

As the shot reverberated down the narrow passage-way, the figure that had stolen from the doorway of Mary's cabin, leaped to the center of the melee with clubbed gun held high as if to end the battle with a single deadly blow. Mary sprang forward to intercept that blow in midair—but with her gun upraised to strike, she shrank back against the shattered woodwork in dazed perplexity. The one whose upraised arm she would have crushed had struck—but not at the masked man. Instead Nina Francisco's gun butt —Mary recognized her now—struck the revolver from Sir Arthur Cumberland's hand. Instantly his opponent seized it and crashed it solidly against the Englishman's temple. Cumberland fell back, limp and senseless.

CHAPTER XIV

THE MYSTERY OF THE S. S. HUMBOLDT

WHAT followed seemed a nightmare of un-
reality. A fourth form, appearing apparently
from nowhere, passed swiftly down the companionway and vanished. The masked victor staggered to his feet and seemingly intent on making more
noise and confusion, raised the unconscious Englishman and dashed him against the door of the purser's cabin, which burst open.

Screams and shouts came from behind stateroom
doors. Mary darted back to her own cabin, slipped
her revolver beneath her pillow and switched on the
lights just as the door was thrown open and Miss
Nina Francisco entered, her clubbed revolver still in
her hand. The girl shot the bolt in the door while
the uproar in the companionway increased and running men poured down from the upper deck.

Without a glance toward Mary, Nina opened a
grip, dropped the revolver into it and locked it. Then
she drew on a pair of stockings, slipped her feet into
shoes and with a calm, quick glance round the room
as if to make sure she had forgotten nothing essential,
threw open the door of the cabin and began to scream
hysterically.

The companionway was lighted now, and ship's officers and seamen, aided by the shaken and white-

faced secretary, were raising the senseless form of Sir Arthur Cumberland.

Mary, peering over Nina's shoulders, saw that the door of the strong-room was open. Blood splotches were everywhere, and Purser Jessen was loudly calling for the ship's surgeon. The doctor and the Captain arrived together.

"What's happened here, Mr. Jessen?" demanded McNaughton, gazing dumbfounded at the bloody, unconscious passenger, the open door of the strong-room, the splintered woodwork.

"Blamed if I know, sir!" gasped his subordinate. "I was asleep when I heard a crash in the companion-way. There was a shot, then another crash. Then this man came through the door of my cabin, tearing away the hinges."

The Captain turned to his first officer.

"Put a guard before every stateroom on the steamer," he commanded. "Let no one leave a cabin until I give permission. Move this crowd back, each to his stateroom,"—motioning to the half-dressed passengers who were pouring out of a dozen doors. "Doctor, take the injured man into Mr. Jessen's cabin and attend him, while I find out what's happening on this ship."

As the passageway was cleared, the Captain picked up from the floor the padlock that had hung on the treasure-room door. It had been opened without leaving even a mutilating scratch.

"The strong-room padlock unlocked!" he gasped.

"Look," cried Jessen, pointing to an object that lay beneath a fragment of splintered wood. The Captain picked it up, turning it over and over in his hand. It was the exact duplicate of the strong-room lock. Near by lay a revolver with blood-stained handle.

"Follow me, Mr. Jessen," McNaughton commanded.

Together they entered the strong-room, piled high with the treasure-chests, and studied it—walls, ceiling and floor. Nothing appeared amiss. One by one they examined the seals on the chests. All were intact.

"They must have been interrupted by Sir Arthur as they were entering," suggested the purser.

"Not as they were entering, but after they had entered," corrected the Captain, sniffing the air.

"Why, sir?" inquired Jessen.

"Cigarette smoke inside," explained McNaughton, still sniffing. "They've broken into the *Humboldt's* strong-room, though it can't be done. And they even dared to keep their cigarettes going while they did it! Thank heavens, Cumberland heard them, for it is evident he must have interrupted the thieves or they would not have struck him down."

McNaughton pushed his way into Jessen's room, where the surgeon was dressing an ugly wound over Cumberland's temple, with the secretary aiding him.

"Is he badly hurt, Doctor?" McNaughton demanded.

The surgeon shook his head doubtfully.

"I can't say yet," he replied. "He took a hard blow. He may come around all right shortly, and he may have a fractured skull—which, from a blow just there, might mean cerebral hemorrhage."

"He may be unconscious for hours?"

"Or even days," said the doctor.

"What do you know of this?" McNaughton asked, turning to McDonald.

"I was asleep," the little Scotchman answered readily. "I heard nothing till a shot awakened me. When I got the lights on and the door open, Sir Arthur was in the purser's arms, wounded. I didn't hear him leave our cabin, and I don't know who struck him, though it is plain he interrupted a robbery of your strong-room."

One by one the Captain visited the nearby cabins, questioning the passengers. None gave information of real value. All had been awakened by the noise in the companionway or the subsequent shot. As they rushed from their staterooms, they had seen the purser raising the injured man within the wrecked cabin door. No one else was in sight except the injured man's secretary, who appeared from his cabin after the trouble was over.

McNaughton came finally to the stateroom of Miss Francisco and Mary.

"What did you ladies see of this?" he inquired courteously. "You first, Miss Whitney."

"I saw more than she did, Captain, for I was

first at the door," interrupted Miss Francisco quickly. "I was awake when I heard the crash in the passageway. Then there was a shot. I jumped from my berth and turned on our lights. I heard a stateroom door near ours bang shut as I threw open our door. I saw the purser with the injured man in his arms. I'm afraid that's all I know. Is poor Sir Arthur badly hurt, Captain?" She spoke with such well-feigned solicitude that Mary, remembering the blow struck in the dark, wondered at the perfection of her duplicity.

"Was the door you heard close to the left or the right of yours?" asked the Captain, seizing the one important bit of information in the girl's story.

"I don't know. I only know it was very close— almost adjoining ours, I judge."

"Can you add anything to what Miss Francisco has told?" asked McNaughton of Mary.

"I heard the shot and the noise; and I think, as Miss Francisco told you, that I heard a cabin door near by close immediately afterward," Mary said, following the other's story with exactness. "That's all I can tell you."

As she heard Nina Francisco's glib invention, Mary, knowing that Blackie's stateroom was far away and around the turn in the companionway, decided instantly to corroborate it. Wittingly or unwittingly, that untruth furnished an alibi for the man whose safety mattered to her. Why Nina Francisco had struck the blow that ended the battle, Mary

could not guess. Why she now imperiled herself
by a bold fabrication was an even deeper mystery.

"Thank you, ladies. I've work before me that
can't wait," said the Captain, bowing himself out
hurriedly.

As the door closed behind him, Nina and Mary
looked at each other with silent lips but questioning
eyes.

"Well, that's over, thank goodness!" said Nina
at last, sighing with relief.

She turned to the dressing-table and dabbed her
powder-puff over her nose.

"You're not a bad sport, after all, Miss Whitney,"
she continued after a long silence. "I beg your pardon for what I've been thinking about you."

"And you're—I don't know what," said Mary.

"Just a woman, my dear," said Nina with soft-
ened voice. "A woman willing to dare anything for
the man for whom she can't help caring."

They smiled across the table at each other, and
though neither asked a question or offered further
explanation, the strange events of the night dissi-
pated, for the first time, the hostility that had divided them.

Morning found Captain McNaughton sitting in
his cabin, perplexed furrows wrinkling his brow.
The steamer had been searched from hurricane-deck
to keel, without result. Not the slightest additional
wisp of evidence came to light to justify even suspicion. The duplicate padlock, the revolver with one

empty chamber, and the injured passenger, were the only bits of evidence left by those who had attempted the daring raid on the treasure.

Investigation showed the electric-alarm wires leading into the strong-room had been cut, and the wainscoting that hid them replaced without leaving even a betraying speck of sawdust. The lead offered by the closing cabin door heard by Miss Francisco proved absolutely barren, for the most minute search of all cabins on the treasure-room companionway revealed absolutely nothing. The duplicate padlock was a duplicate in outward appearance only. It could be opened with the simplest of master-keys.

At daylight a seaman found a pocket flash-lamp rolling on the upper deck with the movement of the ship. It might have been tossed from any one of a dozen cabins. McNaughton locked it away with the padlock and the gun and ascended to the wireless room, where he dictated a message to his company managers telling all that had happened. Until Sir Arthur Cumberland recovered his senses,— the injured man's condition was unchanged,—the Captain had done all that seemed possible. One thought comforted him. The treasure-room gold had not been disturbed, for in the search of the *Humboldt* which had included the personal baggage of passengers, officers and members of the crew, no possible hiding-place for great yellow bars two feet long and weighing thirty or more pounds each had been overlooked. In addition, the chest seals were all intact.

The *Humboldt* was backing slowly from the dock at Victoria—a special stop necessitated by a shipment of British Columbian freight—and had begun the short run down the Sound to Seattle when Mary received a message that brought color back to her white face. A man passed behind her as she sat in the deck-chair and deftly dropped a slip of paper into her lap. Turning as she hid the note with her hand, she recognized Blackie's pal, K. Y. Lewes. Concealing the note in her book, she read at a glance its five words—words that lifted the load that burdened her heart.

"Follow original instructions. Don't worry," was written; and the writing was Boston Blackie's.

Somehow—inconceivably but surely—she knew he had solved the problem of escape at the Seattle wharf. She sprang to her feet, and unutterably content, tossed the now twisted bit of paper overboard and watched it float away on the waters of the Sound as she gayly joined the throng on the decks.

During that last day at sea Purser Dave Jessen watched in vain for an opportunity to speak alone with "Miss Marie Whitney," to tell her he loved her, to ask her to be his wife. Though he admitted to himself his presumption in hoping that she might feel for him even a tithe of the great tenderness in his heart, he did hope, for he was a man and in love.

But never for an instant during the day was Miss

Whitney alone. Among the score of vacation trippers who boarded the *Humboldt* at Victoria for the return trip to Seattle was a party of five—four modestly dressed girls chaperoned by an agreeable, white haired mother—one of whom proved to be a former schoolmate of Miss Whitney's. All day the new-found friends monopolized her attention, and it was not until the nearing lights of Seattle threw their glare against the southern sky that Jessen found the opportunity he sought.

He was distributing the passengers' baggage, which had been intrusted to the safety of the strong-room—baggage that was removed from the stronghold under the personal supervision of Captain McNaughton. Accompanied by subordinates carrying her trunk, he knocked at the girl's door and found her alone. The men deposited the trunk and departed, but Jessen lingered in the open doorway. Mary looked up interrogatively.

"Marie," he said, stepping to her side with a longing, half-fearful look into the face upturned to his. "I love you. Forgive me, only a poor sailor, for daring to tell you, for even daring to hope you would listen. But because I love you, and you are leaving the *Humboldt* to-night, I must speak now. Marie, can you—will you—be my wife?"

There was simple sincerity and great love in the words, the voice and the frank eyes that looked into hers as she slowly shook her head.

"Don't, Mr. Jessen," Mary said gently. "I like

you; I admire you; but what you ask—it can't be."

The bronzed face paled under its tan, and the blue eyes.contracted under the numbing pain of a precious hope suddenly uprooted.

"There is someone else?" he asked unsteadily.

"Yes," said Mary, truly sorry she must so wound the love offered her. "Forgive me, Mr. Jessen," she added, laying a small hand on the man's arm.

Jessen caught and pressed it and hurried with averted face from the cabin as women's voices sounded in the companionway.

CHAPTER XV

MISSING GOLD

WITH a final whining of taut hawsers and a gentle jolt against the long Seattle pier the *Humboldt* had reached the end of her voyage. The gangplank was raised to the deck, and the eager passengers thronged there shoulder to shoulder, pressed backward to let a stretcher precede them to the dock. By the stretcher walked McDonald, grave and silent. On it lay Sir Arthur Cumberland, his head swathed in bandages. He had neither spoken nor given a sign of returning consciousness since the night of the attempted robbery. On the wharf an ambulance summoned by wireless waited to hurry him to a hospital.

The injured man was carried down the gangplank and along the passageway to the Custom House shed. Just inside the entrance four men—two on each side of the doorway—were waiting, keen-eyed and vigilant. Mary, following the stretcher in the van of the crowding passengers, recognized them at once as police detectives. With an apprehensive glance she looked back over her shoulder. Near by, pushing forward, and chatting together as imperturbably as though danger were miles removed from them instead of at arm's length, came Boston Blackie and Lewes.

Captain McNaughton, with President Clancy of the steamship company beside him, was in the Custom House shed. The stretcher was lowered to one of the long tables, and the passengers grouped themselves, silent and expectant about the locked shed as seamen carried in the Englishman's baggage, to which the need of hurrying him to a hospital had given priority of inspection.

"That's Cumberland, who saved our gold," the Captain said in a low voice to the steamship official. "He has an ugly wound and is still unconscious."

"Too bad, but the men who wounded him are enjoying their final moment of freedom," Clancy growled. "The Chief has four men here who will know these crooks the moment they lay eyes on them. They must be bold fellows. The mythical detectives I invented for you by wireless didn't appear even to make them nervous, did they?"

"Scarcely, as they broke into the strong-room notwithstanding the fact that I made it my business to let the news that we had been warned become common forecastle and saloon gossip," the Captain replied sourly.

The inspector ran through the Cumberland trunks and grips rapidly as McDonald unlocked them. The chief inspector watched attentively. The detectives grouped themselves by the side of the litter. Inspection revealing nothing but the ordinary equipment of traveling gentlemen, McDonald was eager to be off to the hospital.

"Come on, my men," he said to the stretcher bearers. "Where's the ambulance? I'll send down later for our baggage."

"Wait," said the chief inspector curtly.

Selecting two of the Cumberland trunks, he emptied them. Then he drew a measuring stick from his pocket and took the outside dimensions of the trunks.

As he comprehended what was being done, the secretary's jaw sagged, and with a furtive glance over his shoulder he began to edge toward a window. At his first movement one of the detectives laid a hand on his arm.

"Don't be in a hurry, 'bo," said the officer. "Anyway, that window's locked."

The inspector jotted down the outside measurements of the trunks, then applied his rule to the inner surfaces.

"Just as I thought," he remarked. "These trunks have double bottoms with a secret compartment between. Give me that hand-ax."

McDonald's face grew ghastly.

A single blow shattered the false bottom, and the inspector dragged it from its place. In the compartment now revealed lay a tiny oxy-acetylene torch —nothing else.

"Queer baggage for a titled English gentleman," said the chief inspector with a glance toward the detective chief.

"Titled English fiddlesticks," cried that officer, stepping to the stretcher and raising the bandages that concealed the injured man's face. Then he called to his comrades with a chuckle of satisfaction.

"Look, boys," he called. "This man calls himself Sir Arthur Cumberland, does he? Well, I've another name for him. I call him 'English Bill' Tatman, and here's how he looks in the clothes he's used to—stripes."

He drew out the photograph of a convict and displayed it to the Captain. Except that it lacked the mustache, it was a perfect likeness of Sir Arthur.

"And you," continued the detective with a grimace toward the secretary, "I've got your 'mug' here too, Mr. McTavish, alias Mac the Scot. A fine pair, you two, parading around the country wearing handles to your names in place of prison numbers.

"It ain't true," shouted the unmasked McDonald. "We'll sue—"

"Stow it, Scotty. The blawsted bobbies 'ave us right as a bloomin' whistle," interrupted a voice from the stretcher as Sir Arthur Cumberland sat up and staggered weakly to his feet. "I'm fit for the 'ospital right enough, but I'd 'ave been missin' with my buddy when the hambulance got there if you bobbies 'ad given me 'alf a chance," he remarked ruefully but with perfect good humor.

"Let's go," he said, holding out his wrists for the handcuffs with the easy nonchalance of a man well used to such situations.

"My 'ead's uncommon sore where that ship chappie sliced it with 'is gun. Cheer up, Scotty, we've less than nothin' to worry over, my lad," he added comfortingly to his companion, and dropping naturally into the broadest of cockney accents. "The bobbies cawn't put us under for bein' willin' to turn a neat trick—and they cawn't say their bloomin' gold ain't just where they put it in the little iron tubs. We didn't lay 'ands near it."

"Cumberland and McDonald!" ejaculated Captain McNaughton. "I never would have guessed it."

Then as a new thought came to him:

"But if they're the crooks we have been looking for, where's the man who stepped in and saved our treasure?"

"It's all a Chinese puzzle," declared the manager. "Just one thing interests me now. I want to see those chests safely into the bank and I want to see the gold that should be in them. Accompany us to the bank, officers, and bring your prisoners."

While the customs men went through the baggage of the remaining passengers with unusual care, and the crowd in the shed gradually vanished in search of hotels and late suppers, bank messengers supported by armed guards loaded the treasure-chests into the waiting auto truck, and with Captain McNaughton, the steamship official, the detectives with their prisoners and a dozen newspaper men following in autos, the *Humboldt's* gold was hauled to the bank vaults for which it was destined.

"English Bill" Tatman—once Sir Arthur Cumberland—looked on with grim humor and a running fire of comment as the boxes were unpacked, one by one, in the sanctuary of the First National's gold-room.

"Look at it, Scotty," he said to his morose pal with a wave of his hand toward the steadily growing pile of gold bars. "There's enough tin to make 'on-est churchmen of us and the bobbies too. Deuced lucky, 'owever, that we didn't 'ave any of the stuff in our luggage."

As the easy-tempered prisoner rambled on with his monologue the bank messengers threw back the lid of another chest. As it opened, they uttered a cry of dismay. Inside, replacing the gold that should have been there, was a neat pile of bars, half of them pig-iron, half of them lead.

Before dawn flaring newspaper extras told the city of Seattle that sixty thousand dollars in gold bars had been stolen from the strong-room of the *Humboldt* and that though two known crooks had been taken at the dock and were safely locked in cells, the missing gold inexplicably had been spirited ashore and safely away, although every piece of baggage on the ship was searched inside and out.

As the enthusiastic police reporters informed their city editors, the story was turning out to be "a whale of a mystery yarn."

While the gloomy conference at the bank was still in progress, Boston Blackie's Mary admitted herself to a modest bungalow on the outskirts of the city.

Within was the white-haired, motherly woman who with her four daughters had been passengers on the *Humboldt* from Victoria.

"All here?" Mary inquired eagerly.

"All but Blackie and Lewes," answered the woman. "There was no 'rumble' at the dock, was there?"

"None. Blackie was through the gate and safely away before I left. It was a wonderful job, wonderfully pulled," asserted Mary, relaxing from the long strain. "Blackie should be here any minute now. Then we have only to put the gold in a safe place and drop out of sight for awhile. You have given up this house regularly, without risking suspicion?"

"I arranged it all yesterday before we left for Victoria, and exactly as Blackie directed me," the woman returned. "The rental agent knows I'm moving in the morning. The girls are gone already. They caught the night train for the south."

The doorbell rang.

"That's Blackie, now," cried Mary, rushing to the door. She flung it open unhesitatingly, an eager, welcoming smile on her face; then as she glimpsed the form outside she stepped quickly forward and barred the entrance.

On the doorstep stood Miss Nina Francisco.

"You!" cried Mary, startled beyond further speech.

"Miss Whitney!" ejaculated the woman, equally amazed. Then she began to laugh, but with a strained, false note in her merriment.

"How stupid of me not to have guessed who you really are during all those days we spent together on shipboard!" she said with a shake of her dark head.

"Why are you here? Where did you get this address?" demanded Mary.

Nina drew a slip of paper from her pocket and handed it to her frankly suspicious friend. On it was written in Blackie's well-known hand the street number, with these words added: "Immediately upon landing."

"Come in," invited Mary reluctantly. "I don't understand all this, but Blackie's note seems to make it all right. Who are you, Miss Francisco? Have we ever met?"

"Never," said the visitor with an elusive half smile. "I never saw you before I boarded the *Humboldt*, though you must have seen a letter I once wrote, I believe—a letter written long ago, Mary Dawson, when your Blackie was risking his life to save a pal from death on the scaffold at Folsom Prison, California. Do you remember that letter? It was signed by a woman called Rita, and it told how she had done for Boston Blackie's sake the one thing he couldn't do himself for his pal because Fred the Count betrayed him. Do you remember now?"

"Rita!" cried Mary. "The woman who saved the Cushions Kid—the woman who—"

She stopped, a quick flush dyeing her face.

"Yes," continued Rita, taking up the interrupted sentence and meeting Mary's eyes with a level, unflinching glance, "the woman who isn't ashamed to admit she would give everything in this world for what she knows you have and will never lose—Boston Blackie's love."

Another ring at the doorbell ended an awkward silence.

Mary recognized Lewes and Blackie in the two forms on the step. As she opened the door, Blackie caught her in his arms and held her to his breast.

"We've won, little sweetheart," he cried joyously. "All here and everything O. K., little girl?"

As Mary nodded, he caught sight of the visitor within.

"Rita!" he exclaimed. "You lost no time in finding the house—which is well, for we're leaving before dawn."

He dropped into a chair and began to laugh.

"Share the joke," demanded Mary.

"I can't help laughing," he cried, "when I think of the paper you wasted warning me against Miss Nina Francisco, detective, while Miss Francisco was equally busy writing notes warning me against the dangerous machinations of Miss Marie Whitney, also a detective. It was better than a farce."

"I saw you the night I boarded the *Humboldt* at Nome, and when I saw parts of that note Mary wrote, with 'Wireless—treasure-room—detectives' so suggestively appearing in it, I suspected her, for the ship's people had managed to let everyone know there were detectives aboard. I knew you wouldn't travel to Alaska for your health; I knew we carried a fortune in gold in the strong-room; and putting two to two, I guessed it was you they planned to trap," the girl explained. "But I was a fool not to know you could and would protect yourself."

"Never!" Blackie denied promptly. "You proved yourself true blue, particularly when you risked everything to knock that revolver from Cumberland's hand. You did do it, didn't you?"

"Yes," said Nina without enthusiasm. "And Mary was just behind, ready to knock my gun from my hand if I hadn't attacked the right man."

"Rita," said Blackie seriously, "we owe you something for that timely blow. It entitles you to a bit with the rest of us. You've earned a share of the gold."

The woman shook her head.

"Not me, Blackie," she said soberly. "I don't want money from you."

Her mood changed with the words, and she smiled up at him.

"There's something I do want, Blackie," she said. "I want to know how it all was done—if you'll trust me."

"Trust you! Of course I do," Blackie assured her. "You're one of us since that night in Sacramento when you saved my pal from the rope. How did we do it? Rita, it was as simple as taking eggs from a hen's nest. Mary's was the only difficult part—getting the wax impressions of the two keys."

"I led the purser on to show me the strong-room on the northbound trip while it was empty, and there was no reason why anyone mightn't be admitted," said Mary in response to Blackie's nod to begin. "I pretended to be amazed that his two tiny keys could protect such a vast treasure as he said the *Humboldt* would carry back from Nome. I picked them up as they lay in his hand—and accidentally, of course —dropped one. As I fumbled about my feet for it, I took impressions of both keys on a circlet of locksmith's wax which was ready on my wrist."

"Of course!" said Rita; then turning to Blackie: "But how did you get the gold out of the strong-room? How did you get it ashore?"

"All much simpler than getting the keys," Blackie said. "On the night of the battle outside the strong-room, I had been inside with the treasure since the previous night. Lewes let me in and locked the door behind me. He had just removed the padlock to release me when the Englishman appeared to try his luck at the game. His idea evidently must have been to saw or burn off the original padlock and substitute the duplicate for which he had keys. He could then have entered the treasure-room and removed the gold when he pleased. Lewes jumped him and with your help put him out. Meanwhile I slipped back to my stateroom."

"But the gold? Surely you couldn't have carried it with you—and besides they searched all the cabins immediately and found nothing!"

"They didn't find any gold outside the strong-room because there wasn't any outside. It was still in the strong-room, and there it stayed until the *Humboldt* was docking."

"I can't guess the answer to that," said Rita.

"No. Well, perhaps you remember that my little pal Mary was on the steamer, and being a woman, naturally she had trunks with her. One of those trunks was turned over to the purser for safe-keeping; so, having been stored in the strong-room, it was inside with me and the gold during the twenty-four hours I spent there. Beastly dull twenty-four hours, too, for it didn't take but one to empty a chest, transfer the gold bars to Mary's trunk and substitute in the chest the iron and lead bars that had been in her trunk. Then I replaced the broken seal with the duplicate Lewes made in Nome as soon as he saw the kind used on the treasure-chests."

"So all the time they were hunting the ship for gold, it was still in the strong-room, but in Mary's trunk!" cried Rita with rapt appreciation. "That's worthy even of you, Blackie. But how did you get it ashore? They searched Mary's trunk with all the rest."

"Certainly—but they found nothing, because the gold was no longer in Mary's trunk when it reached the Custom House men," Blackie said. "Tell her, Mary."

"Do you remember the girls I met on the ship after we left Victoria? My old school friends, you know, to whom I introduced you," began Mary. "Well, those young ladies didn't carry any baggage except ordinary one-night traveling bags; but when they came off the *Humboldt,* each of them—even including their nice white-haired old mother—had one of these contrivances strapped round her waist under her clothes."

Mary opened a closet and dragged from the floor a canvas belt in which, bent to fit snugly against a woman's body, was one of the missing gold bars for which the Seattle police were combing the city.

"I bent them to the proper shape while I was in the strong-room, reproaching myself that I could only allow myself one hundred and fifty pounds from the tons of old Clancy's gold that lay there, mine for the taking," said Blackie. "That's the whole story, Rita, except that when I got Mary's warning that a woman in Seattle had tipped off our game to the coppers, I knew that we hadn't been tipped off, for no one, not even good old Mother Archer or the four girls with her, knew what was wanted of them or what we planned to do until Mary told them to-day on the *Humboldt.* Therefore I naturally concluded there must be another 'mob' on board the *Humboldt* on the same errand as ourselves, and that when we reached the dock at Seattle, the detectives would be waiting for them, not us. And so it turned out. Now you know it all, Rita." He rose and beckoned to Lewes.

"We've work to do," he said. "This stuff has to

be taken to the safe place I prepared for it—immediately too, for it never pays to take unnecessary chances. You'd better do as I suggest and take a share of the stuff for yourself, Rita."

"No, Blackie—nothing for me."

"Good-by, then, and good luck," he answered as he and Lewes staggered out, each laden with belts of gold.

As the men disappeared, Mary and Rita eyed each other throughout a silence palpably heavy with thoughts neither cared to utter.

"I'm going now," said Rita finally, rising and moving quickly toward the door.

Mary made no comment or protest.

As she stood in the doorway, Rita turned and laid both hands on Mary's shoulders.

"Good-by dear," she said gently. "If you were not Boston Blackie's Mary and I were not Rita, a woman who would give her soul to have his love, we could be good pals. But as it is—I imagine the only word we may say to each other in friendship is—good-by."

"Good-by, Rita," said Mary, and watched her guest pass swiftly into the street and vanish in the darkness.

Mary locked the door and began to make coffee for Blackie.

CHAPTER XVI

THE FRAME-UP

THE robbery of the *S. S. Humboldt* grew to be a very nasty thorn in the tender side of the Seattle police.

Larry Rentor, chief of detectives, slammed up his 'phone, chewed the end from the unlighted cigar between his clenched teeth and banged a heavy, hairy fist upon his desk in savage exasperation.

"Wants his gold bars back or my job, does he?" Rentor growled angrily. "It's safe to trust old Jim Clancy to want somebody's scalp if anything happens to singe his hide. Does the doddering idiot think a crook smart enough to make sixty thousand dollars in gold vanish at sea from a steamer's double-locked strong-room is likely to leave it lying around where my bunch of half-witted four-flushers can find it?"

Chief Rentor spat out the mutilated remnant of his cigar and eyed his 'phone speculatively and with growing gravity. Over it but a moment before he had been told by James J. Clancy, aged and irascible president of the Northwestern Steamship Company, that unless the *Humboldt's* mysteriously missing gold was recovered, the resultant police shake-up would jar loose the gold star at present glittering on the breast of Rentor's uniform. The har-

ried Chief knew that Clancy had both the will and
political prestige to uphold his threat.

"It's up to me to get busy or get out, and I'll not
get out—not if I can help it," the Chief said to the
empty room. "I'll get the gold if I can. If I can't,
I'll find a goat and tie this caper to him."

Then, being a shrewd and politic detective well
aware of the undeniable advantage of favorable publicity, Larry Rentor pressed a button and told his secretary to admit the newspaper men waiting impatiently in the outer office. To these he dictated an
interview brimming with assurance, in which he
hinted a solution of the mystery was at hand, predicted the early arrest of the *Humboldt* robber gang
and promised the recovery of the loot "within a few
hours." With the reporters satisfied and out of his
way for the moment, the Chief seized a fresh cigar,
sagged down in his chair and concentrated the full
power of his by no means mediocre mentality on the
problem that confronted him.

Three unbroken days and nights of unmitigated
third degree harrying had developed nothing more
satisfactory than increasingly vehement denials of
guilt from Tatman and his partner; and Chief Rentor, shrewd in judging men of their type, at last was
forced to the conclusion that they spoke the truth.

Who, then, had stolen the gold?

"If Tatman is innocent, as I know he is," Rentor
said to himself, "the man I want is the one who struck
him down outside the strong-room door. No one

on shipboard, passenger, officer or seaman, admits giving the blow. That proves it wasn't struck to protect the gold."

The detective's mind leaped to the logical conclusion.

"One of two things is true," he decided. "There was another crook 'mob' aboard the steamer, and it, not a Tatman, got the gold, or this business was an 'inside job' and the thieves are on the steamer pay-roll. Nothing amazing in that! Gold by the hundredweight will tempt anything human."

Had Rentor guessed that Boston Blackie and Mary, his wife and pal, were among the *Humboldt's* passengers, his summing up of the possibilities would have ended with the first alternative. From the standpoint of a man unaware of this all-important fact, however, Rentor's second theory was far from implausible. The unbroken but open padlock found near the door of the looted treasure-room, and the fact that the missing gold was not found when the steamer was searched immediately after the robbery, or in the baggage of any of the passengers, strengthened the thought growing in Rentor's mind that the vanished fortune might still be hidden on shipboard. Gold bars two feet long and weighing thirty pounds each are not easily hidden within a passenger's cabin.

Rentor touched the button that summoned his secretary.

"McNaughton, captain of the *Humboldt,* is coming down shortly," he said. "When he arrives, bring him in at once and admit no one else till I ring."

As he waited, the gossamer clues upon which he must work expanded in the brain of the detective.

"The strong-room lock was opened by keys made for it," he mused. "The purser had one, the captain the other, and there were no duplicates. That's a fact that means something."

The door opened to admit the big, bluff, white-bearded commander of the *Humboldt*.

"What progress, Chief?" asked McNaughton anxiously.

Rentor studied the face of the visitor silently.

"Considerable, Captain," he said slowly. "More than you would imagine possible. What would you say if I told you I know the *Humboldt* was robbed by men paid to protect her treasure—by men on the ship's pay-roll?"

Rentor watched the effect of his question with keen eyes half concealed by drooping lids. McNaughton, startled by the suggestion, met the Chief's gaze squarely.

"Impossible," he said at last. "No member of the crew had an opportunity; and my officers—well, sir, I know them all. There's not a thief among them."

Rentor leaned across the table and tapped its top.

"And yet," he said, "the padlock was removed intact from your strong-room door by two keys that fitted it. The most expert locksmith in America couldn't have made duplicate keys without the originals as models. That means one of two things;

either the original keys were used to open the treasure-room door, or as patterns for the duplicates that did open it. Which was it, McNaughton? You and the purser are the two men who had the keys in your keeping."

McNaughton leaped to his feet, his face purple with rage.

"Do you dare to accuse me of robbing my own steamer, sir?" he cried, shaking a weather-bronzed fist at the detective.

"I don't accuse anybody—yet," Rentor answered quietly, "but I have just stated a fact you can't deny; and Captain, every man, woman and child who was on the *Humboldt* is under suspicion till this mystery is cleared. Sit down, and we'll get to brass tacks. You have told me that you and the purser together locked the door of the vault immediately after the gold was placed there at Nome, and that your key never left the belt you wear round your waist night and day. Are you absolutely sure that's the truth?"

"Absolutely," said McNaughton.

"Your key was never out of your possession for an instant? No passenger or officer went to you with a story of something to be put in or taken out of the strong-room? Think carefully, Captain, and remember your reputation is at stake in this matter."

"The key never left my body," McNaughton answered without hesitation. "No one asked to have the strong-room opened for any purpose whatsoever, and I wouldn't have permitted it if I had been asked.

It is specially prohibited by the company that the treasure-room be opened at sea when we're carrying the Nome gold, and I obey orders. No, Rentor, from the moment I locked up the bullion, the key never left my belt."

The Captain sat a moment, thinking.

"On the northbound trip when the strong-room was empty—" he began, then paused, suddenly hesitant.

"Yes, yes, on the northbound trip when the strong-room was empty—what happened then?" demanded Rentor eagerly.

"I remember now that Purser Jessen came to me and asked for my key. He wanted to show our treasure-room to some curious passenger," the Captain replied with reluctance. "But that means nothing. We could have left the strong-room door open if we had chosen. There was nothing inside then to be stolen."

Rentor bent over his desk and hid the eager, preying light in his eyes as he fumbled for another cigar.

"How long did this Mr. Jessen have both the keys?" he demanded with the exultant ring of unhoped-for triumph in his voice.

"A half-hour, possibly an hour. I didn't notice particularly." The Captain now was grave and plainly worried. "Don't jump to conclusions because of what I've told you, Chief. I know Jessen. I knew his father, the old captain; and a finer, straighter man never walked a ship's bridge. I've known young Dave since the days when I dandled him on my knee when he wore short breeches. I've seen him grow up and become a ship's officer in line for a command of his own some day. He had no hand in this crooked business; no, sir, Dave Jessen's like his dad, straight."

Rentor leaped up with a scoffing, worldly-wise smile on his lips.

"Because you held this fellow on your knee when he was a boy, that's no reason he mightn't be a crook," he cried belligerently. "If his father was honest, that's no reason he is; and I'll tell you now we'll prove he isn't. While he had your key, he did one of two things; either he made a duplicate of it himself, or he gave it to a confederate who did. Dave Jessen's the man who robbed or helped to rob the *Humboldt,* and in twenty-four hours I'll have his confession."

Captain McNaughton shook his head in firm unbelief.

"Call him down and talk to him," he suggested. "If he knows anything, he'll tell you gladly. But don't do anything to ruin his prospects. Reputation is about all we seafaring men have that we can't afford to lose. If you were to hold him, even on suspicion, he'd never command a ship as long as he lives. Besides, he has a mother old and feeble, and—"

"It isn't my business to worry about men's mothers or reputations. I put men behind bars who belong

there. This young crook is going into a cell, and in
a cell he'll stay till he tells me who stole the *Humboldt's* gold or signs a confession that he did it himself. Where does he live?"

Captain McNaughton gave the address and went
out sorrowfully with bowed head. Ten minutes later
two detectives in a police auto were on their way
to Jessen's home to take him into custody as a suspect
in the bullion robbery.

"Maybe Jessen did this and maybe he didn't,"
Chief Rentor mused as he impatiently awaited the
car's return. "There's better than an even chance
that he's really guilty, but whether he is or not, one
thing is certain: I've found a goat and a bit of incriminating evidence that will justify the pinch in
the newspapers."

One after another he pulled the knuckles of his
big hands until the joints cracked like pistols. That
was Larry Rentor's way of expressing extraordinary
jubilance. He was planning the details of the "third
degree" by which he hoped to extort a confession
that would clear the *Humboldt* mystery. . .

The door of the Jessen home was opened to the
detectives by a sweet-faced little woman with snow-
white hair and age-dimmed eyes.

"My son is at home. I'll call him," she said in
response to the detectives' inquiry.

Dave Jessen, roused from a day dream in which
he stood again on the *Humboldt's* deck beside a dark-
eyed girl with sun-tinted cheeks and wind-blown hair,

appeared behind his mother. Mrs. Jessen vanished.

"Put on your hat and coat, Jessen. The Chief wants to see you," said Mulligan, spokesman of the paired officers.

"Sure. I'll be with you in a jiffy," the purser agreed, dropping the nautical book in his hand.

"Mother," he called, "I'm going down to police headquarters, but I'll be back in time for the dinner you've been fussing over all afternoon so foolishly."

He kissed her and followed the detectives to the auto waiting at the curb.

"What's happened, boys?" he inquired as they climbed into the car. "Have you caught the bullion robber?"

"I reckon we have—now," said one detective pointedly. He drew a pair of handcuffs from his pocket and deftly slipped them over Dave Jessen's wrists.

The first instinctive flush of anger on the purser's cheeks faded, leaving him pale beneath his sea tan.

"You're arresting me?" he gasped in bewilderment. "I'm accused of the gold robbery?"

"Looks that way. What do you think yourself?" replied the detective.

"This is ridiculous. It's an outrage!" cried Jessen, straining his wrists against the steel circlets so hatefully new to them. "I know nothing of the missing gold except what I've told. I'm not a thief."

"Prison is full of men I've heard say those identical words when they were arrested," said the detective. "Save all that guff for the Chief, young fellow. All I've got to say to you is that you're three times seven kinds of a fool to get yourself tangled in a mess like this. A nice old mother you've got, too. It'll go hard with her when she learns what you have been up to."

"But man, I didn't do it. I have neither done nor said anything to justify the faintest doubt of my honesty," cried Jessen. "Who dares say I robbed the *Humboldt?* Who accuses me?"

The detectives smiled at each other knowingly.

"You'll find out soon enough," replied Mulligan's partner. "Take good advice and forget that high-and-mighty stuff before we get to the Chief. He has the real dope on you."

Then though Jessen, outraged, angry, incredulous, asked a dozen fiercely insistent questions, the two officers maintained an omniscient silence until the car stopped at detective headquarters. The prisoner leaped to the sidewalk in advance of his guardians.

"Take me to Chief Rentor, quick," he demanded. "Somebody will suffer for this, for it won't take me ten minutes to clear myself of whatever charge some irresponsible blunderer has made against me."

"Easy lad, easy," cautioned the first of the officers, taking him by the arm and into the building through a private entrance. "You'll see the Chief, all right, but don't be in a hurry. Time is one thing you'll have to spare from now on."

Fretting with rage and impatience, Jessen was taken

into a private room where his name was entered in the "detinue" or "small" book, a police device—unlawful, but that is a mere detail—for holding prisoners against whom the department is not ready to make a public accusation. He was searched and relieved of papers, watch, pen-knife, money and all other trinkets in his pockets. Then he was pushed into a dimly lighted steel cage, and its massive door clanged behind him. A bolt shot into its sockets. The footsteps of the departing officers died away.

Many minutes, each longer than any hour Jessen had ever passed, dragged away while he paced the steel floor.

"It's only a few minutes," he kept assuring himself. "I'm innocent. They can't keep me in this filthy den. It isn't possible."

But the minutes dragged into hours, and no one came.

Meanwhile the arresting officers were reporting.

"How'd he take it?" asked Rentor, cracking his knuckles.

"Mad as a she-bear, and stands pat he knows nothin'," answered Mulligan.

"Naturally he'd do that," said the Chief. "You couldn't expect a man with nerve enough to pull a stunt like this steamer robbery to cough up at the first touch of the cuffs. He'll come across, though. I'll leave him in there alone to sweat awhile. To-night we'll spring the phony identification stuff, and then I'll be ready to talk turkey to him."

CHAPTER XVII

THE THIRD DEGREE

CHIEF RENTOR then climbed into his auto and was driven home to dine leisurely, while at Dave Jessen's bungalow a little old woman who reminded one of a fading flower fretted nervously as she kept an overdone dinner hot for the son who didn't and couldn't come.

It was early in the evening, though Jessen was sure it must be early morning, when a door opened noisily in the corridor and he heard voices nearing his cell.

"At last!" he cried, springing eagerly to the door.

Suddenly his cell was flooded with light, though the corridor beyond remained in darkness. He waited, hot with impatience, for the welcome sound of the jailer's key in the lock. Instead, a wicket in the door was lifted, and a pair of eyes peered in from the outer darkness. There was a moment's silence, then a man's voice spoke.

"That's him," it said. "I could swear to him on a hundred Bibles."

"Good!" replied Mulligan's heavy voice. "We knew we had him right, but this settles it."

The wicket dropped, and the men started down the corridor.

"Come back," shouted Jessen as he realized that they did not intend to release him. "Take me out

184

of this hole. I demand to be taken to the Chief."

Somebody's laugh came back through the darkness as the door at the far end of the corridor closed with a bang. Ten minutes later the same performance was repeated, and a new voice assured the detective that it would "know that fellow's face anywheres."

Again Jessen's shouts and demands remained unanswered, and the lights winked out. For the first time, though the consciousness of innocence buoyed his drooping spirits, a numbing horror of the inconceivable thing that had happened overwhelmed him— exactly as Chief Rentor intended.

Back from dinner, Rentor cracked his knuckles noisily as his men reported the prisoner's shouts and violent demands for a hearing, following the faked identifications.

"Fine!" he ejaculated. "That stuff always jars their nerves, whether they're innocent or guilty. He's ripe now for a friendly, heart-to-heart talk. Bring him in, boys, and see that the detectaphone operator is on my line ready to get every word that's spoken in here. I'll cut out the parts of the talk I don't need, afterward."

"That sympathy stuff you told us to spill about his mother seemed to hit him hard," suggested Mulligan.

"That's a trump card," replied the Chief. "Lead in the lamb and forget the bawling out I'm going to give you, boys. I want him to think I'm a friend."

Jessen, fresh from the gloom of his cell, stumbled at the threshold as the detectives threw open the door of the Chief's office. They pushed him roughly into a chair, his hands still bound by the steel cuffs, and the glare of a desk-lamp full upon his face.

"Who's this?" asked Rentor, looking up from a pile of reports in simulated surprise. "Not Dave Jessen—handcuffed! Take off those bracelets, Mulligan."

"They've had me locked in a dirty cell for hours, Chief," interrupted Jessen. "I demanded to be brought here to you, but they only laughed."

"I told you to bring Jessen here to my office, but I didn't give you permission to treat him like a common crook," roared the Chief angrily at his men. "I knew this boy's father before he was born, and no matter what sort of trouble he is in, he will be treated right while he's in my custody, you blockheads, or I'll know why not."

"I didn't think it safe to take any chances after those two positive identifications, Chief," said Mulligan in mock humility, "and you being out for dinner, I thought—"

"You're paid to do as you're told, not to try to think," interrupted Rentor. "Get those cuffs off his wrists and get out. I want to talk to this boy alone."

As the door closed behind the detectives, the Chief motioned Jessen to draw his chair closer. His manner was grave, sorrowful, deeply sympathetic.

"Dave, you're up against it hard. I'm your friend,

but it's going to take every bit of influence I can swing to keep you out of stripes," he began with the air of a man who regrets his bad news. "Old Clancy wants you prosecuted to the limit. How the devil did you ever come to lose your head and get tangled in a mess of this kind?"

"Prosecute me!" echoed the prisoner. "Surely you can't believe I'm guilty of the robbery on the *Humboldt*, Chief. On my word of honor, I'm as innocent as you. I—"

Rentor interrupted by laying a friendly hand on Jessen's arm.

"Don't, Dave," he cautioned kindly. "It's useless to deny facts. I'm your friend, willing to go the limit for you, but you must be square with me. If there are others in this job and you help to land them and get back the gold, I think I can save you, and I'll do it for the sake of your old mother and your dead father—God bless him! But you must tell me the whole truth. I've brought you in here alone so that no one but me will ever hear what you tell me to-night. It's your one chance, boy, and for the sake of your mother who's worrying herself into hysterics already, don't throw it away."

"Chief, I'm innocent; but it is evident some blunderer has given you reason to believe me guilty," replied Jessen. "I'll clear myself to your full satisfaction in ten minutes if you'll tell me exactly on what grounds you suspect me."

Rentor drew further into the shadow of the shaded

lamps and fixed his eyes on the purser's face to catch the slightest betraying change of expression.

"Evidence against you has been coming in for two days," he began. "But I'll ask one question that will show why we first suspected you."

He paused, then thrust his face close to Jessen's and spat out his question viciously.

"What did you do with the *two* keys of the treasure-room while they were *both* in your possession?"

"I never had both keys," answered Jessen, unperturbed and without hesitation. "From the moment we locked the gold in at Nome, Captain McNaughton—"

"Wait," interrupted Rentor peremptorily. "I didn't say you had both keys *after* the gold was shipped. You couldn't have got them then. But on the way *up* to Nome, Jessen—how about that? Have you forgotten your story to the Captain about showing the strong-room to a curious passenger?"

"You're right about that," admitted the purser slowly. "I did get the Captain's key while we were on the way up. But what of that? The treasure-room was empty then. I borrowed the Captain's key to show the strong-room to —a—a—passenger, one whom I had told of the millions in gold we would carry there on the trip home. How can you connect that with a robbery many days afterward?"

Rentor was cracking his knuckles as he answered.

"Because while Captain McNaughton's key was in your hands, duplicates of it, and of your key as

well, were made for the bullion-robbers, who used
the duplicates later to remove the padlock when there
was something in the strong-room well worth taking."

With growing exultation Rentor saw the blood
drain away from Jessen's cheeks. Instantly he knew
that his bold guess had found a vulnerable mark.

"What happened to those keys while they were
in your possession?" he snapped. "Did you let them
go out of your hands, or did you yourself make duplicates?"

Jessen's eyes wavered and fell. For the first time
doubt of the ultimate outcome of his interview with
the Chief crept into his mind.

"I made no duplicates," he said nervously.
"Neither key was out of my hands except for a single
instant."

He paused and Rentor leaned forward, eager for
the all-important admission to follow.

"While we were in the empty treasure-room," Jessen continued, "the person to whom I was showing it
remarked it was curious such frail bits of metal could
protect such vast treasure as I described. My companion took the keys from my hand and held them
for a second. One dropped. She picked it up from
the floor before I could stoop, and handed both to
me."

"A woman!" cried Rentor, springing triumphantly
to his feet at Jessen's use of the feminine pronoun.
"I might have known there was a woman at the bot-

tom of a job as clever as this! When she dropped the key and stooped for it, she took wax impressions of both of them, of course. That stunt's as old as the hills. Who is this woman? She's the party I want now."

Jessen's chin dropped to his chest. His strong brown hands were clenched. There was a long pause, during which the thought that he had been tricked by the girl he had learned to love on that last ill-fated voyage—the girl whose gentle "no" when he asked for her hand had not lessened his love —seared his brain like molten metal. Could she have been guilty of playing upon that love? Her face, sweet, kind and innocent, rose before him, and because he loved her, denied the accusation convincingly. If he named her, she, a woman, would be subjected to the tortures he was enduring. They might put her in a cell as they had him. Jessen straightened in his chair and met Rentor's piercing eyes squarely.

"I won't tell you her name," Jessen said quietly. "It wouldn't be right. I know she isn't a crook, but you won't believe that. You would do to her what you are doing to me. I won't name her."

"You'll go to the penitentiary if you persist in protecting this woman crook. You understand that, don't you?" asked Rentor.

"If necessary, I'll go," replied Jessen wearily.

"If this girl's innocent, I won't harm her. If she is guilty, unless you are her accomplice, why should you be willing to do time to protect her?" Rentor asked, probing the one phase of the situation that still puzzled him—Jessen's apparently quixotic determination to sacrifice himself for a casual steamer acquaintance.

"I'm innocent, and you've harmed me," the purser answered.

The pair studied each other eye to eye.

"Chief," began Jessen at last, with a note of boyish appeal in his voice, "I can understand how my refusal to name the girl who, unfortunately, has been dragged into this case, may seem suspicious to a man like you, whose business makes it necessary to suspect everybody. Even so, there's a spark of humanity in you, I'm sure. For her sake and mine, I'm going to tell you everything, and then I know you'll not demand her name."

"Go on," said Rentor encouragingly.

"She was a passenger on the *Humboldt* making the round trip to Alaska with us," Jessen continued. "She was alone, and I tried to make the trip pleasant for her, first for duty's sake and, then, when I grew to know her, because I treasured every moment I could be near her. Long before we reached Nome, I knew she is the one woman I want and always shall want for my wife."

"Ah!"

"On the return trip, I asked her to marry me. She told me there is someone else, and"—Jessen raised a hand to shield himself from the coldly piercing eyes that never wavered from his face—"I'm glad she is going to be happy. That's all there is to tell, Chief. Now you'll understand why I can't let the unlucky chance that led to the incident of the keys permit me to involve her even remotely in such a case as this. No decent man could do that. I know she is not a crook. Such a girl couldn't be."

Rentor pressed the button that summoned the waiting officers.

"Now I've got you just where I want you, my bucko!" he exclaimed gleefully. "The one thing I lacked to make my case complete was a motive that would explain why you try to protect the woman. You have just given it to me—the oldest and best motive in the world. Will you give me the name of this she-crook?"

"Never," said Jessen.

'Take him away, boys," Rentor ordered as his men appeared in the doorway. "Tell Clark to take this fellow's Bertillon measurements and to mug him the first thing in the morning so I can give the afternoon papers his pictures to-morrow. This has been a neat piece of work, if I did do it myself."

Jessen, as he rose to follow his guards, looked down on burly Larry Rentor half in hatred, half in scorn.

"I understand now how crooks are made," Jessen said, in a voice whose evenness failed to hide the tempests of bitter anger that shook him from head to foot. Larry Rentor merely laughed.

When Jessen had been lodged again in his cell, the Chief called in four of his best men and gave his instructions for the continuation of the third degree.

"Handcuff him to a chair and keep at him without a second's let-up all night," he ordered. "Never let him close his eyes. Never let him rest. Keep up a perfect stream of questions and drag answers out of him any way you can. Play on his love for his mother. Pretend that we have taken over the house to search it and turned her out. Pretend that we think she herself may be implicated and that she is to be brought down here in the morning for the same kind of a deal he's getting. We'll take her through one of the cells for an instant to-morrow and let him see her there. That'll fetch him. Now go to it, boys. By the way, someone better go out and talk to the old lady. She might tell something worth knowing."

The men filed out. The result was a night of horror that Dave Jessen never forgot and never recalled without a shudder.

While the stenographer was transcribing those portions of Jessen's statement in which he admitted having both strong-room keys, admitted that he had given them momentarily into the possession of a woman passenger and in which he flatly refused to give her name, Chief Rentor analyzed the results of his night's work.

"Jessen has told the truth from beginning to end,"

he decided. "First, he was this unknown woman's goat, and now he is mine. It's a hundred to one, without takers, that she made impressions of the keys during the moment he left them in her hands. She had pals aboard, and of course they turned the trick."

The Chief chewed his cigar reflectively, and his thoughts brought a look of shrewd and ruthless cunning to his eyes.

"It's the luckiest thing in the world that this fellow is fool enough to refuse me the girl's name," he thought. "If he had not done that, he would practically have cleared himself and put me up against the problem of finding the girl. As things stand now, I've almost got enough on Jessen to make a showing in court, and if I never find the woman or the gold, he gets all the blame. Anyway, it's a safe bet now that old man Clancy will be satisfied I'm big enough for my job."

The fox-like cunning in the eyes beneath Rentor's shaggy brows deepened.

"If Tatman would say Jessen is the man who hit him in front of the strong-room door,—it was directly opposite Jessen's own door, too,—my case would look good even before a jury," he reflected. "That would be the final link in the chain. I'll have a talk with him."

He ordered Tatman up from his cell.

"Tatman," said Rentor when they were alone, "Purser Jessen has been booked for complicity in the bullion robbery. He took both the keys to the

strong-room on the northbound voyage, and admits
he allowed them to go into the hands of a woman on
board. He refuses to give her name. Were there
any crooks on the *Humboldt,* either men or women,
that you knew?"

The ex-convict shook his head. The Chief continued:

"You're likely to stay inside a cell a long time,
Tatman. I am fairly well satisfied you weren't in
on this, but I can't let you go until I've cinched somebody—you understand that."

Tatman grinned without replying. He was an old
hand at the game and knew the Chief's sudden con-
sideration had an explanation.

"I've just been thinking, Tatman, that if you had
caught a glimpse of the face of the man who hit
you, and that man happened to be Purser Jessen,
I wouldn't have any object in keeping you after you
had identified him in court," continued Rentor insin-
uatingly. "It would be a mighty lucky break for you,
old timer, if you happened to be able to make that
identification."

"I get you, Chief," said the convict. "Lead me
to 'im when you like. Hit might 'ave been 'im, for
all I know; an' anyway, 'e's only a square shooter.
Lead me to 'im; that's my hanswer."

"You understand I want only the truth," cautioned
the detective.

Tatman grinned knowingly.

"I hunderstand," he repeated. . . .

CHAPTER XVIII

AN ANSWER IN GRAND LARCENY

THE following morning the papers told of Jessen's arrest in flaring headlines. Boston Blackie's Mary, in the seclusion of a friend's flat in in which she was awaiting the day when Blackie, now out of town, judged it safe to return for the *Humboldt's* gold, felt a sickening sense of guilt grow with each line she read.

"Poor boy! What a shame!" she murmured with deep regret. "What hopeless bunglers the coppers are."

When she read the account of her visit to the strong-room under Jessen's guidance, and Rentor's assertion that she had taken wax impressions of the keys during the brief moment they were in her possession, the furrows in her brow deepened into wrinkles of concern.

"A shrewd guess that hits the mark but that doesn't involve the purser," she thought.

Then she came to a paragraph that brought a mist of tears to her eyes. It was the paragraph that quoted Jessen's statement to Rentor that he declined to give her name—that he would go to prison himself rather than involve her.

"Oh, oh, tell them! Tell them," she cried, as if the accused man were within hearing. "It can't harm me. Surely you must guess now that the name and address I gave you were both fictitious."

Then in a flash, because she was a woman with womanly intuition, she understood why Jessen had answered "Never!" to the police demand for her name.

"He believes me innocent," Mary murmured, awed by the proof of what principle may cost those who have it. "He still thinks I am what I seemed—an innocent girl, a girl about to be married, who would be ruined by a breath of scandal such as this. And because he believes that, he is sacrificing himself to save me."

She sprang to her feet and paced the room with clenched hands and cheeks wet with tears of compassion.

"It's the rightest act I ever knew," she sobbed. "They sha'n't railroad this poor, loyal boy. Oh, how I pity his distracted, broken-hearted old mother! What have Blackie and I done? What shall I do?"

Like an answering message, the thought of Judge Mortimer Garber came to her.

Judge Garber was an attorney of long-proved ability, whose specialty was criminal law. He was a trusted neutral in frequent negotiations between the police and the crook-world, for he never betrayed to either the secrets of its warring adversary. He despised police chicanery and hated thug brutality. He was respected, feared and trusted by both classes.

As Mary was ushered into his office, he was frown-

'ng over the newspaper accounts of the Jessen identification by Tatman.

"Well, well, Mary!" the Judge exclaimed cordially. "It has been a long, long time since either you or Blackie paid me a visit. Sit down and tell me all about it. I can see you are in trouble."

Mary slipped a hundred-dollar bill from her purse and pushed it across the table.

"I want you to take a case for me, Judge Garber. There's a retainer."

The lawyer handed back the money.

"Tell me the case first," he said. "We'll discuss the fee later."

"It's the *Humboldt* bullion-robbery," began Mary.

"I thought so the moment I saw you at the door," interrupted Garber. "It's fortunate I am a lawyer instead of a detective, Mary. When I read the first accounts of this affair, which for sheer ingenuity stands alone, I said to myself: 'The one man I know who might have done this is Boston Blackie.' Was this boy Dave Jessen mixed in it with you?"

"He was not, Judge. That's why I'm here. Rentor is trying to frame him," said Mary.

"I suspected that, the moment I read that this tame crook Tatman has suddenly recovered his memory and identified Jessen. I'm glad the lad isn't implicated. Old Captain Jessen was my good friend for many years, and the boy has the dearest old mother in the world. Tell me the story from the beginning."

Mary told it, omitting nothing, mitigating nothing. The old Judge was muttering angrily to himself long before she finished.

"So this rat Rentor, who is getting rich on the graft he is collecting from gambling houses and red light dens, thinks he'll make a reputation by railroading to prison a boy whose only crime is that he is too decent to ruin a girl's reputation!" growled Garber. "He won't succeed as long as I keep my Southern blood and remain a member of the Seattle bar."

He looked across the table at Mary with shrewd but kindly eyes. "Well, what do you and Blackie want to do about it?" he demanded.

"Blackie isn't here," said Mary. "If he were in town, he'd know what should be done, but I'm alone. That's why I came to you. I thought that when I told you the circumstances, you might be willing to take Jessen's case and clear him. We'll stand all expenses if you will. I can't see that boy Jessen ruined, Judge," added Mary.

The attorney pondered with half-closed eyes and touching finger-tips.

"With the information you have given me, I can acquit him without a doubt before any jury that can be dragged together in the State of Washington," he said at last. "But Mary, my dear, has it occurred to you that a mere acquittal won't do? If Jessen even goes to trial on this charge, it will wreck his career and probably send his mother to her grave. You've shouldered a heavy responsibility, girl."

"I know," she cried, "and I'm frantic with remorse. What can be done? If you went to Clancy of the steamship company and told him you know positively that Jessen is entirely innocent of any connection with the robbery, he would believe you; and Clancy is a man important enough to have his way at detective headquarters. He could have Jessen set free within an hour with an apology from Rentor to take home with him."

"Clancy could do that, but he wouldn't," said Garber. "He would never see any man free whose stubbornness was costing him a chance to get back sixty thousand dollars—stubbornness due to what Clancy would think a silly scruple. My judgment is that if he knew all you have just told me, he would wring your name from Jessen or see him hanged if he had his way. Jim Clancy is a man with a soul dead to all feeling that cannot spring from a dollar-mark, Mary."

"That's true, and I hate him," said Mary furiously, letting long-nourished resentment reveal itself. "He sent my father to prison wrongly, Judge, and Dad died there. Afterward, when the truth was discovered and Clancy was forced to admit that he had blundered he stated to the papers that the mistake was 'less regrettable' because poor old Dad was 'no benefit either to himself or to society.' The principal reason Blackie and I attempted this robbery is because Jim Clancy owns the *Humboldt*."

"That's Clancy, with photographic accuracy," assented Garber. "Well, Mary, Jessen's predicament is a hard proposition. Shall we abandon it as hopeless now and content ourselves with doing something when he goes to trial?"

"No, no," she said. "Wait, Judge, please. I'm trying to decide something."

Ten, fifteen, twenty minutes passed.

"It's all right now, Judge," she said resignedly at last. "I've decided. If you will trust us for your fee until Blackie gets money, you can call up Jim Clancy and tell him you know where his gold bars are and that you will return them to him ten minutes after Mr. Jessen is free and in possession of a written document from the Northwestern Steamship Company that admits his innocence and guarantees his position on its steamers. It's hard to give up the day of righteous reckoning for which you've waited and prayed year after year; but"—with a wry smile—"it's worth even that price to feel as content as I do since I decided to forego revenge for a clear conscience."

A faint glow of gratification flushed the old lawyer's cheeks.

"Child, have you thought what Blackie will say to this?" he suggested gently. "Do you realize that you are planning to give away sixty thousand dollars that, according to his code, rightfully belongs to him?"

"Neither Blackie nor I care about the money. The two things that worried me most were the debt I owe

Clancy and can't pay now, and the fact that all of the sixty thousand dollars doesn't belong to us. We owe fourteen thousand, five hundred to those who helped us get the gold safely ashore. But we have enough banked to pay that off. I've just figured it up. We'll have just twenty dollars left when we're done. That's why I told you you would have to wait for your fee."

The old Judge wiped his glasses.

"Will Blackie approve this, Mary?"

"Of course. Blackie always does right, no matter what the cost," she answered, utterly unconscious of the naivete of the verdict she so confidently pronounced upon a man with a nation-wide reputation as a criminal. "He would never forgive me if I let a boy who had proved himself 'right' ruin himself for my sake. Call up Clancy, Judge. I want to feel sure that Jessen will be at home before night."

Garber reached for his 'phone with a hand that was tremulously eager.

"By the way," he said, "you haven't told me yet where these trouble-making bars of gold are to be found."

Mary opened her purse and tossed a bit of metal across the table.

"There's the key of the safe-deposit box Blackie rented months ago for the gold," she said, smiling. "It's in Jim Clancy's own vaults."

"Ho!" chuckled the man delightedly. "That's a joke on the old skinflint that will be told on him to the last day he breathes, even though he out-ages Methuselah. I wouldn't miss the sight of his face when I show him the missing gold stored in his own deposit vault, for all his millions."

"What's your fee, Judge?" asked Mary, rising.

"Fee!" shouted Judge Garber wrathfully. "Get out of my office, young woman, before I call my stenographer and have you thrown out. When I take a fee for an afternoon's work like this, I'll change my name to *Clancy.*"

Suddenly he stooped and kissed her gently on the forehead.

"Permit an old man that privilege, my dear," he said with the graceful deference of the old-school gentleman. "I'm honored in calling you and that mad scapegrace husband of yours my very dear friends."

A quick answer to her S. O. S. to Blackie, bade her take the night train to Spokane. The following afternoon in Spokane, looking into Boston Blackie's face from the stool beside his chair, as she finished relating how old Jim Clancy's wandering bars of gold had found their way back to his covetous fingers, she entreated, "Tell me I did right, dear. Tell me I did what you would have done."

"Right! Of course you did right. My girl never did anything else. She couldn't," declared Blackie, echoing the words Mary had spoken of him to Judge Garber. "Always remember, Mary, that an honest crook can afford anything but crooked honesty."

The smile of happiness in Mary's eyes just then was worth more to Boston Blackie than all the gold the *Humboldt* ever carried.

Blackie gravely flicked the glowing end of his cigarette.

"How much money have we in bank, dear?" he asked. "We must give the others their bit on the day I named. We can't give away their money."

"Enough," said Mary. "But we will have only twenty dollars left."

"Twenty dollars and a crystal-like conscience," corrected Blackie jubilantly. "Why, Mary dear, we're rich."

"IT'S good to be home again, dear," said Mary sinking wearily into a chair as Blackie dropped suitcases and put an arm caressingly about her shoulders.

"Home again, broke but not broken, little girl," he answered. "Let's check up on that bankroll and then I'll get busy."

He emptied his pockets.

"Ten dollars and thirty cents," he counted. "We owe Frank Cavaness $100 we borrowed for the trip home, too. Well, what does it matter? I'll go down to Old Mother McGinn and borrow a thousand and then we'll go out and get enough in a night to give us a good long rest. I'm better satisfied since you gave back that $60,000 than I have been in ten years. It's proof to myself that we really live up to the code we preach. I'm off to Mother McGinn. I'll be back for dinner. Rest, meanwhile, little sweetheart."

* * * * *

* * * *

No one ever knew how or where Alibi Ann found the Glad-rags Kid. She had been absent from her haunts in San Francisco for a fortnight—nothing unusual, for Ann was accustomed to make solitary pil-

grimages out of town that invariably caused consternation and frenzied but futile activity in the detective department of the Jewelers' Protective Associa-
tion. Then, unexpectedly as always, she appeared
one night before the barred doors of the Palms
Hotel—rendezvous and sanctuary of the elect among
the Powers That Prey—and whistled up the speak-
ing-tube to the cage-like cubby-hole where old Mother
McGinn, knitting interminably, had sat for many
years answering such summonses from the strange
and furtive company that frequented her house.

"It's me, Mother," said Ann softly into the tube.
At the sound of her voice the door swung open. Ann
and her companion entered, and the doors closed
behind them. As they climbed the stairs, Mother
McGinn's quick ear detected the double step, and
she appeared suddenly on the floor above them, gazing down suspiciously.

"It's all right, Mother," said Ann quickly. "He's
with me."

Mother McGinn stared in speechless amazement.
There was a new and strangely buoyant quality in
Alibi Ann's voice, and with her was a man. No wonder Mother McGinn almost unbelievingly watched
them ascend the dingy, ill-lighted stairway. For
many, many years Ann's proudest boast had been
her solitary spinsterhood. During the eventful double decade that had passed since Ann, then a young
girl, had first been admitted to the Palms, many
men of many kinds had made love to her in many

ways. Some she had scorned silently; some she had laughed at gayly; some she had withered with the biting sarcasm of a ready tongue and a fertile wit. And to none had she ever listened. Yet now she was climbing the stairs of the familiar old hotel with a stranger—one who, had he appeared alone, might have whistled out his lungs without gaining admittance. It passed belief.

Alibi Ann dropped her suitcase at the door of the tiny office. Her companion dropped another beside it, and as the light fell full upon him, Mother McGinn in one quick, curious glance sought to appraise him. She saw a youth who manifestly tried to belie immaturity beneath a self-conscious swagger that accentuated it. He was good-looking in a way, though a weak chin and self-indulgent mouth marred an otherwise attractive face. But Mother McGinn forgot his features in her wonder at his clothes—the last word in exaggeration as to both style and pattern. A mammoth diamond horseshoe scintillated from his tie. His Panama hat was one of the kind that is weighed by the ounce and priced by its weight in gold. He wore spats.

Alibi Ann laid a trembling hand on the old womans' shoulder, and Mother McGinn, looking at her for the first time, saw that her eyes were bright and eager and her cheeks flushed as they never before had been.

"Mother," said Ann with a queer little break in her voice, "meet my husband, Tom Coyne. Mitt her, Tom. Mother McGinn's the pal of all the gang."

The old woman stuck out a gnarled and withered hand and clasped the newcomer's palm.

"Gracious Peter! Your husband!" she ejaculated turning to Ann. " 'Gratulations, folks." Then in an aside to the girl: "We'll all have to hand it to you, Annie my dear. You were a long time picking one, but when you did, you sure grabbed the original glad-rags kid."

Right there Tom Coyne ceased to exist. From that moment, in the world of Alibi Ann and her kind, he was the Glad-rags Kid. Mother McGinn had given him his "moniker."

"Are Boston Blackie and the bunch upstairs?" asked Ann.

"Sure! Smoking in the Chink room," answered the old woman. "Take your man up and let them give him the double O. The Kid and his clothes will astonish 'em, all right. He'll give the crowd something to chew about all night."

"Not to-night, Mother," said Ann. "But I wish you'd slip Blackie the news about me, and tell him I'm going out to the flat tomorrow afternoon to see his Mary. I want a long talk with her. And send old Crowder, the fence, down. We've brought back a swell bunch of stones, and we want dough. We're going to scatter some, Tom and me."

Mother McGinn, chuckling hoarsely, made a gesture indicating the pulling of a champagne cork.

"No, no," corrected Ann. "Nothing like that for us. We've a better way than that to blow our coin."

" 'We—us—our!' " echoed the old woman pointedly, for Ann until now had always prided herself on making her money alone and spending it as she made it—alone.

" 'We' is right," said Ann softly. "It's fifty-fifty between Tom and me. Fifty-fifty now and always—in good luck or bad, eh, Tom?"

"That's it, fifty-fifty in good luck or bad," repeated the Glad-rags Kid with whole-hearted enthusiasm.

Alibi Ann's eyes, as she looked up at him, revealed the possibilities that lie latent and hidden—except for one man—in all women's eyes. But the Glad-rags Kid missed their message. He was too young, too self-centered, too unthinking even to perceive the heights to which love had raised the woman the world called Alibi Ann.

Next day Ann called on her friend Mary.

"Yes, it's like that with me, Mary," said Ann as she told of her marriage, "and I'm so happy that sometimes I wake in the night shivering with dread for fear it's only a dream."

Ann's words answered the thought in the mind of Boston Blackie's Mary, who realized from the moment of her visitor's appearance at the little apartment that a new and vastly altered Alibi Ann had taken the place of the self-sufficient, cynical diamond thief she knew so well. "A new and different world is opening itself to Ann," Mary thought.

"Love is a whole lot like the measles, Mary," Ann continued after a pause. "The longer you escape it, the harder it hits you when it does come. Until I met the Glad-rags Kid, I never knew how empty and lonely my life was. I never knew what I was missing. I never knew how ignorant I am. Say, Mary, if you turn me loose at the diamond counter of a swell store, I can handle myself. But in a kitchen I'm as helpless as a three-year-old kid. But I'm going to learn—quick. Any half-wise flapper can steal for a man, but it takes class to cook for one so he'll like it. Am I right or am I wrong, Mary?"

"You've learned a lot about life and the road to happiness in—how long is it, Ann?"

"A week. Just one little week, and it's worth more to me than all the years that went before it. When I think that maybe there are hundreds of such weeks ahead, I begin to tremble. I know I don't deserve them, and it don't seem possible there can be that much happiness in this world. How long have you and Blackie been together?"

"Seven years and a month."

"Seven years, each three hundred and sixty-five days long, and on every one of those days you've known you've had the love of the man you love. You're the luckiest girl living, Mary."

There was a long silence in which a faintly troubling thought slowly furrowed Ann's brow.

"Do you know how old I am, Mary?" asked Ann at last.

Mary shook her head.

"In my thirties—well along in them," said Ann almost defiantly.

Mary made no comment.

"And the Kid is twenty-four and doesn't look even that."

Alibi Ann gave the information with deeper—far deeper—anxiety than she would have made the announcement that police were breaking in the door. Then she added:

"Mary, do you think that need make any difference in the years to come?"

"It doesn't matter if you really love each other," Mary answered. And she slipped an arm around her friend and drew her closer. The unspoken message of sympathy and understanding reopened the flood-gates of Alibi Ann's overfull heart.

"Can you guess what we are planning, the Kid and I?" she began reverently as one approaching a sacred subject. "You will understand, Mary, for you love Blackie. We're planning a home—a real home—one like this. We're not going to have fuss and frills and things made for show instead of for comfort. The Kid and I want a place to live in— just for us two. It's going to have big, deep easy-chairs and cushions everywhere and an open fireplace that we can enjoy together in the evenings. All the little comforts a man wants and enjoys without knowing what they are, will be there. And when it's all ready,—I'm not going to let Tom set his foot inside the door until it is ready,—then I'll show it all to him, and we'll sit down to dinner at our own table." She clasped her hands and looked up with glowing eyes. "And then, Mary, there'll be a little bit of Heaven right here in old 'Frisco."

"And what will there be for you, Ann, in this bit of Heaven?" asked Mary, tightening her clasp about the shoulders of the woman the newspapers had often called "the most dangerous and incorrigible of professional criminals."

"For me? Why, for me there's going to be a cook-stove—the best I can buy," replied Ann, laughing happily as a child. "I'm going to get a cook-book to-day—which is the best, Mary?—and learn it by heart. I've got to, for when the Kid and I decided on a home of our own, he asked me if I could cook, and I said: 'You just wait and see, Tom, after you eat the first dinner I give you.' Pure bluff, Mary, but I'll deliver the goods, believe me, even though I never made a cup of coffee or fried a steak—"

"Broiled a steak," corrected Mary.

"You see! What a simp I am about things that are really worth knowing! I don't even know what the difference is. That's one reason I'm up here now. I want you to help me make a list of things I'll need, and tell me where to get them. I'm going to plan it all just as if it were the biggest diamond job I ever tried to put over. It's the biggest job of my life, Mary."

Long after Alibi Ann had gone, list in hand, flushed and radiant with the excitement of her great adventure, Mary sat weighing the chances of her friend. Her face betrayed indecision.

"Ann is right. It's the biggest job she ever undertook," Mary murmured to herself.

A key turned in the lock, and she jumped up to throw her arms around Boston Blackie and drag him to a chair while she drew up a footstool from which she could look into his face.

Alibi Ann has been up here all afternoon," she began, "and she's bound up heart and soul in the plans she's making for a wonderful little home—just like this," she added with the little smile that meant more than words to her husband.

"Her new husband has been down at the Palms all afternoon, and he's bound up heart and soul in the plans he's making to corner the diamond market of the world—with Ann's help," said Blackie.

"What sort is he, Blackie?" asked Mary anxiously. "He's going to make Ann as—well, as happy as I am or as wretched as I would be without you."

Blackie caught her hands and held them with a caressing touch.

"He's a ten-dollar-check passer, loose-tongued and vain, who got his growth up here"—tapping his forehead—"about the time he went into long trousers. X-Y-Z is where I rate him."

"Poor Ann!" murmured Mary.

"Poor Ann!" echoed Blackie with deeper regret than if she were on her way to prison.

Alibi Ann spent two happy days in finding a flat exactly to suit, and five other days even more deliriously happy in selecting furniture.

Then she was ready for the great event—the evening on which she would proudly give the Glad-rags Kid his first glimpse of their new home and cook his dinner for the first time with her own hands. With Mary's assistance she planned and replanned every detail of that dinner. It was to be her great triumph —a fitting culmination of all her dearest hopes, a suitable beginning for the new life that promised "a little bit of Heaven in old Frisco."

After an afternoon spent in helping Ann with her final preparations, Mary was back in her own apartment recounting the events of the exciting day to Blackie, for she had caught from Ann the spirit of the occasion.

"The Glad-rags Kid is there now. He was to come at six," Mary said, glancing at the clock. "Oh, I wish I could be there just for a second to see Ann's face when he sees all she's done."

A taxicab swung round the corner on two wheels and stopped before the door. There was a hurried ring at the bell.

"Something has happened," cried Mary as Blackie opened the door.

"Here's a package and a note," said the taxi chauffeur. "It's from Mrs. Coyne over on Lyons Street, and she promised me a five-dollar tip if I'd get here quick enough for you to answer her over the 'phone in five minutes. Four minutes is up already, lady, and I need that five-spot."

Mary tore open the note and read its scribbled contents; then she tore away the paper from the package. Within was a yellow pellet as thin and hard as a board.

"Oh, look, look, Blackie," she cried, midway between tears and laughter. "It's supposed to be a biscuit." She handed Blackie the note, and he read it aloud with occasional pauses for laughter.

" 'Dear Mary: Tom is here and has asked for hot biscuit with dinner. I've made them twice exactly as the cook-book says, and they're all like the thing in the package. Dinner is ready and waiting, but I've got to have biscuit. For the love of Mike, what's wrong? 'Phone me quick, or I am disgraced —and everything else has been going so beautifully. Quick, Mary. Ann the Simp.' "

Blackie dropped the biscuit to the table. It struck with a resounding thud, bounced to the floor and rolled away like a silver dollar.

"Oh, oh, oh, this is too good!" he cried, collapsing into a chair, helpless with laughter. "She's making ammunition, not biscuits."

"Don't laugh, Blackie," said Mary reprovingly. "It's serious to poor Ann."

She recovered the sample of her friend's cookery

and broke it open. It was as yellow as a grapefruit. Mary ran to the 'phone. Ann, evidently waiting, answered instantly.

"It's yellow Ann, and it didn't rise at all," Mary cried. "It looks as if you had used baking soda. What? No—no, the book doesn't say baking soda; it says baking powder—the little red can you put on the second shelf in the pantry. A teaspoonful and a half, Ann, and mix the dough just as it tells you in the book. Yes, hurry. Call me after dinner."

Two hours later the 'phone rang.

"Oh, Mary," said Ann's voice softly over the wire, "the biscuits were fine, and the dinner was just perfect, the Kid says. When he finished, he said: 'No more restaurants for me, Annie—you're some cook!' He's sitting before the fire in the big chair with his feet on a footstool, and oh, Mary dear, I'm so happy."

Mary repeated Ann's words to Blackie as they sat together before their own fire. Her hand slipped itself into his.

"All Ann's eggs are in one basket," she murmured. "I pray from the bottom of my heart that the bottom doesn't fall out."

CHAPTER XX

DURING the months that followed, the Glad-rags Kid became a conspicuous figure in petty police circles in San Francisco—so conspicuous that the newspapers discovered him and made the most of the discovery. He developed a perfect genius for publicity, the one indulgence a crook may not permit himself. After a trip with Ann to a Puget Sound city,—a trip from which they brought back a palmful of gems that made the eyes of old Crowder gleam avariciously,—the Kid bought a bright vermilion racing car which a salesman solemnly assured him was an exact duplicate of Barney Oldfield's. His first taste of newspaper publicity followed the day on which he was arrested for speeding slightly over fifty miles an hour along a crowded driveway in Golden Gate Park. He appeared before the police judge next morning bedecked with diamonds and in apparel that made the room gasp, and gave reporters a chance to comment humorously on the descriptive justice of his nickname. The judge fined him fifty dollars. The Glad-rags Kid peeled a hundred-dollar bill from a thick roll and tossed it to the court clerk.

"Buy yourself a smoke with the change," he said carelessly. "I haven't time to wait."

In a second he was gone, and an amazed courtroom

through open windows heard the staccato reports of his giant motor fading away in the distance at a speed that caused the judge to remark: "I hope to have the pleasure of fining that debonair young gentleman again."

A reporter with a real gift for fiction discovered that the Glad-rags Kid was a New York gunman (and the Kid, though he had never seen the eastern slopes of the Sierras, tacitly confirmed the charge) and wrote a page story for his paper's Sunday magazine called "New York's Mankillers Invade the Wild West." It was profusely decorated with photographs of the Kid in his newest and most startling examples of the tailoring art, and contained a circumstantial account of "My Bloodiest Street-battle" over the Kid's signature. The Glad-rags Kid clipped that page from the paper and carried it about in a wallet from which he offered it for inspection at the slightest provocation. Also he began to carry a gun, slung under his armpit, crook-fashion, where by carelessly throwing back his coat he could display it in cafes and saloons when opportunity offered.

"He's a thoroughbred notoriety hound," said Blackie disgustedly to Mary. "His one joy is to be the spectacular figure in the center of the calcium. It will take all of Ann's cleverness to keep them out of prison if he keeps on. Also he's becoming a familiar figure at the downtown restaurants and the beach dancing pavilions. Sometimes Ann is with him, and more often she isn't. I'm afraid her little bit of

Heaven is going to be no more than that."

"I know," answered Mary mournfully. "She never says anything, but I can see the truth in her face. She never comes over here any more and very seldom calls up. She don't even go downtown or to the Palms. I'm afraid she spends many a lonely evening beside a big chair that's vacant by the fireplace. I never see her with the cookbook any more."

The next evening Ann called up Mary to ask if she and Blackie would dine with them at an Italian restaurant noted less for food than for its dancing.

"Let's go and try to cheer her up a bit," suggested Mary to her husband. "There was something in her voice over the 'phone that it hurt me to hear."

All through the dinner the Glad-rags Kid monopolized the conversation, dividing his time between discussing clothes and diamonds and berating the waiter for faulty service. The men were dawdling over cigarettes and a liqueur when the orchestra began an old waltz. The Glad-rags Kid turned to Alibi Ann.

"Come, honey," he said, "let's dance."

Ann rose quickly, and they glided away.

"Did you see the light that came into her eyes when he asked her to dance?" asked Blackie of Mary.

"Yes," said she, "I saw it. Poor Ann! She's clinging desperately to the remnants of her happiness, and she asks so very little and gives so very much. What would he be without her?"

"Just what he is anyway—nothing," answered Blackie.

As Ann, flushed and happy, returned to the table and sank into her chair with the last strains of the waltz, the Glad-rags Kid glanced across the dining-room to a table where a young girl sat alone.

"I see Dessie Devries, the dancer, across the room," he said. "I'm going to invite her over to our table. She's good company, and besides, she's anxious to get on here as an entertainer, and I'm going to introduce her to Williams, the manager."

For just a second Alibi Ann's body stiffened. Then with a forced lip-smile that revealed in an instant the utter soul-weariness of a woman consciously losing a vital struggle, she looked up at her husband.

"Yes, do bring her over, Tom," she said. "I would like to meet her."

The Glad-rags Kid threaded his way between the tables to the one where the girl sat. She looked up at him with a confident, welcoming smile; they talked a moment, and started back to the now silent table from which Ann with half-shielded eyes was studying every detail of the newcomer's appearance.

Alibi Ann saw in Dessie Devries a slender girl, young, attractive and vivacious, with great coils of golden hair low on her head. If the dancer was conscious of the atmosphere of constraint, she ignored it, and in a moment was chatting across the table to Ann and Mary—but particularly to Ann— with the easy familiarity of assured acquaintanceship. Ann, if she felt hostility, masked it beneath a concealing but thin veneer of cordiality.

During a lull in the conversation the orchestra began the jazziest of fox trots.

"Bully time! Let's dance," cried the Glad-rags Kid, rising.

Ann, her pale face warmed by a flush of becoming color, half rose eagerly and then, as she looked up, saw Dessie Devries also rising. There was an awkward moment as their eyes met. They both looked toward the Kid.

"Dessie and I will dance this," he said, flushing slightly as he made the choice. Then with a clumsy attempt at playfulness and utterly unconscious of the dagger in his words, he added to Ann:

"The time's too fast for you, Grandma."

"Of course it is—sonny," said Ann with a laugh.

The Glad-rags Kid whirled away with Dessie Devries in his arms. Alibi Ann poured a glass of champagne—her first of the evening—and drank thirstily.

"Youth turns to youth," she said, looking across the table to Blackie and Mary. "It's always been so, but until now, I never realized how inevitable it is."

She snapped her fingers with a reckless gesture, vividly expressive, and began to talk of inconsequential things with a careless gayety that might have deceived less keen observers than the two opposite her.

* * * * *

The ferryboat *Piedmont* was making her final trip across the bay from Oakland to the San Francisco shore. The few passengers she carried had found shelter from the chilling night-wind within the brilliantly lighted cabin—all but two. One of these was a woman who from the moment the boat had left the Oakland slip had been standing alone, motionless and silent, against the after-deck rail. The other was Boston Blackie, who from concealment in the shadow of the deck-house was watching her curiously.

Not until the *Piedmont* had passed Goat Island did the woman raise her eyes from the inky blackness of the water. Slowly she straightened herself and turned for a moment toward the distant San Francisco shore, a bright flare of light against the black background of the night sky. The cloak that had been drawn high about her neck slipped to the deck, and Blackie, leaning forward, caught the glint of something in her hand that she had drawn from beneath the discarded garment. Without making a sound, he stepped quickly to her side and laid a hand on her arm.

The woman trembled under the pressure of the unexpected fingers, and turned a white and haggard face toward him.

"Ann!" cried Blackie, and reaching down, he took a bottle from between ice-cold fingers that surrendered it without resistance. A thin beam of light from his pocket flashlamp revealed the label.

"'Cyanide of potassium,'" he read. "So, Ann, it has come to this with you—you, Alibi Ann, the gamest of them all!"

The woman turned away her face.

"Why not?" she said at last in a faint, far-away voice. "Other tired ones have. Why not I?"

She felt the pressure of the firm fingers on her arm tighten.

"Because, Ann, you never were and never can be a quitter," he said quietly.

"A quitter," she cried wonderingly. "I don't understand."

"You wouldn't leave a pal in prison," said Blackie. "You wouldn't abandon a pal lying sick. No! But without knowing it, you were thinking of doing just that."

She shook her head.

"He doesn't need me. He doesn't want me. Youth turns to youth." For the first time her voice trembled.

"Yes, and turns into old age, too, before it finishes paying for its folly," Blackie answered. "The Gladrags Kid hasn't brains enough to know it, I admit, but he needs you as no one else ever did or will."

Alibi Ann turned to him instantly, with something like faintly kindling hope in her eyes.

"You know him better than anybody," Blackie went on. "Alone he couldn't steal milk bottles from doorsteps without landing himself behind bars. He has trained himself to spend money—lots of it. He has a faked reputation as a gunman to uphold—or thinks he has. Well, easy money and that reputation, what's the answer? You've played the game long enough to know, Ann. It's prison."

"If you quit the Glad-rags Kid in this or any other way, I'll tell you just what will happen. He will spend all the money you've left him. Then when he has to have more money to live as he wants to, he'll try one brainless caper and land himself in prison for the rest of his days. You've undertaken something, Ann, that you can't pass up You say the Kid doesn't need you. I say you know better."

Boston Blackie laid the vial of cyanide in her hand.

"There's your bottle, Annie," he said gently. "It's up to you."

For a second the bottle lay in the hand that rested on the deck-rail. Then the fingers slowly opened and let it slip overboard, to splash faintly as it struck the water and vanished. Alibi Ann seized Blackie's arm.

"You're right, dear old pal," she whispered between sobs. "I'd have been a quitter if I'd gone where that bottle is now. I'm going back to the flat, and I'll wait with a smiling face for him to come. I'll play the game out, Blackie."

Just before daylight Boston Blackie was awakened by the telephone. Ann's voice, very low and frightened, replied to his "Hello!"

"It's happened already, Blackie," she said. "All that you predicted came true to-night. Tom has killed a man at the Trocadero Pavilion. The coppers have him, and it looks like a hard case. Thank God—and you—I'm still here to save him. Will you and Mary come over now, oh, quickly!"

The morning newspapers carried the news in flaring headlines. At last the Glad-rags Kid, much-advertised gunman, had justified his newspaper reputation by committing deliberate murder. It had been an unusually dramatic crime, done on the crowded dancing floor of the Trocadero, under the eyes of scores of diners. The papers agreed on all the essential details. The Glad-rags Kid had come in from his racing car alone and at once appeared to resent the fact that Miss Dessie Devries, cabaret entertainer, was dancing with the manager of a downtown dining place. As the music had ended and the dancer and her escort started toward the table from which they had ordered supper, the Glad-rags Kid intercepted them.

There had been a quick, angry exchange of words between the men, and the older had roughly shouldered the "gunman" aside. Instantly the Kid had drawn his automatic and covered his adversary. But he did not shoot. His experience in gun-play ended when he had drawn his revolver—the cue for his opponent to fade out conveniently through the nearest door and leave the "gunman" a spectacular figure in the spotlight.

This particular antagonist, however, knew what the San Francisco crook-world had always known— that the Glad-rags Kid was a gunman on paper only. Instead of retreating precipitately as the Kid expected, the girl's escort had faced him.

"Put up that gun, you four-flusher, before I stuff

it down your throat," he had commanded. "A kid's popgun is all a cheap bluffer like you ought to be allowed to carry."

Then, for the first time since he had owned it, the Glad-rags Kid's pistol had spat forth a jet of flame, and the man who had said "four-flusher" crumpled to the floor with a bullet through his heart—the price of forgetting that even a four-flusher may become the real thing when his vanity is sufficiently stung.

The diners and dancers had fled the room, hysterical with fright—foremost among them Miss Dessie Devries—and left the Glad-rags Kid, very white and very frightened, standing above the man he had killed and wondering dully how and why it had happened.

He had been still staring down at his victim when a policeman tapped him on the shoulder.

Long before the police auto reached the City Prison, the Glad-rags Kid was begging like a frightened child for someone among his blue-coated captors to telephone for Alibi Ann to come to him at once. He needed her now.

It was late afternoon before Ann reached the City Prison where her husband was confined. All day she had stifled a frantic desire to rush to him with the comfort of her love and loyalty, for she knew instinctively his state of utter despair and fright. But there were other matters vastly more important that must first be arranged if the Kid was to have a fighting chance for life. Already the prosecuting attorney had announced publicly that he intended "to stamp out 'gunmanism' in San Francisco by insisting that the so-called Glad-rags Kid, a notorious criminal, be given the extreme penalty of the law—death on the scaffold."

Drennan, shrewdest of criminal lawyers, for whom Ann was waiting when he appeared at his office, listened to the story and read the papers with steadily growing gravity.

"It's a tough case, Ann," he said solemnly when he had gathered all the facts, "and it's been made a hundred times worse by this cursed reputation as a gunman he has allowed the papers to build up against him in the past. It is established that his victim was unarmed. That knocks out self-defense. Insanity doesn't go with juries any more—it's been badly overdone. There were a dozen, maybe twenty witnesses. We can't get them all out of town. I tell you frankly we're going to be mighty lucky if we can save this kid's neck."

Ann shuddered.

"It looks," the lawyer continued, "as if we are up against proof of what obviously is the truth—that this young gentleman committed deliberate murder in cold blood."

"He's only a boy," pleaded Ann, "just a poor, foolish boy."

"What the devil did you marry such a fool of a boy for?" demanded the lawyer in exasperation, for he knew and liked Ann, and her voice told him how deeply she was suffering.

"Because I loved him," she answered. "And now that he needs me, I love him even more."

Boston Blackie, who was with her, jumped to his feet.

"Drennan," he said, "play for time. Delay every move as long as possible. Have the inquest continued, the preliminary continued, everything continued. Every week gained is an advantage; every month is a victory. Anything will happen, you know, if you wait long enough for it, and something may; even in this case."

The attorney looked up with shrewd understanding.

"I don't know but you're right," he said. "I don't see a chance in the world to save him if he ever goes before a jury."

It was after a long day of such discouragement that Alibi Ann was at last admitted to the visitors' room at the prison, where the Glad-rags Kid was waiting. He rushed to her with outstretched hands and reproachful eyes.

"Oh, Ann," he cried brokenly, "you've left me here for the whole day without a word. I thought you were not going to come at all. I've been half crazy with worry. Have you seen the papers? Have you read what the prosecutor says? He says he will insist that they—hang—me—me!"

He broke down completely over the dreaded words.

"Never, Tom, never," said Ann, drawing the bowed head close against her breast with a movement inexpressibly tender and protecting. "They'll never —do that," she faltered, her lips refusing the word she meant. "Never while I live, Tom."

She told him of the employment of Drennan and of their plans to delay and postpone each step in the preliminaries to the actual trial.

"And meantime, Ann, what am I going to do?" he asked. "Can I get bail? Can you buy me out?"

"There is no bail for murder," she answered regretfully.

"Then I've got to stay in the dirty, rotten hole for days, weeks, months," he cried in resentful amazement. "I can't do it. I won't. There must be some way to release me if you'll take the trouble to find it. You've never had to lie in jail yourself, but now that I'm in, you don't care. You're willing to let me stay in here through days of hell like this."

Ann dared not tell him that her one hope was that the subtlety of the shrewdest of lawyers might win him the privilege of remaining in a prison cell instead of being carried, still and silent, to one narrower, darker, lonelier and eternally permanent.

That night Alibi Ann, who had neither tasted food nor rested since the murder, worked alone in her flat on a list she was making of every diamond and jewel and marketable possession she owned. She was turning everything into cash to make a fight for the Glad-rags Kid's life.

At the same hour Dessie Devries was posing before the camera of a newspaper photographer who had promised her his paper would treat her "beautifully" and that he would send her enlarged copies of her photograph.

CHAPTER XXI

THE LOVE OF A WOMAN

WEEKS passed—weeks in which the Glad-rags Kid fretted and fumed and raged at Ann because she did not take him from his cell and restore him to liberty and "life." During those weeks Ann grew so old and haggard and worn that Mary, alarmed, begged her to come to Blackie's flat, where at least she would have care and companionship. Ann refused.

"I would rather stay in my own little place," she said. "You know, I must sell it soon, and I want to be there as long as I can, for I was happier there than I will ever be again. It is all there is left of my dream."

At the preliminary hearing the Glad-rags Kid, as was inevitable, was held for trial before the higher court and was moved from the City Prison to the County Jail, located on the outskirts of the city. On the next day Blackie summoned Ann.

"I have waited until now," he said, "to tell you a plan."

"Tell me quickly, Blackie," cried Ann, rising excitedly.

"You know the Black Maria in which prisoners are taken back and forth from the County Jail to the downtown courtrooms," Blackie began. "Well, as you know, it is a closed machine, boarded up all round, and with a door opening at the rear. In that door is a barred window big enough for a man to get through if the bars were sawed out and then cemented back into place to hide the cuts until the time for the get-away came. A copper is supposed to ride outside on the steps behind the door on the trip downtown, but it is a long trip and tiresome work standing on the steps; so three times out of four the coppers ride on the seat with the chauffeur until they get downtown. Well, Ann, if those bars were sawed through some night while the Black Maria is standing in the old jail stables, which are unguarded, and the Glad-rags Kid pulled out the sawed bars and climbed out just where the County Jail drive joins the Ingleside Boulevard, a fast car could pick him up and race him away to safety before anyone could interfere, even if some snitch in the Maria gave the alarm."

"You will saw those bars for me, Blackie?" Alibi Ann was trembling from head to foot.

"Of course," he said.

A week later the Glad-rags Kid was scheduled to appear in court to have his case set for trial. Ann visited him on the day before and explained Blackie's plan. Instantly the Kid's bravado and swagger returned. He threw back his shoulders immediately.

"Gee, but it will be great to be on the street once more," he said. "This will be some little sensation for the town, won't it! You're all right, Annie."

At midnight Blackie returned to the flat where Mary and Ann were waiting, and reported the bars cut and everything ready.

A big touring car idled along the Ingleside Boulevard in the bright sunshine the following morning as the Black Maria began its daily journey into the city. Blackie was at the wheel, with Ann beside him. In the tonneau was a grimy suit of workman's clothes —the disguise in which the Glad-rags Kid was to attempt an escape from the State after his rescue.

The prison car and Blackie's, approaching each other diagonally, drew nearer together. The junction of the roads at which the escape was to be made was at hand. There was no policeman on the rear step. As the cars drew abreast Blackie saw that the bars of the wicket were out and the way to escape open. Then a head appeared through the aperture —a helmeted head—and a hand holding a revolver.

"A copper!" cried Blackie. "He's riding inside and guarding the open wicket. They're wise to the job, Ann. It's all off."

Ann made no sound, and except for her ghastly pallor she might not have heard or understood. The Black Maria disappeared around a curve, and Blackie turned his car back toward the city, driving slowly on the trip that was to have been a wild race to freedom for a man now doomed.

"Mary and I and you and the Kid himself knew of this," said Blackie. "Did you mention it in any way to anyone?"

Ann shook her head.

"It's strange," Blackie continued. "There isn't one chance in a million that the coppers would discover the cut bars without information. And yet they did."

Ann neither cried, spoke nor gave outward indication of the bitterness of her disappointment. She sat silent and still and very white, staring straight ahead with eyes whose far-away look reminded Blackie of what he had seen in them on the night she stood on the deck of the *Piedmont* with a bottle of poison in her hand and said "Why not?"

Blackie returned to the Palms and sent old Mother McGinn out to the County Jail to investigate. She came back toward night with the explanation:

"The Kid snitched on himself," she reported. "He bragged to his cellmate during the night that he'd be free and on the street before the Black Maria got downtown, and that the papers would be full of it. His cell-partner tipped it off to the guards the first thing in the morning, and they frisked the Maria from top to bottom and finally found the cut bars. They're going to take him downtown in a special car with gun-guards from now on. The Glad-rags Kid has let his tongue put a rope round his neck."

"I thought he had done it himself," said Blackie to Ann, who sat staring into the street with dull, glazed eyes. "I'm afraid it's all off now, little woman. They'll guard him as if he were the Kaiser every moment he's out of his cell. There's not a chance on earth to save him now."

"Not a chance on earth now, Blackie," repeated Ann in a lifeless monotone. "Not one! Well—"

She stepped to Mother McGinn's mirror and smoothed her hair and straightened her hat. Then she began to talk as if her mind suddenly were freed of a crushing burden.

"That was some diamond stunt that was pulled the other night out at the Pullman mansion, eh, Blackie!" she began, and then chatted on, discussing the "big job" with all the zest of a crook-woman without a care or a worry. "Well, I've got to get downtown and see Drennan before he closes up for the night," she said finally. "I'll see you to-morrow or next day, Blackie. Be good to yourself, old pal, and thanks."

She was gone, leaving Blackie staring after her in perplexity.

"I don't get her idea this time," he said to himself. "But whatever it is that's on her mind, it worries me."

The next day Alibi Ann was missing. Frequently both Blackie and Mary called her 'phone number without getting a reply. They called at her flat and found it locked and deserted.

"Probably gone on one of her diamond hunts. She was trying to raise a big bunch of money for the Kid's defense," conjectured Blackie; but somehow this explanation did not satisfy, and he was distinctly uneasy.

Other days passed without any word from Ann,

and then from prisoners discharged from the County Jail, San Francisco's crook-world heard startling news. It was that Ann had "quit" the Glad-rags Kid.

"She sent him a note by her lawyer tellin' him she was beatin' it," Reddy the Rube reported. "He's ravin' like a lunatic and callin' her copper-hearted and a rat and so on. She didn't even pay his mouth-piece" (lawyer), "and the Kid had to hock all his stones to make good. It's the right dope, folks. I heard the Kid tell it with my own ears."

"It's a lie, even though that fool Kid is telling it. It will take better evidence than his to convince me that Alibi Ann has turned 'wrong,' " Blackie answered angrily.

But notwithstanding his denial, Boston Blackie was worried. He called at Drennan's office.

"Some of the gang just in from the 'County' are spreading the news that Ann has quit the Glad-rags Kid," Blackie began. "They say she sent him a note by you saying she was going. I know it isn't true—"

"It is true, Blackie," Drennan interrupted. "I delivered the note myself. She came here and told me what she was going to do. She surprised me, I'll admit. After he finished raving over it, the Kid gave me the note to keep for him. I'll show it to you if you like."

He drew an envelope addressed to her husband in Ann's writing from his desk and handed it to

Blackie, who took it with the air of one disbelieving
his eyes. This is what he read:

> Dear Tom:
>
> Good luck and good-by. I've done all I can for
> you, but there isn't a chance in the world, and I'm
> on my way. You'll have to sell your diamonds and
> car to pay Drennan. I would, but I haven't the
> money.   ANN.

Blackie was stunned by the note's revelations. This
thing wasn't possible, he felt, and yet it was true.

"She must have worried herself crazy," he insisted. "In her right mind Alibi Ann never could
have written that note to a husband facing the gallows. Why, it's downright yellow."

"She was in her right mind when she wrote the
note," the lawyer replied gravely.

On the day that the Glad-rags Kid went to trial
for the murder at the Trocadero, Boston Blackie
and a few others were in the Chinese room at the
Palms, when Mac the Gun came bursting in with
an afternoon paper.

"Pipe the news, fellers!" he cried excitedly.
"Glad-rags has copped a plea" (pleaded guilty) "an'
got off with a life jolt. That's only half. Alibi Ann
was grabbed las' night for the big jewel-job up at
the Pullman house. The bulls has her dead to rights.
They found all the sparks and even the clothes and
wig she wore when she was in the Pullman place.
The old lady has identified her, and Ann sees it's
all off and comes clean with a confession to the dicks"
(detectives).

"What!" cried Blackie, snapping the paper from his hand.

It was all there as Mac had related it. Ann, whose cunning in evading the best efforts of the police had supplied her moniker of "Alibi Ann," had been tripped at last. And no less surprising was the sudden change in heart of the prosecuting attorney, who after stoutly asserting for weeks that he would insist on the death penalty for the Glad-rags Kid, had at the last moment permitted him to plead guilty and take a prison sentence.

The paper passed from hand to hand, and as each read it, the men looked at one another questioningly, but hesitated before voicing something evidently in all their minds. Halsted Street Al was the first to speak:

"There's something rotten in Denmark, boys," he said slowly, "and something else rottener yet right here in Frisco. Glad-rags saves his neck and gets let off light, and Alibi Ann is grabbed with the goods all in the same day. What for did that prosecutor let the Kid off with a stir jolt after bragging he would hang him—which he sure could have done? Not for nothing, believe me. Boys, somebody snitched on Alibi Ann, and that somebody is the Glad-rags Kid."

"Ann had quit him, and he was sore, anyway," spoke up another. "She done wrong to blow him when he was up against it, but that don't give him no license to turn copper. He's plain rat, folks."

Blackie rose and put on his coat.

"I'm going down to see Ann right now and find out exactly what has happened," said Blackie.

Alibi Ann greeted Blackie eagerly. He was amazed at her appearance. She looked almost happy—almost like the Ann who had lavished all her love on the now-desolate little flat on Lyons Street.

"Oh, Blackie, I'm so glad you're here!" she cried delightedly. "I was going to send for you, for there is something I want you to do for me."

She hesitated for a moment.

"I suppose the gang are all saying the Kid snitched on me to save himself," she went on, studying Blackie's face as she talked.

"Isn't that what they ought to be saying?" demanded Blackie. "Isn't that the truth?"

"That's the reason I wanted to see you, Blackie. I don't want that said of Tom. I want you to tell everybody you know in town that it isn't true."

"I won't do it, Ann," Blackie answered angrily. "I won't give a rat like that a good name even for you."

"But he didn't do it," Ann asserted, and Blackie all at once realized that she spoke the truth. "As far as I know, Tom never heard of the Pullman jewels, and anyway, he couldn't have snitched on me, because,"—she glanced cautiously over her shoulder and lowered her voice,—"because, Blackie, I didn't steal them."

"You didn't!" cried Blackie. "Then why have

you confessed that you did? Explain it, Ann, explain it. I can't make even a guess at the answer."

Ann drew closer to him and spoke in a whisper.

"You and Drennan are the only two in the world who will ever know the truth, Blackie. He'll never tell, and I know you won't," Ann said. "On the day when the rescue failed, you told me there wasn't a chance in the world to save the Kid, and there wasn't, except one. That one chance was that the prosecutor would consent to let him take a plea and a prison sentence. The prosecutor wouldn't consent —he wanted a hanging. Well, I had a plan of my own to change his mind.

"He and the police department are at outs. I knew he would do almost anything to clear up the Pullman mystery and show up the police by getting back the jewels himself. I knew who pulled that job. It was Baltimore Ben and his Mollie. I followed them to Seattle, and there, Blackie, I bought the Pullman jewels of them.

"When I got back, I sent Drennan to the prosecutor to hint that he might be able to fix it for him to get back the Pullman jewels. The 'cutor bit. He wanted those jewels bad. Drennan told him Tom knew where they were and might agree to tell if he could get a prison sentence. The 'cutor spluttered for a while, but finally agreed, except that he insisted that he must have the thief as well as the Pullman jewels—somebody has to do time for that job, he declared, or the Kid must hang.

"Drennan came back, thinking it was all off and that he would have to go to trial with the Kid's case, but I told him to agree to the 'cutor's terms—the jewels and the thief too, in return for the Kid's life. And that's why, Blackie, I'm going to take a jolt at last—my first one and for a job I didn't do!"

"Ann! Ann!" murmured Blackie, divided between admiration for her gameness and sorrow for her fate. "You are buying the Kid's life with yours."

"It's cheap as dirt at the price," she said, and she meant it.

"But the note to the Kid saying you had quit him," said Blackie. "You wrote that and let him believe it was so. Why?"

"Camoufake, Blackie. Pure camoufake. You know it isn't safe to trust Tom to keep anything to himself. And yet we had to convince the prosecutor that all this was absolutely on the square and that Tom had a real reason for hating me and wanting to see me in trouble. That's why I wrote the note and let everybody think it was on the square. Up in the prosecutor's office they'll always think that Tom did the snitching, but I want you to be able to tell the gang he's right and no snitch. When you say you know it's so, they'll all take your word for it."

"You're a wonder, Ann," Blackie said.

"Oh, yes, I did the job up right with all the trimmings," Ann admitted with a trace of pride. "I had Mollie describe exactly how she was dressed

when she got into the Pullman house and conned
the old lady while Ben turned the trick. I dupli-
cated her costume—hat, dress, shoes and all—and got
a wig that matches Mollie's hair. All this junk was
in the flat ready for the 'cutor's men to find when
they pulled their raid and got me and the jewels.
Of course, they dressed me up in the clothes this
morning, and Mrs. Pullman identified me immediately. It isn't half hard to alibi yourself into jail."

"How much time are they going to give you,
Ann?" asked Blackie, turning his head to hide his
eyes.

"The limit—twenty years," she answered calmly
and without regret. "That's the deal we made. The
'cutor was to be free to do his worst to the Pullman
thief."

"Twenty years! Oh Annie," ejaculated Blackie,
"this is awful!"

"It's a long time, Blackie, an awful long time, but
it was the best I could do," said Ann, growing suddenly grave.

"Do you know how old I'll be in twenty years?"
she asked after a long pause. "Nearly sixty! A
white-haired old woman fit for nothing but the poor-
house."

The weary, haggard look was stealing back over
her face.

"There is one last favor I'm going to ask you,
Blackie," she said unsteadily. "Tom is upstairs in
the anteroom waiting to be taken back to the County.

If I don't see him now to say good-by, I never will see him, Blackie—never again as long as I live. Will you try to fix it for me to be taken up there just for one moment?"

"I won't try to fix it; I'll do it," Blackie answered.

The Glad-rags Kid was sitting with his back toward her, when Ann caught her first glimpse of him. Beside him, and with her hands clasped in his, sat Dessie Devries.

Alibi Ann, as she caught sight of the girl, caught her breath in a quick, choking gasp. Then slowly she managed to force back to her lips the smile that had been on them when she entered.

"I've come to say good-by, Tom," she said gently.

"Oh, it's you, is it?" answered the Glad-rags Kid, looking up with a sneer. "Now that I've got myself out of danger, you turn up like a bad penny that's not wanted anywhere. It strikes me you have your nerve with you to be here at all."

His anger and disdain grew as he talked.

"That was a swell little note you sent me," he continued. "That showed you up for what you are. I'd be headed for a death-cell by now if I had depended on you for anything. Didn't even have the dough to help pay my lawyer, did you? But now when you're in trouble yourself, you come sneaking back looking for sympathy. Nothing doing with me."

With the fear of death now safely behind him, the Glad-rags Kid was his old swaggering bullying self again.

Alibi Ann stood looking down at him for a full minute with immeasurable love in eyes that seemed to be searching and memorizing every line in his face. Suddenly she stooped and kissed him.

"Good-by Tom dear," she whispered softly. "It's the last time we will ever see each other in this world."

She was gone before his jeering reply reached her.

"Why didn't you tell him you have paid for his life with twenty years of your own?" demanded Blackie as the door clanged shut behind them.

"I didn't want him to know," Ann answered in the detached, far-away tones he had heard on the deck of the *Piedmont*. "It will be easier for him to think of me as he does now than to know that I'm doing time for his sake. I hope that girl will be decent enough to visit him. Prison life is going to be hard on him, poor boy.

"No, I won't let myself be sorry she is up there with him now," she continued, speaking as if to herself alone. "No matter how kindly he felt toward me, we could never, never meet again, anyway. I'll be a woman of sixty when I come back—if I do come back. It's all over forever."

For the first time Ann let the grief and loneliness in her tortured heart sweep away all self-control. Even crook women are women beneath their masks. Dropping her head, Ann sobbed as women do when the first clods of falling earth touch the caskets of their dead.

After many minutes the flood of tears gradually ceased, and Ann looked up at Blackie with eyes that were resolutely courageous behind their wet lashes.

"Two lines of a poem I read years and years ago have been running through my mind for days," she said. "Listen, Blackie:

"The sins ye do two by two
Ye shall pay for one by one.

"That comes home to me now, Blackie, particularly that last line. It is 'one by one' that Tom and I are going to pay—yes, one by one—apart."

Again her eyes flooded with tears, but she brushed them aside.

"Anyway, I have something precious to take across to the prison with me, Blackie," she said with a smile on her lips and her eyes that was not forced. "And it's something no one and nothing—not even penitentiary walls—can take away from me. It's the memory of the little home out on Lyons Street —the home that was a little bit of *Heaven* while it lasted."

Alibi Ann took Boston Blackie's hand in hers.

"Anyway, old pal," she said, "I've played the game, haven't I?"

CHAPTER XXII

COMING in with the dripping sea fog which San Franciscans love clinging to him in glistening crystals, Boston Blackie found Mary crouched over the open fire. As she smiled up at him he saw new and deep emotion in her eyes.

"What's happened, little woman?" he asked solicitously.

"Blackie, I've been over to San Quentin prison to-day to visit Alibi Ann, and I found her——."

The unfinished sentence ended in a sob.

"Found her how, dear?"

"Happy—absolutely happy, Blackie. Think of it! The fact that she's sacrificed herself for The Glad-rags Kid has brought her peace and contentment even behind the walls of that gloomy old penitentiary. Blackie, that's the truest and best love in the world."

"Sacrifice is the rock upon which real love is built," said Blackie reverently. "And yet—poor Ann."

"Her only thought still is for him," continued Mary, with glistening eyes. "Mitt-and-a-half Kelly owes Ann some money. What do you suppose her only request was?"

"That I collect it and send it to that worthless young rotter," guessed Blackie.

246

"Exactly. Poor, poor Ann! And yet at last she has found happiness—far more perfect happiness than there ever was for her in the little flat on Lyons Street when he was with her."

"I'll have to do as Ann has asked, but I hate to," said Blackie grudgingly. "Kelly lives at the Carteret. I'll see him to-night after the theatre."

Blackie and Mary spent the evening at the Orpheum theatre. A supper at a downtown restaurant after the performance kept them until just midnight. Then Blackie sent Mary home in a taxi.

"I may have to wait quite a while for Kelly," he said as they parted. "He's a nighthawk, and besides he and his 'mob' have been planning a stunt for some night this week, unless I am mistaken."

At a quarter past twelve Blackie entered the dingy south-of-Market-Street lodging house, frequented by crooks not welcomed at Mother McGinn's. The place was dimly lighted and apparently deserted. Blackie climbed the worn stairs to the second floor and, with the freemasonry of his craft, opened Mitt-and-a-half Kelly's door and entered when there was no response to his knock. No one was within.

"He'll surely be back soon," thought Blackie, settling himself in a chair and picking up a paper.

Half an hour passed. Then Blackie heard the street door open and close with a bang. Listening intently he heard staggering steps slowly climbing the stairs.

A groping hand clutched the door knob. A fumbling key sought the lock. The door opened and Mitt-and-a-half Kelly stood on the threshold.

Blackie sprang to his feet with a low cry of alarm. Blood was streaming from Kelly's clothes. His left arm swung helplessly at his side.

"A 'rumble' and a bad one, from your looks, Kelly," ejaculated Blackie, seizing the wounded man's arm and leading him to a chair. "What happened?"

"We made a try for the Buffalo Brewery safe," groaned Kelly. "We got the box open and the 'dough' packed up. Then as we were leaving a 'harness bull' turned the corner. He saw us and drew his gun. We got him. He's dead I think, but he got me. The worst of it is I've left a clear trail of blood all the way here. The others got away but the 'coppers' will follow me here sure. I've got to get out quick."

Blackie slipped the man's coat from his shoulders and slit his shirt with the skill of experience.

"I'll stop this bleeding and then you had better go," he agreed. "This looks like a bad night's work, Kelly, if the 'copper' is dead."

Deftly he bound the wound. Then he threw off his own coat and slipped the wounded crook's uninjured arm into it.

"That will keep you until you can get out of town and to a doctor to-morrow," he said. "And now, Kelly, it's leaving time for you."

The man pressed Blackie's hand.

"Thanks, pal," he said. "I'm going by the alley. They may be at the front door any minute."

As the door closed behind Kelly, Blackie looked at himself in the mirror. His hands, face and arms were covered with blood.

"Bad business," he ejaculated. "This shows the result of using bullets instead of brains. Kelly and his bunch never did have any judgment."

As he turned toward the washstand he heard the street door open again and heavy feet tramped up the stairway.

"The coppers!" cried Blackie.

He looked about him. Kelly's bloody coat lay on the floor. Blood was everywhere. Blackie glanced toward the window, weighing its possibilities as a means of escape. Then he straightened up, folded his arms and waited.

"What's the use of running," he thought. "They can't tangle me in this business."

There was a knock at the door, plainly from a heavy gun butt. Blackie threw it open.

"Here he is," cried the leader of the group of policemen that stood outside. "We've got him, boys."

Blackie, unarmed, was powerless to resist, even had he wished to. A policeman's club crashed against his skull and he dropped to the floor, unconscious, with a thousand scintillating points of light flashing through his brain.

When Boston Blackie recovered consciousness he

was in the hospital with a policeman on guard at
either side of his cot. His bandaged head ached
horribly.

"Ho, ho, me bucko, yer're comin' round, eh," said
one of the officers vengefully as Blackie opened his
eyes. "Better fer ye, me lad, if yer head hadn't been
so hard. Now ye'll live to be hanged. McManus,
the boy ye shot, is dead."

"I shot nobody. I wasn't even armed, as you
know. I wasn't in on this brewery job. If I had
been nobody would have been killed."

"Ye've a mighty good idea what happened fer a
mon what wasn't there," persisted the policeman
slyly. "Th' Chief will be after wantin' to see ye
soon."

That afternoon Blackie was led to the office of detective chief Jim Moran. Meantime he had read
the papers in which the police exultingly announced
the capture of the famous cracksman, Boston Blackie, after a safe robbery in which a policeman had
been shot to death.

"So, Blackie, we've got you right, at last," began
Moran. "You'll swing for last night's work."

"Listen Chief," said Blackie. "I had no more
to do with this job than you. I'm going to tell you
exactly what happened."

He did, while Moran watched him from beneath
gradually contracting brows.

"You dressed this fellow's arm, you say," Moran
interrupted. "You knew him. Who was he?"

Blackie's shoulders straightened. He looked squarely into Moran's eyes.

"I thought you knew me better than to ask that question, Chief. You'll never find out from me."

Moran's heavy fist banged the table.

"You'll tell," he cried belligerently. "You'll tell, unless you want to do his time for him. If we don't get him we'll get you," the detective paused and lowered his voice while he shook his clenched fist in Blackie's face,—"even if we have to railroad you."

"You're capable of it, but it can't be done," said Blackie quietly. "The bloody coat with the bullet hole in the shoulder will acquit me. I've no bullet hole in my shoulder. The only wound I have is on my head where your 'coppers' struck me down while my hands were up. That coat will acquit me, Chief."

"We'll see," said Moran with an evil smile. "We'll see, Blackie. I believe your story but—unless we get the right man—we'll get you. Take your choice."

"It's made," answered Blackie. "Do your worst, you 'framer.' "

Three months later Boston Blackie, charged with murder and safe robbery, faced a jury. He was defended by a skillful lawyer. The prosecutor presented his evidence. Policemen told how at the sounds of the shots at the brewery they had rushed to the scene and found the dying policemen. They told of the trail of blood leading from the spot and that they followed it to the Cartaret and up the stairs

to the door of the room in which they had found
Blackie blood-spattered and dishevelled. His reputation as a safe-cracker was skillfully interjected by
the prosecutor. The state rested.

Blackie took the stand in his own behalf and told
the complete story of the evening.

"Who is this mythical person whose wound you
say you dressed?" demanded the prosecutor on cross-
examination.

"I decline to answer," was the reply.

The prosecutor turned toward the jury with a triumphant smile.

"That's all. We want facts, not fairy tales," he
said.

Mary told how the evening had been spent at the
theatre and of the supper that followed it—a supper which ended at midnight, ten minutes after the
robbery was committed. The waiter remembered
serving them, but was not positive as to the time.
Then Blackie's lawyer played his strongest card. He
demanded the bloody coat with the bullet hole in the
shoulder. The police denied all knowledge of it.
They had never seen such a coat, they testified. The
prosecutor waved aside the incident as pure fiction.

In rebuttal for the state the policeman who rode in
the ambulance with the dying officer was called. He
swore that the victim's last words were that Boston
Blackie was one of the safe-robbers he had surprised.
He knew him and recognized him by the flash of the
guns.

"Didn't McManus tell you that this defendant is the man who fired the shot that struck him down?" persisted the prosecutor.

The witness twisted uneasily in his chair as he glanced toward Blackie whose black eyes were fixed on him as though they would wring the truth from his perjured lips. The policeman was willing to lie to send his man to prison, but his conscience rebelled at swearing away his life.

"He didn't say who fired the shots. He only said he saw this man, Boston Blackie, in the bunch."

"That's all," snapped the prosecutor disgustedly.

The jury, impressed by the straightforward, sincerely told story of Mary and Blackie himself refused to convict him of murder, but found him guilty of safe-robbery.

"This Boston Blackie's story sounded like the truth," the foreman said to his wife when he was eating his dinner that night. "Those policemen might have lied; I don't know. But anyway the man is a safe-cracker and even if he wasn't guilty of this he is guilty of other robberies, so we compromised and acquitted him of murder but sent him across for robbery. The Judge roasted us for it, too."

Boston Blackie was sentenced to fifteen years in San Gregorio.

"It's hard, Mary, but it can't be helped," he said tenderly as his wife clung to him on the morning he was leaving her for fifteen long years of a living death. "I'm taking a clear conscience with me, anyway. Some day I'll be back and then— "

Their tears dropped together as Mary sobbed hysterically on his breast.

And so the police at last rid themselves of Boston Blackie, first among cracksmen.

CHAPTER XXIII

THE REVOLT

THE great jute mill of the San Gregorio penitentiary was called by the board of prison commis-
sioners "a marvel of industrial efficiency." The
thousand stripe-clad men who worked there—hopeless, revengeful bits of human flotsam wrecked on the
sea of life by their own or society's blunders—called
the mill "the T. B. factory"—"T. B." of course
meaning "tuberculosis." Both were right.

The mill was in full operation. Hundreds of shuttles clanged swiftly back and forth across the loom-
warps with a nerve-racking, deafening din. The jute-
dust rose and fell, swelled and billowed, covering
the floor, the walls, the looms and the men who
worked before them. Blue-clad guards armed with
heavy canes lounged and loitered through the long
aisles between the machines that were turning out
so rapidly hundreds of thousands of grain-sacks, destined some day to carry the State's harvest to the four
corners of a bread-hungry world.

To the eye everything in the mill was as usual.
Every convict was in his place, feverishly busy, for
each man's task was one hundred yards of sackcloth
a day, and none was ignorant of what happened in
"Punishment Hall" to any who checked in short by
even a single yard. Outwardly nothing seemed amiss,

and yet the guards were restless and uneasy. They gripped their canes and vainly sought this new, invisible menace that all felt but none could either place or name. Instinctively they glanced through the windows to the top of the wall outside, where gun-guards paced with loaded rifles. The tension steadily increased as the morning dragged slowly away. Guards stopped each other, paused, talked, shook their heads perplexedly and moved on, doubly watchful. Something was wrong; but what?

If they could have read the brain of one man,—a convict whose face as he bent over his loom bore the stamp of power, imagination and the ability to command men,—they would have known. They would have seen certain carefully chosen striped figures pause momentarily as they passed among the weavers delivering "cobs" for the shuttles. They would have guessed the message these men left—a message that would have been drowned in the roar of the machinery had it been shouted instead of spoken in the silent lip-language of the prison.

The word went out through the mill in ever-widening circles, leaving always in its wake new hope, new hatred and desperate determination. Those who received it first passed it on to others near them—others chosen after long study by the convict leader; for a single traitor could wreck the great scheme and bring upon all concerned punishment of a kind that the outside world sometimes reads about but seldom believes.

Trusted lieutenants, always approaching on legitimate errands, reported back to their leader the acceptance of his plans by the hundred men selected for specific tasks in the first great *coup*. Each had been given detailed instructions and knew precisely what was required of him. Each, tense, alert and inspired by the desperate determination of their leader, awaited the signal which was to precipitate what all knew was truly a life-and-death struggle, with the cards all against them.

A convict with a knife scar across his cheek and sinister eyes agleam with excitement approached the loom at which worked the one man in the secret whose face betrayed nothing unusual. The convict emptied a can of "cobs" and spoke, though his lips made no perceptible movement.

"Everythin' sittin' pretty, Blackie," he said. "Everybody knows w'ats doin' and w'at to do. Nobody backed out. Give the high-sign any old time you're ready, an' there'll be more mess round this old T. B. factory than she's ever seen."

Boston Blackie looked quickly into the eyes of his lieutenant.

"You told them all there's to be no killing?" he questioned with anxiety, for none knew better than he that bloodshed and murder ride hand in hand, usually, with the sudden mastery by serfs about to be unleashed.

"Told 'em all w'at you said, word fer word," replied the man, "though I don't get this no-blood scheme myself. Give 'em a taste of w'at they give us, fer mine. But I done what you told me. Let 'er go w'en you're ready!"

Boston Blackie looked up and glanced around the mill. Covert eyes from a hundred looms were watching him with eager expectancy. The guards, sensing the culmination of the danger all had been seeking, involuntarily turned toward Blackie too, and reading his eyes, started toward him on a run.

Instantly he, high above the sea of faces beneath him, flung up both arms, the signal of revolt.

One convict seized the whistle cord of the mill siren, and out over the peaceful California valley beyond the gray prison walls there echoed for miles the shrill scream of the whistle. Another convict threw off the power that turned the mill machinery. The looms stopped. The deafening noise within the mill ceased as if by magic.

The guards rushing toward Blackie with clubs aloft, were seized and disarmed in a second by squads of five convicts each who acted with military precision and understanding. Ropes appeared suddenly from beneath striped blouses, and the blue-coated captives were bound, hands behind their backs. Two squads of ten ran through the mill armed with heavy wooden shuttles seized from the looms, and herded to the rear scores of their fellows who, because of doubtful loyalty, had not been intrusted with the secret.

The guards' phones connecting with the executive

offices of the prison were jerked from the walls, though there was none left free to use them. The great steel doors of the mill were flung shut and bars dropped into place on the inside, making them impregnable to anything less than artillery.

In three minutes the convicts were in complete control of the mill, barred in from outside assault by steel doors and brick walls.

The gun-guards on the walls surrounding the mill-yard turned their rifles toward its walls, but they held their fire, for there was no living thing at which to shoot.

Calmly, with arms folded, Boston Blackie still stood on his loom watching the quick, complete fruition of the plans that had cost him many sleepless hours on his hard cellhouse bunk.

Of all the officers in San Gregorio prison, Captain Denison, head of the mill-guards, was hated most. He was hated for his favoritism to pet "snitches"— informers who bought trivial privileges at usurer's cost to their fellows. He was despised for his cowardice, for he was a coward and the convicts instinctively recognized it. When he was found hiding behind a pile of rubbish in a dark corner of the mill and dragged, none too gently, into the circle of captive guards, a growl of satisfaction, wolfish in its hoarse, inarticulate menace, swelled through the throng that confronted him. What Captain Denison saw as he turned his ashen face toward them would have cowed a far braver man than he—and he fell on his knees and begged piteously for his life.

Boldness might have saved him; cowardice doomed him. As he sank to his knees mumbling inarticulate pleas, a convict with a wooden bludgeon in his hand leaped to his side and seized him by the throat.

"We've got you now, damn you," cried the volunteer executioner, called "Turkey" Burch, because of the vivid-hued neck beneath his evil face. "Denison, if you've got a God, which I doubt, talk to Him now or you never will till you meet Him face to face. Pray, you dog, pray! Do you remember the night you sent me to the straight-jacket to please one of your rotten snitches? I told you when you laughed at my groans that some day I'd get you. Well, that day has come."

Burch stooped toward his victim, his lips curling back over his teeth hideously.

"In just sixty seconds," he snarled, "this club is going to put you where you've put many a one of us—underground."

The prostrate mill-captain tried to speak, but fear choked back his words. The convict's grip on his throat tightened like a vise. A roar of approval came from the stripe-clad mob. Someone leaped f ward and kicked the kneeling form. Burch raised his club, swinging it about his head for the death-blow.

"Stop!"

The sharp command was spoken with authority. Involuntarily Burch hesitated and turned.

Boston Blackie sprang from his vantage-point on the loom and snatched the club from Burch's hand. He flung it on the floor and roughly shouldered his fellow-convict from the man he had saved.

"I said no blood, and that goes as it lays, Turkey," he said quietly but with finality.

The convicts, being human,—erringly human but still human,—screamed their protest as Blackie's intervention saved the man all hated with the deep hatred of real justification. Turkey Burch, encouraged by the savage protest from his mates, caught up his club.

"Get out of my way, Blackie," he cried. "That skunk on the floor has to die, and not even you are going to save him."

"Listen," said Blackie, when the howl of approbation that followed this threat died down: "He's not going to die. He's going out of this mill without a scratch. I planned and started this revolt, and I'm going to finish it my own way."

Burch was a leader among the men scarcely second in influence to Blackie himself. He sensed the approval of the men behind him. The blow Blackie had intercepted would have been compensation, to his inflamed mind, for years of grievances and many long hours of physical torture. He swung his club.

Boston Blackie seized an iron bar from a man beside him.

"All right," he said, standing aside from the kneeling Captain Denison. "Croak him whenever you're ready, Turkey, but when you kill him, I kill you."

The two convicts faced each other, Blackie alert and determined, Burch sullen and in doubt. For the first time the crowd behind was stilled. Thirty tense seconds passed, in which life and death hung on balanced scales.

"Why don't you do something?" Blackie said to Burch with a smile. Then he threw his iron bar to the floor. "Boys," he continued, turning to the crowd, "I hate that thing on the floor there wearing a captain's uniform more than any of you. I didn't stop Burch from croaking him because he doesn't deserve it. I stopped him because if there is one drop of guards' blood shed here to-day we convicts must lose this strike. If we keep our heads, we win. Now it's up to you. If you want to pay for that coward's blood with your own, Denison dies. But if he does, I quit you here and now. If you say so, he goes unharmed and we'll finish this business as we began it —right."

He turned unarmed to Burch, standing irresolute with his club.

"You're the first to vote, Turkey. What's the verdict?" he asked.

Burch hesitated in sudden uncertainty. Denison cowered on the floor with chattering teeth. Then the convict tossed aside his club and stepped away from the prisoner.

"You've run this business so far, Blackie," he said slowly, "and I guess it's up to us to let you finish it in your own way. If you say the dog must go free, free he goes, says I."

There was a chorus of approval from the convict mob.

"Fine!" said Blackie. "I knew you boys had sense if I only gave you a chance to use it. Now, we've work to do. The first thing is to boot our dear Captain out those doors, and I nominate Turkey Burch to do it."

Action always pleases a mob. Joyous approval greeted the suggestion. Denison was dragged to the doors. They were unbarred, and then, propelled by Turkey Burch's square-toed brogan, Captain Denison shot through and into the yard, where he was under the protecting rifles of the guards on the walls. One after another the captives were treated similarly.

"Take this message to Deputy Warden Sherwood," said Blackie as the last of the bound bluecoats stood ready to be kicked past the doors. "Tell him we control this mill. Tell him all his gun-guards and Gatling guns can't touch us in here. Tell him that unless within one hour he releases from Punishment Hall the ten men he sent there yesterday for protesting against the rotten food, we're going to tear down his five-million dollar mill. We're going to wait just one hour, tell him, for his answer. Now go."

The man shot out. The doors were banged shut and barred behind him, while the mill resounded with the joyous shouts and songs of the convicts, hugging each other in the unrestrained abandonment that followed the first victory any of them had ever known over discipline.

CHAPTER XXIV

DEPUTY WARDEN MARTIN SHER-
WOOD, disciplinarian and real head of the
prison management, sat in his office gripping
an unlighted cigar between his lips. The screaming
siren had warned him of trouble in the mill. Wall-
guards reporting over a dozen 'phones had told him
all they knew—that the men had seized the mill and
barred its doors against attack and were ejecting the
guards one by one.

"Any of them hurt?" Sherwood inquired.

"Apparently not, sir," the subordinate answered.
"Their hands are tied, but they don't seem to be
harmed. Captain Denison is out and on his way
up to you."

"If Denison is out unharmed, nobody needs a doctor," Sherwood said with a glint in his eyes that
just missed being disappointment. "If they had
spilled any blood, his would have been first. Strange!
Twenty men at the mercy of a thousand uncaged
wolves, and nobody dead, eh? I wouldn't have be-
lieved it possible, and I thought I knew cons."

He turned and saw a nervous assistant buckling
on a revolver.

"Take off that gun and get it outside the gates
quick," he commanded. "Don't leave even a bean-

shooter inside these walls.   This is no ordinary riot.
There's headwork behind this.   It looks as if we
might have real trouble."

Deputy Sherwood reached into his desk, struck a
match and lighted his cigar.   When Martin Sherwood lighted tobacco, he was pleased.   The whole
prison knew this habit.   Among the convicts the sight
of the deputy smoking invariably sent a silently spoken warning from lip to lip.

"The old man's smoking.   Be careful.   Someone's going to hang in the sack" (straightjacket) "to-
night," they would say, and the prediction seldom
was unfulfilled.

It was true that Martin Sherwood took grim, silent delight in inflicting punishment.   He hated and
despised convicts and took pleasure in making them
cringe and beg under the iron rod of his discipline.
Somewhere well back in his ancestry there was a
cross of Indian blood—a cross that revealed itself in
coarse, coal-black hair, in teeth so white and strong
and perfect they were all but repulsive, and lastly in
the cruelties of Punishment Hall—cruelties that made
San Gregorio known as "the toughest stir in the country."

There was a reason for this strange twist in the
character of a man absolutely fearless and otherwise
fair.   Years before, he had brought a bride to his
home just outside the prison walls.   She was pretty
and young and weak—just the sort of girl the at-
traction of opposites would send to a man like Mar-

tin Sherwood. There were a few months of happiness during which Sherwood sometimes was seen to smile even among the convicts.

Then came the crash. A convict employed as a servant in the deputy's home completed his sentence and was released. With him went the Deputy's wife, leaving behind a note that none but the deserted husband ever saw. He never revealed by word or look the wound that festered in his heart, but from that day he was a man unfeeling as iron—a man who hated convicts and rejoiced in their hatred of him. Punishment Hall, when he could use its tortures with justice, became his instrument of revenge.

This perhaps explains why Martin Sherwood sat in his office calmly smoking a cigar when Captain Denison, white and shaken, rushed in and tumbled into a chair. His superior read in a glance the story of the scene in the mill.

"They might as well have killed you in the mill as to send you up here to die of fright in my office," the Deputy said with such biting sarcasm that Denison, terror-stricken as he was, flushed.

A few quick, incisive questions brought out the facts about the revolt. "Deputy, there is serious trouble ahead," Denison warned in conclusion. "Those cons have a leader they obey like a regiment of soldiers. He is—"

"Boston Blackie, of course," interrupted Sherwood. "There isn't a man down there who could have planned and executed a plot like this but Blackie. I should have⸲known better than to put him where he could come in contact with the men."

The guard who had been given the convict lead-er's ultimatum to the deputy warden rushed in.

"He says he wants the men out of Punishment Hall and your promise of better food from now on, or he'll tear the mill down in an hour," the man reported.

The Deputy Warden tossed away his cigar and stepped out into the courtyard, bright with a thousand blossoms of the California spring.

"Sends an ultimatum to me, does he?" he repeated softly to himself. "He's a man with real nerve and real brains. There is no way for me to reach the men while they're inside the mill. I must get them out and up here in this yard where the Gat-lings and rifle-guards will have a chance. And then I'll break Mr. Boston Blackie and the rest of them in the jacket—one by one."

His eyes gleamed at the thought. He turned to the men in the office.

"I'm going down to the mill," he said. "Have a Gatling gun ready in each of the four towers that cover this yard—ready but out of sight, do you understand?"

"Down to the mill?" cried Denison in amazement. "Deputy, you don't realize the spirit of that mob. You won't live five minutes. They will murder you as surely as you put yourself in their power. Don't go."

"If I am not back in half an hour, your prediction will have been fulfilled," Sherwood said. He took his pocket-knife and a roll of bills from his pocket and locked them in his desk. "If I am not back in half an hour, Denison, call the Warden at his club in San Francisco, tell him what has happened and that they got me. Say my last word was for him to call on the Governor for a regiment of militia. But for the next half-hour do nothing except get your nerve back—if you can."

Sherwood pulled a straw from a whiskbroom on his desk, stuck it between his teeth, from which his lips curled back until the abnormally long incisors were revealed, and started for the mill-yard as calmly as though he were going to luncheon.

White-faced guards at the last gate tried to stay him. The uproar from within the mill was deafening. Songs, curses and cries of frenzied exultation came from behind the steel-barred doors.

"Open the gates," commanded Sherwood. "Lock them behind me and don't reopen them again, even if you think it's to save my life."

Still holding the straw clenched between his teeth, the Deputy crossed the yard, neither hurrying nor hesitating. Nothing in his face or demeanor gave the slightest indication that he knew he was delivering himself, unarmed, into the power of a thousand crazed men, every one of whom had reason to hate him with that sort of undying hatred that grows from wrongs unrevenged and long-suppressed.

Sherwood hammered on the door with his fist. The clamor inside suddenly died.

"Open the door," he commanded. "I'm coming in to talk to you. I'm alone and unarmed."

The man on guard at the door raised the iron wicket and looked out.

"It's the Deputy," he whispered. "He's alone, too. Once we get him inside!" The man sank his teeth into his lip until the blood streamed across his chin. Primeval savagery, hidden only skin-deep in any man, reverts to the surface hideously among such men in such an hour.

With hands trembling with eagerness, the convict unbarred the door, and Martin Sherwood stepped quickly in and faced the mob.

For five seconds that seemed an hour there was dead silence. It was broken by an inarticulate, un-human, menacing roar of rage that rose to a scream as the men realized the completeness of their power over the man who to them was the living embodi-ment of the law which denied them everything that makes life livable.

A man in the rear of the mob thrust aside his fellows, rushed at the Deputy and spat in his face. As calmly as though he were in his own office, Sher-wood drew out his handkerchief and wiped his cheek, but never for an instant did his eyes waver from the men he faced. His teeth, whiter and more animal-like than ever, it seemed, gleamed like a wolf's fangs as he chewed at the straw between them.

"I'll remember that, Kelly, when I get you in the jacket," he said slowly to the man who had spat upon him. The convict laughed, but pressed backward, cowed against his will by the fearless assurance of his antagonist.

Boston Blackie was in the rear of the mill when the sudden silence warned him of new developments at the front door. Forcing his way through the crowd, he was within ten feet of the Deputy Warden before he saw him. The striped leader's face paled as he recognized Sherwood—paled with fear, not of him but for him. If the official were killed, as there was every probability he would be, he knew it meant the gallows for himself and a score of the men behind him. He had risked everything on his ability to prevent bloodshed. The lives of all of them depended on the safety of the hated autocrat who stood before him calmly chewing a broom straw in the midst of hundreds of men hungering for his life.

Blackie caught the Deputy War .n by the shoulder and turned him toward the door.

"Go," he said. "Get out before they kill you."

Sherwood threw off his hand.

"You may be able to command this convict rabble, Blackie," he said in a voice perfectly audible in the new silence which had fallen on the mob, "but you can't command me. I came to talk to these men, and I'm going to do it."

From somewhere in the rear came a metal weight:

which missed Sherwood's head by inches and crashed
against the door behind him. The screaming blood-
cry rose again. One struck at the Deputy's head
with a shuttle, but Blackie, quicker in eye and hand,
hit first and laid the man senseless at his feet. Then
he jumped to the top of a loom.

"Men, if you want to hang," he cried, his voice
rising even above the bedlam about him, "I'll go
along with you, if you'll listen to me first."

The outcry died down for a moment, and Blackie
talked to them. He made no pleas, asked no favors.
He told them their situation and his plan to attain
the ends for which they had revolted—the release
of the prisoners in Punishment Hall and better food
for themselves. He pointed the futility of the hope
of escape, ringed about as they were by Gatling guns
and rifles in a score of watch-towers, even if they
could force the walls as one suggested. Gradually,
by sheer force of mind, he dominated the crowd;
and when at last he called on them to follow him to
the end, their cheer was that of soldiers to a recognized leader.

All through this harangue Sherwood stood listening, his face as inexpressive as the walls behind him.

"Deputy," said Blackie, turning to him, "we have
been told you said you would keep the men in Punishment Hall in the straightjacket until they die, if
necessary, to find out who smuggled out the letter
complaining about the rotten food. Is that true?"

"It is," said Sherwood, who never lied.

"We make three demands, then," said Blackie:
"first, the release of all the men undergoing punishment; second, your promise that no man concerned in this revolt shall be punished; third, your guarantee that henceforth we get the food for which the State pays, but which the commissary captain steals."

"And if I refuse, what then?" asked Sherwood.

"At noon we will destroy the mill."

"Boys," said the Deputy, "I have listened to your spokesman. You know I can't grant your demands without consulting the Warden, who is in San Francisco. I will do this, however. I will declare a half-holiday. It is almost dinner time. Come over to the upper yard, have your dinner as usual and we'll watch a ball game in the afternoon. Before night I will give you your answer."

With the thought of the Gatling guns and rifles that covered the upper yard in his mind, Sherwood smiled grimly. The men cheered and made a rush in the direction of the doors, thinking the victory won.

"Wait," cried Blackie, barring the way with uplifted arms. "Nobody is going to stir out of this mill until you, Mr. Sherwood, have given us a definite promise all our demands are granted. You would like well enough to get us into the upper yard away from these protecting walls and where we couldn't do a dollar's worth of damage, but we're not going. When the men in Punishment Hall are free and you, who have never been known to lie, have told us we'll be fed right and no one harmed or punished now or in the future for this morning's work, we'll go into the upper yard—not before."

"Boys," said the Deputy, still hoping to urge the men into the trap, "do as I suggest. Why should you let this man"—contemptuously indicating Blackie—"order you around. He's only a con like yourselves. Come on up to the yard, and I'll issue an extra ration of tobacco all round. Are you going to go along with me or stay here with him?"

"We'll stay," answered Blackie for the men. "It's no use, Deputy; the game doesn't work this time."

A shout from the men proved Sherwood's defeat. He wasn't a man to delay or lament over a beaten hand.

"You're quite a general, Blackie," said the Deputy slowly, a flicker of admiration in his eyes. "I'll give you an answer in fifteen minutes. But"—he looked straight into Boston Blackie's eyes with steely determination—"don't think you are always going to have all the cards as you have to-day. The next time you and I clash, I'm going to break you like this."

He jerked the straw from his mouth and twisted it apart; then he walked out of the mill.

A quarter of an hour later ten pain-racked prisoners from the punishment chambers were welcomed back to the mill with an outburst of exultation such as San Gregorio Penitentiary had never seen. With them came the Deputy Warden's acceptance of Boston Blackie's terms. The men rioted joyously in an abandonment of happiness. In the midst of the turbulent jollification a half-witted, one-armed boy nicknamed "the Squirrel" climbed to the top of a loom, drew out his one treasure, a mouth-organ, and tried to express his joy in the one way he knew—and his dismal interpretation of "The Star Spangled Banner" floated out over the crowd.

"Cut out the bum music," cried a burly convict to whom the spirit of the hour had given a wanton impulse to command. "Where d'you figger in this, you nutty Squirrel?"

The boy's eyes filled with tears, and his notes faltered and died in the middle of a bar.

Boston Blackie, always sensitive to the feelings of others, stopped the lad as he slunk from his perch on the loom and lifted him back.

"Go ahead. Play, little Squirrel," he said encouragingly. "Your music is as good as a band. Go to it. You're one of us, you know, and we're all happy."

Intuitively Blackie had salved the wound caused by the gibe. Radiant now, the Squirrel pressed his mouth-organ to his lips and played on and on with a light in his dull eyes that made Blackie mutter: "Poor kid! A pardon wouldn't make him any happier."

And the convicts, only one degree less childish than the Squirrel, celebrated and sang in their cells that night until at last they settled into silence and carefree sleep. No thought of a to-morrow disturbed them; but Boston Blackie, quiet and wakeful, lay on his cell bunk anxiously probing the future. In his mind he still saw the broken bits of Martin Sherwood's broom straw fluttering to the mill floor and heard his threat:

"The next time you and I clash, I'm going to break you like this."

CHAPTER XXV

BOSTON BLACKIE'S MARY

F OR Mary the days were the longest and saddest she had known. Her father, Dayton Tom, had done his bit,—but this was different. She was a "prison" widow now, who never missed a visiting day at the San Gregorio Penitentiary. Twice each month she crossed the bay from San Francisco to the prison. Twice each month, with others like herself beside her, she rode from the station to the prison gates in the rickety old stage and waited in the reception room aquiver with impatience and longing for the first glimpse of the man she loved. When he came, when he caught her in his arms and kissed her, looking into her face with eyes that answered the love in hers, then for a pitifully short half hour both forgot prisons and the law and separations and were happy.

Boston Blackie and his Mary reckoned time from visiting day to visiting day. Those half hours together, separated though they were by thirteen long blank days, made life endurable. Neither ever spoke of the long years that must elapse before Blackie would walk out through the gates and go home a free man with Mary. Blackie reckoned them at night in his cell, and Mary checked off each day on a calendar in her rooms, but when they were together, they let no evil thoughts mar their happiness.

Ever since the strike, Blackie had been apprehensive and watchful. Deputy Warden Sherwood had made no attempt to punish any of the men concerned in the revolt. He was not a man to break his word, but when any of the men involved in it transgressed a prison rule, even in a trifling matter, the punishment that followed proved that Sherwood neither forgave nor forgot.

On a bright Saturday afternoon Blackie was impatiently pacing the yard, awaiting the summons to the reception room and Mary. It came at last, and he hurried through the gates, pass in hand. She was waiting for him and sprang to his side, hands outstretched and trembling with eagerness, in her fear of losing even one second of their thirty precious minutes. Their kiss was interrupted by the gruff voice of Ellis, the reception room guard. "Wait a minute there, Blackie," he commanded. "Who is this woman?"

"Who is she?" repeated the convict in blank amazement. "Why, she is Mary, my wife. You surely know her well enough. She has been here every visiting day."

"I know she has managed to slip in here on visiting days," Ellis said. "But what I ask you is, who and what is she? We're told she's an ex-con herself. If so, she can't visit you. The rules don't permit it."

The man turned to Mary.

"Isn't this your picture?" he asked sneeringly as he handed her a photograph of a woman with a prison number pinned across the breast.

It was Mary's picture. Years before, Mary Dawson, daughter of Dayton Tom, a professional crook, had been sent to the penitentiary because she declined to clear herself at the expense of one of her father's pals, and her past now had suddenly risen up to deprive her of the single treasure that life held— her half hour visits with Blackie.

"It's my photograph," she said in a voice choked with anguish, for she knew prisons too well not to realize what the admission meant. "But Mr. Ellis, please, please don't bar me because of that. I did time—yes; but I wasn't guilty. For God's sake, don't take our visits away from us. They're—they're— all we—have." The girl's voice was broken by her sobs.

"Of course you weren't guilty! That's what they all say," the guard answered. "You better beat it, woman, while you've got a chance. You're lucky the Deputy don't put the city dicks (detectives) on to you. There's a bunch of them over here to-day, too."

Boston Blackie, white as a marble image, glared into the guard's face with eyes that narrowed dangerously. The man's reference to the Deputy made everything clear. This was Sherwood's revenge.

"Did the Deputy tell you to bar Mary from visiting me?" he demanded of the guard.

"What's that to you?" the man answered with pointed insolence. "I don't want her here, and she's barred—that's all. She's got nerve to come here anyway among decent women, the—"

The word never left his lips. Boston Blackie's blow caught him on the chin, and Ellis sprawled across the room and toppled to the floor. In a second Blackie was upon him again, grasping his throat in a frenzy of savagery.

The whole reception room was in an uproar. Women screamed; convicts shouted encouragement. Blackie's vise-like grip was strangling the all-but-unconscious guard. Mary's voice, pleading with him frantically, restored the convict to sanity.

"Don't kill him! Don't kill him!" she begged. "For your sake and mine, let him go, dear. Think what it means to us both!"

Slowly Blackie's grip loosened. He dropped the man and took Mary in his arms.

"Good-by, dear one," he said. "I've tried to get by here without trouble, but Sherwood won't let me. From now on I've just one purpose. I'm going to beat this place. I'm going to escape. Watch and wait for me. It may be a month; it may be a year—but some day I'll come."

Guards summoned by the uproar rushed in, and one struck Blackie over the head with a club, laying him bleeding and senseless.

Blackie, still unconscious, was carried inside the gates and to the Deputy's office, where Sherwood was informed that Boston Blackie had committed the most heinous of prison crimes: he had struck an officer.

"Take him to Punishment Hall and leave him there for to-night. Don't give him punishment of any kind. I'll attend to that in the morning," the Deputy ordered.

As the guards carried Boston Blackie across the yard toward the punishment chamber, Martin Sherwood took a match from his desk and lighted the cigar he had been chewing.

Boston Blackie lay on the floor in Punishment Hall trussed up in the straightjacket as tightly as two able-bodied guards could draw the ropes. Great beads of perspiration stood on his forehead. A thin trickle of blood showed on his chin, beneath which his clenched teeth bit into the flesh. The man's eyes betrayed the torture he was suffering, but no sound came from his lips.

Martin Sherwood stood above him, looking down at the helpless form in the canvas sack. He was smoking.

A prison straightjacket on a wall is nothing alarming to the eye, but in operation it is an instrument of most fiendish torture. The victim stands upright, arms straight down before him and hands on the front of each leg. The jacket itself is a heavy canvas contrivance that extends from the neck to the knees with eyelets in the back in which ropes make it possible to cinch it to any degree desired,

as a woman's corset can be tightened. When
the jacket is adjusted over the arms and body,
the man is laid face downward on the floor
and guards tighten the jacket by placing a foot on
the small of the convict's back and drawing in the
ropes with their full strength.

Fully tightened, the jacket shuts off blood circula-
tion throughout the body almost completely. For
the first five minutes, oppressed breathing is the only
inconvenience felt. Then the stagnating blood com-
mences to cause the most excruciating torture—a
thousand pains as if white-hot needles are being
passed through the flesh run through the body. The
feet and limbs swell and turn black. Irresistible
weights seem to be crushing the brain.

Four hours in the jacket made one convict a para-
lytic for life. Some men have endured it for a half
or three-quarters of an hour without crying out, but
only a few.

Boston Blackie had been in the jacket for an hour
and five minutes, and as yet Martin Sherwood had
waited in vain for groans and pleas for release.

The prison physician stood nearby looking on
anxiously. One man had died after the jacket had
been used on him in San Gregorio, and the newspapers made quite a fuss about it. The doctor didn't
want a repetition of that trouble, and yet he knew
the man on the floor had been under punishment
fully twenty minutes too long. Still the Deputy gave
no indication of an intention to release him.

Five minutes passed. Blackie's face was a ghastly purple. Blood oozed from his nostrils. He rolled aimlessly to and fro on the floor, but his lips still were clenched, and no sound came from them.

The doctor grew more and more nervous. At last he called the Deputy Warden aside.

"He's had enough—more than enough, Deputy," he urged. "Hadn't we better call it off?"

"Never till he begs," said Sherwood, biting off his cigar in the middle and tossing it away. Perspiration stood on his brow too.

Five more minutes passed, and the form on the floor, too horrible now to be described, ceased to roll and toss. The doctor stooped over him quickly.

"He's out," he announced. "You've got to quit now, Sherwood. A few more minutes are likely to kill him, and anyway he's unconscious and you're not doing any good."

"Release him," said the Deputy Warden curtly. "Take him over to the hospital and bring him round. We'll try it again to-morrow."

Hours later Boston Blackie, slowly and painfully, came back into what seemed a blurred and hideous world.

"He didn't break me," he said over and over to himself. "I've beaten him again. I'll do it just once more, too. Nobody has ever escaped from this place since Martin Sherwood has been deputy, but I will."

The relieved doctor gave Blackie a drink that

sent him off into an uneasy slumber in which he was climbing an interminable ladder to a garden from which Mary stretched down her arms to him, but when he seized her hands, the fingers shriveled into cigars, and her face changed to Martin Sherwood's, whose white teeth bit into his flesh until he clenched his lips to keep from crying out.

"When Blackie gets out of the hospital, put him in charge of the lawn in front of my offices," said Sherwood to the assignment captain the following morning. "I have decided not to give him any more of the jacket."

The captain wonderingly obeyed. It was the first time he had ever known the Deputy to deviate from his inflexible rule that a convict once sent to the jacket stayed until he begged for mercy.

CHAPTER XXVI

"PLAY FOR ME, LTITLE SQUIRREL"

MARTIN SHERWOOD, from within his office, stood fixedly studying Boston Blackie, who was spraying the courtyard lawn with a hose. The convict was more like a skeleton than a living man. His striped coat hung sack-like across his emaciated shoulders. His cheek bones seemed about to burst through the crinkled, parchment-like skin that covered them. His eyes were dull, deep-set and haggard, his movements slow and languid like a confirmed invalid's.

"He's ill, without a doubt," mused the Deputy Warden. "The doctor's evidently right about the stomach trouble. No man could counterfeit his appearance; and yet—" Sherwood's brow was wrinkled with perplexity as he studied the convict. "Everything may be as it seems. If he were any man but Boston Blackie, I should be wasting my time thinking about it. But because he is Boston Blackie I'm puzzled. It's three months since I barred his wife from the prison and gave him the jacket—three months in which he has been docile as a lamb, though I know such a man must have murder in his heart every time he lays eyes on me. Why this calm?"

The perplexed furrow in the Deputy's brow deepened. For ten minutes he stood studying Blackie without making a movement or a sound.

"One of two things is true," the Deputy concluded. "Either he is just a common con after all and I did break him in the jacket, or else he's getting ready to cover my king with the ace of trumps. Suppose his plan, whatever it is, requires him to sleep in the hospital. He'd have to be sick to get there, of course —really sick, too."

Just then Boston Blackie, unconscious of the Deputy's scrutiny, turned toward him, and the sunlight fell full on his emaciated face.

"Gad, he looks like a corpse now," was Sherwood's thought. "It's impossible that this sickness is a trick, and yet nothing is impossible to a man who can stand the jacket without a murmur. I'm going to play safe. I'm going to move him out of the hospital, though there isn't a surer place to keep a man inside the walls, as far as I can see. I'll move him, anyway. If he tries to get back there again, I'll know I'm right."

Sherwood turned to his clerk.

"'Phone to the doctor to come over," he said.

The physician protested strongly against the Deputy Warden's order to transfer Boston Blackie from his cell in the hospital to one of the dormitories in the cell-house.

"The man's nothing but a living corpse now, Deputy," he argued. "He has a stomach complaint I haven't been able to diagnose. He isn't likely to live another three months. He hasn't eaten a thing but bread crusts for weeks. Let him die in the hospital."

"Move him over to C dormitory to-morrow morning," Sherwood commanded with finality. "I'm going to put him in with Tennessee Red, who'll keep me informed of what he does nights. I've got a hunch, Doctor, that Mr. Boston Blackie is framing another surprise party for us. I'll find some excuse to move Red's present cellmate out by to-morrow."

The doctor went back to the hospital shaking his head at the strange vagaries of his superior concerning Boston Blackie. He sent his runner, the half-witted, one-armed boy Blackie had protected on the day of the strike, for the turnkey.

"The Deputy has ordered Boston Blackie out of the hospital," he said when the messenger returned with the officer. "He thinks Blackie is framing something. I told him the man won't do anything worse than die, but he's set on moving him and so we'll have to do it. Look's to me as if Blackie's sort of on the old man's nerves since the affair of the jacket. I never knew him to worry so much about any man in the prison. He's going to put him in with Tennessee Red, his chief stool-pigeon, and see what he can find out. The Deputy won't have Red's cell-partner out till to-morrow, so don't say anything to Blackie to-night."

The officers separated. The Squirrel climbed back on his stool and looked out through the barred windows to the lawn, where he could see Boston Blackie laboriously dragging his hose across the grass. There was new grief in the Squirrel's dull eyes. He had heard what the doctor told the turnkey. They were going to take Blackie away from the hospital dormitory—Blackie, who gave the Squirrel tobacco and the inside of a loaf of bread each night—Blackie, who always protected him when the other men teased him—Blackie, his friend. The boy's eyes filled with tears. Blackie was the only one who liked to hear the Squirrel play his mouth-organ, and now they were going to take him away. But Blackie was smart. The doctor had said "not until to-morrow." Maybe if the Squirrel told Blackie at dinner time what he had heard, Blackie would find some way to make them let him stay in the hospital. Slowly the ideas filtered through the haze that clouded the dull brain.

Boston Blackie was sitting in his dormitory cell slowly chewing the crust of a half loaf of bread, from which he had hollowed out the soft inner portion that his tortured stomach couldn't digest, when the Squirrel slipped into the cell. The boy laid his finger on his lips as Blackie started to speak.

"They mustn't know I'm here," he said. "I heard what the doctor told the screw" (turnkey). "They're going to take you out of the hospital."

Boston Blackie's loaf fell to the floor.

"When, little Squirrel, when?" he whispered hoarsely, gripping the boy by the shoulder. A great fear showed in the convict's eyes.

"To-morrow, when the Deputy gets a place ready for you with Tennessee Red," the boy answered.

"Thank God, I've one more night. One night must be enough." Blackie, scarcely aware that he was voicing his mind, sank back in relief so intense it left his whole body dripping with perspiraton. A new danger occurred to him.

"What else did the doctor say, little Squirrel?" he asked.

"He said the Deputy thinks you are framing something, but it isn't so because you're going to die in three months. Are you going to die in three months, Blackie?"

"No, not in three months, little Squirrel," answered Blackie, and then softly to himself he added: "—but maybe to-night." He turned again to the boy, his mind swiftly grappling with the details of the task before him, which must be done now in a single night.

"Will you play your mouth organ for me to-night, Squirrel?" he asked. "Will you play it *all* the time from lock-up till the lights go out? All the time, Squirrel, and loud so I can hear it plain. Here's a sack of tobacco for you. You won't forget? All the time, and loud."

"Yes, all the time and loud," the boy repeated, dog-like devotion in his eyes.

Boston Blackie mopped a forehead dripping with cold perspiration. All his hopes of freedom depended on a half-witted boy and his mouth-organ.

Boston Blackie's mind that afternoon was a jumble of torturing doubts, painstaking calculation and unflinching resolution. The Deputy Warden's intuition had not misled him. Blackie had planned an escape, and his every act for weeks had been taken with that sole purpose in view. His plan required that he sleep in the hospital dormitory used for tubercular patients and others unfit for the cell-houses, but not bedridden. To accomplish this he diluted prison laundry soap, strong with lye, and drank it day after day until it ruined his stomach and left him unable to digest any food but hard baked crusts of bread. The lye caused him excruciating anguish, but in ten days it accomplished its purpose. Blackie had been ordered to the hospital dormitory to be put on a diet and given treatment for his puzzling stomach trouble. He had been there two months and was still using the lye to prevent the possibility of being turned back to his old quarters. He had wrecked his physique, but each night saw him a step nearer his goal.

He wasn't ready to make his bid for freedom, but the Deputy with uncanny divination had given him no choice. He must make the attempt that night or never.

First he took a spade and laboriously began to dig around the rose bushes that flanked the lawn. No one saw him uncover a rudely improvised saw made with his hoe file from a steel knife stolen from the kitchen. The saw and a tobacco sack containing a single five dollar bill were quickly hidden in his blouse. The bill had come from Mary in the cover of a book sent him according to instructions delivered by a discharged convict.

Next he asked permission to air his blankets on the clothesline in the lower yard. The toolhouse in which his garden implements were kept was nearby. From beneath its floor he took the treasures that had cost him the hardest work and greatest risk—a civilian pair of trousers, a blue shirt and a mackinaw coat made from a blanket, and a cap. It had taken him one full month to steal them from the tailor shop where the clothes of the new arrivals were kept after they received their prison stripes. The trousers Blackie put on under his striped ones, pinning up the legs well out of sight. When his blankets went back to his cell, the coat, shirt and cap were hidden in them.

A half hour before lock-up time Blackie rolled up his garden hose and carried it to the toolhouse. Once within its doors and alone, he cut off six feet of the hose and wound it around his body, tying it securely in place. Next from a pile of rubbish he unearthed a single rubber glove which he had filched one day from the hospital dispensary. He had tried in vain to get its mate. Two hundred feet of heavy twine from the mill completed the list of his preparations.

It would have puzzled even a man as shrewd as Martin Sherwood to determine how Boston Blackie planned to escape from San Gregorio Penitentiary with the motley array of contraband he had gathered together. The hospital dormitory where he celled was on the top floor of a detached building that stood alone in the yard, fully a hundred feet from the wall that surrounded the prison. It was conceivably possible for a man with even such a makeshift saw as Blackie's to cut the bars of his window and escape from his cell, but freedom from his cell was a long step from real freedom. There still remained the thirty-foot wall to be scaled—a wall guarded on top by a gun-guard in a watch tower and patrolled at the bottom all night by other armed guards.

At five o'clock Boston Blackie and the other hospital inmates were locked in their cells for the night. Thereafter, twice each hour, a guard was scheduled to pass and inspect the cells. At five minutes past five the Squirrel, faithful to his promise, began to play on his mouth-organ.

And as the boy played, Blackie chipped away the soap and lampblack with which he had plugged a half-sawed window bar and cut at it with his pitifully inadequate saw in frantic haste. The noise of the mouth organ drowned the gentle rasping of the saw, a vitally necessary precaution.

A mirror hung on the wall near the door warned Blackie of the approach of the guard each time he made his rounds. Hour after hour the Squirrel played, and hour after hour Blackie sawed. He had spent a month and a half sawing through the first bar and halfway through the second. To-night in four hours he must complete the task, for at nine o'clock "lights out" would sound throughout the prison, and silence would settle over the dormitory, making further work on the bar impossible.

The saw blade cut into his hands and tore his finger tips. His arms were numb with pain. The sing-song rasping seemed like a voice crying out a warning to the guards. The saw grew hot, and again and again he had to cool it in the water bucket. Often it seemed as if he couldn't drive his tortured muscles another second, but he conjured into his mind a picture of Martin Sherwood's face with the teeth gleaming in a white line as he bent over a form in the straightjacket. Sheer will power kept the saw moving then, and so slowly it was almost imperceptible; but surely, nevertheless, it bit through the steel that seemed a living thing bent on binding Blackie to years of prison slavery and punishment.

At last it was done! With fifteen precious minutes to spare, the saw grated through the outer rim of rust and left the bar severed. With two bars cut and bent outward, Blackie knew he could squeeze his body through the window to the wide ledge outside and four stories above the guarded courtyard below. He swept the glistening filings into his water bucket, hid the saw, worn now smooth as a knife, and tumbled on his bunk a quivering wreck.

The prison bell tolled out nine; the lights winked out; and silence settled over the dormitory.

At one o'clock Blackie waited for the guard to

pass, and then, with a half hour at his disposal, slipped out of his convict clothes and fashioned them into a dummy which he covered with blankets to resemble a sleeping man.

He dressed in his civilian clothes, with his six-foot length of hose still coiled about his body. He tucked his one glove carefully into his breast beside the ball of twine. Then he pulled out one of the heavy legs of his stool and tied it across his back. His preparations were complete. He took another stool leg and, using it as a lever, bent the severed bars straight out. A moment later he stood outside on the window ledge.

Below him the wall fell away sheer for four stories. Six feet above his head the rain-gutter marked the level of the flat roof. So far, Blackie had followed in the footsteps of other men who had tried to escape. But the others, once free from their cells, had gone down, each to be shot to death as he lurked in the courtyard vainly seeking a means to cross the towering wall that barred him in.

Instead of going down, Blackie went up. He took off his shoes and hung them about his neck. With fingers and toes clutching the bricks that jutted out a few inches around the window coping, he climbed slowly and with infinite caution upward. A single slip, the slightest misstep, and Martin Sherwood would smile and light a cigar in the morning when they carried his body in.

Inch by inch Blackie raised himself, pressing his

body close to the wall to keep from overbalancing. For the first time he realized his physical weakness. His arms were like dead things, and unresponsive to the iron will that commanded them. Again and again, in the agony of forcing his wasted muscles to obedience, he thought of releasing his clutch and falling to a quick death—relief. But always, in the wake of that thought, Martin Sherwood's face danced before his eyes, and the cruel satisfaction of the Deputy nerved Blackie to climb on.

At last his groping, bloody fingers clutched the edge of the roof gutter. He faced the last crucial task. He must now swing his feet clear and raise himself to the roof by his arms alone—no great feat for a well man but, to the ill and exhausted convict, one that taxed even his iron resolution to the last atom of its resource.

Somehow he did it and lay at last safe on the roof, blinking back at the stars, which hung so low it seemed he could reach up and touch them. He lay still, thoughtlessly content, until the chiming prison bell forced on his wandering mind the realization that a precious half hour was gone, leaving him still 'inside the walls that barred the road to Mary.

Blackie rose and crept silently to the edge of the roof nearest the wall. He was high above that stone barricade, from which he was separated by a full hundred feet of space. Nothing, apparently, spanned that impassable gap, and yet when one looked again, something did span it—two glistening copper wires that ran down from the roof at a sharp angle to a pole outside the wall above which they hung a full twenty feet. They were uninsulated, live wires which fed the prison machinery and lighting system with a current that was death to whatever touched them— yet they were the key to Boston Blackie's plan of escape.

Carefully he unwound the length of rubber hose from about his body. Carefully he laid the insulating rubber over the strands of shining metal. With infinite pains he bound and rebound the stool leg to the dangling length of rubber that hung beneath them. The result was a crazily insecure trapeze which swung under wires, the touch of which was fatal.

Then Boston Blackie pulled out his ball of jute twine and attached it to a brick chimney, the only thing upright and secure in sight. He glanced toward the wall far beneath him, where a sleepy guard dozed in his tower; then Blackie unhesitatingly seated himself on the bar of his improvised trapeze. With his back toward the wall, he swung clear of the roof and began to slide down the wires, regulating his speed with the cord on the chimney.

The light wires swayed and sagged but supported his weight. Yard by yard he let himself down. Half the perilous journey through the air was accomplished, and he was directly over the wall, when the chimney cord that kept him from shooting madly backward down the incline, suddenly snapped. The hose trapeze shot downward at headlong speed. Instinctively Boston Blackie reached up with both hands to seize the wires and check his fall.

Even as he reached, realization of the certain · death they carried flashed through his brain. He stayed one hand within inches of the wires. With the other—the one covered with his single rubber glove—he caught one of the wires and gradually checked his fall. Slowly he slid over the wall and down toward the pole outside the prison inclosure. When its shadow warned him he had almost reached it, he stopped himself and turning his head, studied the network of wires with deep caution. Seeing no way of avoiding their death-dealing touch if he tried to work his way through them and clamber down the pole, he slipped from his seat on the trapeze, hung by his hands for the fraction of a second and dropped.

The fall jarred him from head to foot but left him crouching by the light pole—uninjured and outside the walls.

For five minutes he lay motionless, watching for any sign of an alarm from the walls. None came; he was free.

Slowly and on his stomach, Indian fashion, Blackie worked his way out from San Gregorio and across the sweet smelling fields that led toward the world of free men. When the last watch tower was behind him, he rose to his feet and raised his arms toward the blinking and kindly stars in a fervent but unspoken prayer of thanksgiving. He had done the impossible. He had escaped from the hitherto un-beatable prison ruled by Martin Sherwood.

CHAPTER XXVII

TRAPPED

JUST as the morning bell was rousing the sleepy cell-houses at San Gregorio to another weary day of serfdom, a gaunt wraith of a man climbed a rear stairway to a tiny apartment on Laguna Street, San Francisco. The early morning fog added to his ghostlike appearance as he softly rapped at the bedroom window with the knock that is the open sesame of the underworld. The woman sleeping within awoke instantly with a start, but lay quiet, fearing she still dreamed, for in her dream she had been with Boston Blackie, her husband.

Again she heard the soft rap at the window. She sprang to the sash, looked out and threw it open, seizing in her arms the scarecrow of a man who stood there and dragging him inside.

"Mary!" he cried.

"Blackie!" she answered.

All the endearments of all the languages accentuated a hundredfold were in the two words.

"God in Heaven, I thank you," she whispered, falling to her knees with Blackie's stained and haggard face clasped to her breast.

* * * * * *

"Boston Blackie is missing from his cell in the hospital, sir. He sawed two window bars and got

299

out during the night. He left his clothes rolled into a dummy on his bunk, and the night guard didn't discover it until the morning count a moment ago. But he can't be far away. He couldn't have got over the wall and must be hidden somewhere about the prison, the night captain thinks. He has ordered the whole force out to make a search."

The hospital turnkey saluted the Deputy Warden and stood awaiting his orders. There was no surprise in Martin Sherwood's eyes, and no excitement in his manner.

"And so he's gone," he said. "His convict suit in his bunk, you say?" The guard nodded.

"Tell the captain he needn't bother to search the prison yard or buildings. He's wasting his time," Sherwood continued. "Blackie has five to seven hours' start at least, and he's miles away from here now."

"But he can't be. He must be inside the walls. He couldn't have got over them," protested the guard.

"He's over the walls, safe enough," Sherwood returned with conviction. "Boston Blackie isn't a man to saw his way out of a cell and then hide in a dark corner of the prison and wait for us to find him. He's gone, without a doubt."

The Deputy pulled his 'phone toward him and called the chief of police of San Francisco at his home.

"Boston Blackie, the safe-blower, has escaped," he

said when a sleepy voice answered him over the wire "What? It's the first time, yes, but there has to be a first time for everything, you know, particularly when you are dealing with a man like Blackie. Now, Chief, he's bound to go straight to Mary Dawson, a woman who is living somewhere in your town. I wish you would put your best men out quick to locate her. It ought to be easy, for every crook in town knows them both, and somebody will be sure to tell where she is living. You haven't a second to spare, for both she and Blackie will drop out of sight before night so completely we never will find them. We'll offer five hundred dollars reward for Blackie. Sure! All right. I'll be over."

Martin Sherwood hung up the 'phone and turned to the work before him with something akin to pleasurable anticipation in his face. Like all truly strong men he found satisfaction in a battle with a worthy foeman.

Meanwhile, in Mary Dawson's Laguna Street apartment, Boston Blackie was no less alert than Martin Sherwood.

"Does anyone know this address?" he asked the woman who sat on his knee stroking his hair and running gentle, loving fingers sadly over the deep lines left in his haggard face by pain and illness.

"I moved only a month ago when you sent me word," she said. "Scarcely anyone knows. I met Diamond Frank and Stella last week, and they were up here to dinner.

"We must get away from here at once," Blackie said. "We've got to disappear so completely it will be humanly impossible to trace us. One overlooked clue—the slightest in the world—will lead the Deputy Warden to us. He's no ordinary copper. It's a hundred to one he has half the detectives in the town out hunting this flat now, for he knows, of course, that I'd go to you. But little sweetheart, I'll promise you this: whether he finds us or not, he'll never take Boston Blackie back to San Gregorio. Have you my guns?"

Mary nodded, shuddering, and began to throw clothes into a trunk.

"Never mind packing the trunk, Mary," Blackie corrected. "Just throw together what you can get into a couple of suitcases, dear. We'll leave everything else behind. We're not going to use any transfer man in this move, little woman."

Mary sighed as she obeyed without question. Little feminine trinkets are dear to a woman, and she hated to leave them, but Blackie's word was the only law she knew.

There was nothing to distinguish the man and woman carrying suitcases, who took a car near Mary's apartment and crossed to the other side of the city, from scores of other passengers who traveled with them—except the man's emaciation. They rented a room in a modest lodging house on the edge of a good residence district.

"Mary," said Blackie the moment they were alone,

"there's work for you to do quickly. We're safe here until to-night, but no longer. Go downtown to Levy's theatrical shop. Tell them you're playing a grandmother's part in an amateur play and get a complete old woman's outfit—white wig, clothes, shoes, everything. Get a cheap hat and a working girl's hand-me-down, too. You're too well dressed not to attract attention where we're going. Draw every dollar we have in the bank just as soon as possible, for every moment you are on the street is a danger. You better bring something to eat, too—just a loaf of bread, for I ruined my stomach with lye to get into the prison hospital, and I can't eat anything but crusts. Above everything, be careful no one recognizes you and trails you out here. Every copper in town must be looking for us by this time."

He drew two revolvers from the suitcase, looked carefully to their loads and laid them on the bed.

"I'm going to sleep while you're gone. I didn't get much rest last night," he said, smiling happily.

At noon that day, while Boston Blackie lay sleeping in the crosstown lodging house, the police located Mary Dawson's Laguna Street apartment. Diamond Frank had casually mentioned the address to another crook, who happened to mention it to a bartender who was a stool-pigeon; and so, deviously but surely, it finally reached headquarters.

The chief of police called in a dozen of his best men, armed them and sent them out in two autos.

"Take no chances with him, boys," the chief warned. "When he's lying dead in a morgue, it might be safe to walk in on him, but I wouldn't gamble on it then unless I had seen him killed. He's a bad one. Take care of yourselves."

The chief's men did so to the very best of their ability. They put officers with drawn guns at every door and window—outside. When everything was ready and not even a mouse could have escaped from the house without being riddled by a dozen bullets, the captain in charge of the expedition asked who would volunteer to enter the apartment and arrest the escaped convict. The policemen shifted uneasily on their feet and glanced expectantly at each other, but no one spoke. Somebody had an inspiration.

"Let's send the landlady to the door with a phony letter," he suggested. "When the girl comes to the door, we'll grab her and bust in on Blackie before he knows we're in the joint."

The plan was adopted. The landlady knocked on the door, with four brawny men behind her ready to seize whoever opened it. There was no response. Finally the landlady herself opened the door.

"Gone," chorused the detectives as they saw the empty rooms.

"The girl's out somewhere, probably to meet him. Then they'll come back here, both of 'em," the captain declared. "They haven't blowed. Look at the trunks and clothes. Now we'll get 'em dead to rights. We'll just plant inside here and cover them when they come back."

But the guards in Mary's flat stayed there three days ready to pounce on the man—who never came. Meanwhile Sherwood started a canvass of every hotel and lodging house in the city. On the third day a detective brought in the information that a landlady, when shown Blackie's picture, identified it as that of a man who came with his wife and rented a room on the morning of the escape. They had two suitcases. The woman went out and came back with some packages. The next morning when she went to collect her rent for the second day, the couple had gone. That was all the landlady knew.

"I thought so," Sherwood mused when the news was 'phoned him. "He's hidden somewhere he thinks is perfectly secure. Every exit from the city is guarded, but that's pretty much wasted effort, for Boston Blackie, if I know him, won't stir from his place of refuge for weeks, maybe months. The man who finds him now will have real reason to compliment himself. And," he added with unalterable determination, "I'm going to be that man."

Sherwood turned the management of the prison over to a subordinate and spent his time directing the investigation of the hundreds of clues the reward brought to the police. But all proved futile. Fewer and fewer clues came in. A newer sensation crowded stories of the hunt for Boston Blackie from the first pages of the newspapers. The police frankly were beaten. Only Martin Sherwood kept at the task.

Sherwood puzzled and pondered for days without finding the clue he sought. Every detail of the escaped convict's appearance as he last saw him on the prison lawn was graven photographically on his brain. He remembered the emaciated face, the too-brilliant eyes, the shrunken shoulders from which the flesh had fallen away during his illness in the hospital.

"The doctor said that illness was real," he pondered. "Stomach trouble, he said, and he's not a man to be fooled. Blackie was really sick, without doubt, and yet that sickness couldn't have been mere chance. He hadn't eaten anything but outer crusts of bread for weeks. Even the night he escaped he left the inside of a loaf—and he always did that—always threw away the inside of bread loaves because he couldn't digest them."

Martin Sherwood sprang to his feet more nearly excited than he had been in years.

"It's a long chance," he said to himself. "But it is a chance. He'll be more than human if he has thought of that too."

The Deputy Warden ordered his car and drove out to the city incinerator where garbage wagons of the city consigned their ill-smelling burdens to a cleansing flame. Sherwood explained to the superintendent.

"Tell every garbage collector in the city," he said, "that I'll pay the man who finds the hollowed out insides of loaves of bread in a garbage can one hun-

dred dollars for the address from which that can
was filled."

* * * * *

"In three days, Mary, just three short days, we'll
sail out through the Golden Gate. You and I will
be together with a new world ahead, and Martin
Sherwood behind, nursing the bitterness of defeat!"

Mary, with a better, sweeter happiness in her eyes
than Boston Blackie had ever seen there, clung to
him as he spoke. They were in the two small rooms
—kitchen and bedroom—in which they had lain securely hidden during the ten days which had elapsed
since Blackie's flight from prison. Their landlady,
who scrubbed office building floors at night to support herself, lived alone on the floor below. The
house was an attic cottage with a garden, in San
Francisco's sunny Mission. Boston Blackie and his
Mary sat hand in hand planning a future without
a flaw—a future as rosy-hued as the girl's cheeks.
The realization of their hopes was very near now. In
three days a steamer sailed for Central American
ports. Their passage was paid. The hunt for
Blackie had died down. Once aboard the steamer
and out of the harbor, a matter of little risk now,
they would be safe and free and unafraid.

So they sat and planned in happy whispers,—
for caution still bade them be low-voiced while their
landlady was in the house,—while just below them,
low-voiced and cautious too, Martin Sherwood questioned that landlady.

CHAPTER XXVIII

MAN TO MAN

"I HAVE no roomers but a Miss Collins and her mother, who is an invalid, poor soul. They .have the two rooms in the attic," she was telling the Deputy. "The girl is learning shorthand and don't go out much. The old lady is crippled with rheumatism and can't leave the rooms. Oh, they are nice, quiet, respectable people, sir."

Sherwood was deeply puzzled. From the garbage can behind this house had come a half-dozen loaves of bread in three days, with the crusts—and only the crusts—eaten off. He had come to the house after painstaking preparation, feeling that Blackie and victory were within his grasp. The landlady's story of the girl who studied shorthand, and an invalid mother, found no place in his theory of what he would find there, and yet it was evident the woman spoke the truth.

"What does the girl look like? What is the color of her hair?" he asked.

"Red, sir—a beautiful red like a polished copper kettle."

Mary's hair was coal black. For the first time Martin Sherwood's confidence was shaken.

"When did they come here?" he asked.

"Why, let me see." The woman reckoned on her

fingers. "It was a week ago Thursday, sir, in the evening. They saw my advertisement in the paper and came just before I went to work—which is nine o'clock, sir."

Blackie had escaped early on the morning of the day she mentioned. On that Thursday night he and Mary had disappeared from the lodging house which was their first place of refuge. The date and hour of their arrival decided Sherwood. He would have a look at this red haired girl and her invalid mother.

"I would like to go up and see them for a moment," he told the woman. "I'm an officer." He showed his star. "Oh, no, nothing wrong at all. I just want to see them. I like to keep track of people in the district."

"Certainly, sir. I'll call Miss Collins and—"

"No, no—that isn't necessary," hastily interrupted Sherwood. "I'll just step upstairs and knock."

Though he tried to step lightly, as Sherwood's tread sounded on the uncarpeted stairway there was a sudden shuffling of feet on the floor above. He smiled, for that augured well, and he felt for the gun slung just inside his coat. Then he rapped.

Muffled sounds came from behind the door. A chair squeaked as it was pushed across the floor. A few seconds of silence; then, plain and unmistakable, came the sound of a woman sobbing hysterically. Sherwood tried the door, found it locked and knocked again peremptorily.

The door suddenly was flung wide open, and in

the flood of light from within a woman faced him—
a woman with a wealth of bronze hair that should
have been black, a woman with tears on cheeks that
were as bloodless as death, a woman whom he instantly recognized as Boston Blackie's Mary.

Martin Sherwood sprang inside with drawn revolver ready to answer the stream of lead he expected
from some corner of the room. None came. Instead he saw a woman, white haired and evidently
feeble, sitting beside a bed with bowed head while
her body shook with convulsive sobs. On the bed,
covered with a sheet that was drawn up over the face,
lay a silent, motionless form that told its own story.

Sudden disappointment gripped Martin Sherwood's heart. Had the man he had rated so highly
cheated him of his long-coveted triumph only by the
coward's expedient of suicide?

"Where's Boston Blackie?" he demanded, his gun
still covering the room.

Mary pointed silently to the still figure on the bed.

"Dead!" exclaimed the Deputy Warden. "When?
how?"

"An hour ago," she sobbed. "You starved him
to death in your prison." She dropped to her knees.
"God have mercy on us now!" she prayed.

Sherwood strode to the bed, beside which the
aged woman still sat sobbing, and leaning over, lifted
the sheet. As he did so his gun for the first time
failed to cover all the room. Beneath the sheet, instead of the face he expected, he saw a roll of blank-

ets carefully molded and tied into the semblance of a human form. Before he could turn, cold steel was pressed against the base of his brain.

"Drop that gun, Sherwood," said Boston Blackie's voice from behind him. "Drop it quick. Raise it one inch and you'll be as dead as you thought I was."

Sherwood hesitated as a full realization of the new situation flashed through his mind; then he smiled as he thought of the posse he had thrown around the house and let his revolver slip through his fingers to the bed. Here was a worthy antagonist—a bit too worthy, as the cards lay just then! But the deal was far from done.

"Pick up his gun, Mary, and lay it on the table in the corner, well out of the Deputy's way," directed Blackie. "Then see if he has another. I don't care to move the muzzle of my gun from his neck just yet. Now," he continued, "slip off these skirts. I'm not overly well used to them, even though I've worn them for ten days, and if Mr. Sherwood should forget the company he's in and get suddenly reckless, they might be in my way."

"Now turn round, Sherwood, and face the music," ordered Blackie a moment later.

The Deputy Warden turned and faced the convict behind whom lay a discarded white wig and an old woman's garments. He met his captor's eyes without a tremor, and smiled.

"Well done, Blackie, I must admit," he said. "But

I should have known that when you didn't shoot as I came in, things weren't what they seemed."

"I didn't expect you, Sherwood," Blackie replied, "but as you see, I made preparations to receive you in case you came."

The convict's face grew pale and suddenly grave. His grip on the gun leveled at the Deputy's head tightened.

"You understand, of course, Sherwood, I've got to kill you," he said then.

"As matters stand, naturally it wouldn't surprise me," the Deputy answered. His voice was absolutely calm and unshaken, his eyes without the remotest trace of fear.

"If you have anything to say or do or think, be quick," said the convict.

"I haven't—thank you."

The men stared into each other's eyes, the silence broken only by Mary's sobs.

"I hate to kill a man as brave as you in cold blood," said Boston Blackie slowly. "You're a brave man, Sherwood, even when you don't hold all the cards in the game as you do inside your prison. I hate to kill you, but I've got to. I can't tie and gag you. You'd get free before we could get away from the city. I can't risk that.

"Naturally not," said Sherwood.

"I couldn't trust your promise not to bother me, in a life-and-death matter like this, if I let you go alive," continued Blackie with troubled eyes.

"I wouldn't give it if you did." There was no hesitation in the answer.

"Well, then." The gun that covered the Deputy Warden's head swayed downward till the muzzle covered his heart. "Are you ready?"

"Any time," said Sherwood.

The hammer rose under the pressure of the convict's finger on the trigger. Mary Dawson, crying hysterically now, turned away her face and covered her ears.

"Do you want to go, Mary, before I—I do what I must do?" asked Blackie, realizing what the scene with its inevitable end must mean to the girl. "It would be better for you to go, dear."

"No, no," she cried. "I want to share with you all blame for what you do. I won't go till you do."

Sherwood turned his eyes curiously on the woman. Sherwood knew what he would have risked for such a woman and such love.

Boston Blackie's face was strangely gray. The hammer of the revolver rose, hesitated, fell—then rose again. The Deputy, his gaze returning from the woman's face, looked into the gun unflinchingly and in silence. Another pause freighted with that sort of tension that crumbles the strongest; then slowly the convict let the muzzle of his weapon drop below the heart of the man he faced.

"Sherwood," he said in a voice that broke between his words, "I hate you as I hate no living man, but I cant kill you as you stand before me unarmed and helpless. I'm going to give you a chance for your life." He stepped backward and picked up the Deputy Warden's revolver. He pushed a table between himself and the man he couldn't kill. He laid the revolvers side by side on it, one pointing toward him, the other toward Sherwood. The clock on the mantel showed three minutes of the hour.

"Sherwood," he said, "in three minutes that clock will strike. I'm exactly as far from the guns as you. On the first stroke of the clock we'll reach together for them—and the quickest hand wins."

Martin Sherwood studied Boston Blackie's face with something in his eyes no other man had ever seen there. He glanced toward the guns on the table. It was true he was exactly as near them as the convict. Nothing prevented him from reaching now, and firing at the first touch of his finger on the trigger. Blackie deliberately had surrendered his irresistible advantage to give him, Martin Sherwood, his prison torturer, an even chance for life. For the first time the Deputy's eyes were unsteady and his voice throaty and shaken.

"I won't bargain with you, Blackie," he said.

"You're afraid to risk an even break?"

"You know I'm not," Sherwood answered, his gaze turning once more to the woman who stood by the door, staring panic-stricken. It was plain that the issue to be decided in that room was life or death to her as well as to the men.

Boston Blackie reached toward his gun, hoping the

Deputy Warden would do likewise and end, in one quick exchange of shots, the strain he knew was breaking his nerve. Sherwood let Blackie recover his weapon without moving a muscle. Once more the convict's revolver rose till it covered Martin Sherwood's heart. They stood again as they had been, the Deputy at the mercy of the escaped prisoner.

Seconds passed, then minutes, without a word or a motion on either side of the table over which the triangular tragedy was being settled not at all as any of those concerned had planned. The strain was unbearable. The muscles of the convict's throat twitched. His face was drawn and distorted.

"Pick up that gun and defend yourself," he cried.

"No," shouted Sherwood, the calm which his mighty will had until then sustained snapping like an over-tightened violin-string.

"You want to make me feel myself a murderer," cried Blackie in anguish. "Why didn't I give you bullet for bullet when you came in the door? I could have killed you then. Now I can't unless you'll fight. Once more I ask you, will you take an even break?"

"No," cried Sherwood again.

With a great cry—the cry of a strong man broken and beaten—Boston Blackie threw his gun upon the floor.

"You win, Sherwood," he sobbed, losing self-control completely for the first time in a life of daily hazards. "You've beaten me."

He staggered drunkenly toward Mary and folded her in his arms.

"I tried to force myself to pull the trigger by thinking of the life we hoped for together, dear, but I couldn't do it," he moaned brokenly. "I'll go back with him now. Everything is over."

"I'm glad now you didn't, dear," she cried, clinging to him. "It would have been murder. I don't want you to do that, even to save our happiness. But I'll wait for you, dear one, wait till your time is done and you come back to me again."

Boston Blackie straightened his shoulders and turning to Sherwood, held out his wrists for the handcuffs.

"Come, come," he urged. "For God's sake, don't prolong this. Don't stand there gloating. Take me away."

Martin Sherwood, with something strangely new transfiguring the face Boston Blackie knew and hated, reached to the table and picked up his gun slowly. Just as slowly he dropped it into his pocket. He looked into the two grief-racked faces before him, long and silently.

"I'm sorry to have disturbed you folks," he said quietly at last. "I came here looking for an escaped convict named Boston Blackie. I have found only you, Miss Collins, and your mother. I'm sorry my misinformation has subjected you both to annoyance. The police officers who are outside"—the Deputy Warden opened a crack in the window curtain and

pointed out to the dim shapes in the darkness—
"and who surround this house, will be withdrawn at
once. Had Boston Blackie been in this room, and
had he by some mischance killed me, his shot would
have brought a dozen men armed with sawed-off shotguns. Escape for him was absolutely impossible.
I saw to that before I entered here alone to capture
him. But it all has been a blunder. The man I
wanted to take back to prison is not here, and I can
only hope my apology will be accepted."

Blackie stared at him with blazing, unbelieving
eyes. From Mary came a cry in which all the pent-
up anguish of the lifetime that had been lived in the
last half-hour found sudden relief.

"Good night, folks," said Martin Sherwood, offer-
ing Boston Blackie his hand. The convict caught it
in his own, and the men looked into each other's
eyes for a second. Then the Deputy Warden went
out and closed the door behind him.

Mary sprang into Blackie's arms, and they dropped together into a chair, dazed with a happiness
greater than either had ever known.

"He is a man," said Blackie. "He is a man even
though he's a copper."

Martin Sherwood let himself out of the house and
beckoned the cordon of police to him as he looked
back at the windows of the attic rooms and spoke
softly to himself.

"He is a man," he said. "He is a man, even

though he is a convict."

It was the greatest praise and the greatest concession either had ever made to another man.

Three days later a steamer passed out through the Golden Gate. On the upper deck were a man and a woman, hand in hand, with eyes misty with happiness—Boston Blackie and his Mary.

THE END